PRAISE FOR B

Michael L. Printz Award Winner
National Book Award Finalist
ALA Best Fiction for Young Adults Top Ten
ALA *Booklist* Editor's Choice
SLJ Best Book of the Year
***Publishers Weekly* Best Book of the Year**
ew York Public Library Best Book for Teens
Chicago Public Library Best of the Best

's a novel about actual changes in world view,
nd all its science and myth and realism and
gic are marshaled, finally, to answer crucial
uestions about empathy and difference,
and the way we see people we love."
—*New York Times Book Review*

"*Bone Gap* marks Laura Ruby as one of fiction's most original voices. She is capable of moving you to tears, terrifying you on deep and dreamlike levels, and making your heart shout with happiness. This book is magic realism at its most magical."
—E. LOCKHART, author of *We Were Liars*

"Violence and social pressures mixed with a hefty dose of myth and magic may feel like a too-many-ingredients stew for one novel to tackle. Ruby accomplishes this seemingly impossible feat with an original, well-constructed plot scary enough and honest enough to satisfy teens as well as adult readers."
—*Chicago Tribune*

"Ruby weaves powerful themes throughout her stunni novel: beauty as both a gift and a burden; the differen between love and possession; the tensions between what lies on the surface and what moves beneath; the rumbling threat of sexual violence; the brutal reality o small-town cruelties. She imbues all of it with captivatin snowballing magic realism, which has the dual effect of making the hard parts of the story more palatable to read while subtly emphasizing how purely wicked and dehumanizing assault can be. But in Ruby's refined and delicately crafty hand, reality and fantasy don't fall neatly into place. She compellingly muddles the two together right through to the end. Even then, after she reveals many secrets, magic still seems to linger in the real parts of Bone Gap, and the magical elements retain their frightening reality. Wonder, beauty, imperfection, cruelty, love, and pain are all inextricably linked but bewitchingly so."
—ALA *Booklist* (starred review)

"Told from the viewpoints of multiple Bone Gap citizens, this inventive modern fable whimsically combines elements of folklore, mythology, romance, and feminism. Both Roza and Finn's love interest, Priscilla, develop over the course of the magically real journey into strong women to be reckoned with, while the secondary characters, including a sassy beekeeper, wise chicken farmer, and self-aware horse, are charming and memorable. Cleverly conceived and lusciously written."
—*Kirkus Reviews* (starred review)

"*Bone Gap* bewitches with indelibly real characters, beautiful prose, and fearless refusal to bow to convention. A thoroughly unforgettable experience."
—FRANNY BILLINGSLEY, author of *Chime*

"The author defies readers' expectations at every turn. In this world, the evidence of one's senses counts for little; appearances, even less. Heroism isn't born of muscle, competence, and desire, but of the ability to look beyond the surface and embrace otherworldliness and kindred spirits. Sex happens, but almost incidentally. Evil happens, embodied in a timeless, nameless horror that survives

on the mere idea of beauty. Ruby's novel
deserves to be read and reread.
It is powerful, beautiful, extraordinary."
—*SLJ*

"*Bone Gap* is an imaginative corkscrew of a mystery about a town full of surreal and sinister secrets. Laura Ruby blends a fairy-tale atmosphere with the heart-stopping grip of a thriller in this exquisite world you can't—and won't want to—escape."
—NOVA REN SUMA, author of
Imaginary Girls and *17 & Gone*

"Ruby raises incisive questions about feminine beauty, identity, and power in a story full of subtle magic that is not compelled to provide concrete explanations. A haunting and inventive work that subverts expectations at every turn."
—*Publishers Weekly* (starred review)

"One part magical realism and two parts fantasy, *Bone Gap* is a story of whispering corn, buzzing bees, and glimpses of magic in parallel universes. Like in so many classic small-town stories, the town of Bone Gap becomes an integral character. Its collective judgment influences each main character; its magic is both the question and the answer to this very complex, emotional puzzle. Through understanding the importance of trust, Ruby defines the essence of love. The real magic in Bone Gap is the discovery of love, an idea many stories misrepresent but *Bone Gap* explores with the utmost honesty and truth."

—*VOYA* (starred review)

"A novel that carries you away from its first word into a world that is beautiful, unsettling, magical, and powerfully real all at once. Once you've been to Bone Gap, you won't forget it."

—COURTNEY SUMMERS, author of *Cracked Up to Be*

"With lyrical and often stunning prose, Laura Ruby delivers a magical love story and chilling thriller with a cast of characters both surprising and endearing. *Bone Gap* will haunt you."

—STEVE BREZENOFF, author of *Guy in Real Life*

Bone Gap

Laura Ruby

FABER & FABER

First published by Balzer + Bray,
an imprint of Harper Collins Publications US, in 2015
First published in the UK in 2016
by Faber & Faber Limited
Bloomsbury House, 74–77 Great Russell Street
London, WC1B 3DA

Typeset by M Rules
Printed and bound by CPI Group (UK) Ltd, Croydon, CR0 4YY

A CIP record for this book
is available from the British Library

ISBN 978-0-571-33275-5

2 4 6 8 10 9 7 5 3

For Steve, who sees.
And for Anne, who believes.

The nice part about living in a small town is that when you don't know what you're doing, someone else does.

—ANONYMOUS

Contents

July: Thunder Moon

August: Green Corn Moon

The People of Bone Gap

The people of Bone Gap called Finn a lot of things, but none of them was his name. When he was little, they called him Spaceman. Sidetrack. Moonface. You. As he got older, they called him Pretty Boy. Loner. Brother. *Dude.*

But whatever they called him, they called him fondly. Despite his odd expressions, his strange distraction, and that annoying way he had of creeping up on a person, they knew him as well as they knew anyone. As well as they knew themselves. They knew him like they knew that Old Charlie Valentine preferred his chickens to his great-grandchildren, and sometimes let them roost in the house. (The chickens, not the children.) The way they knew that the Cordero family had a ghost that liked to rifle through the fridge at night. The way they knew that Priscilla Willis, the beekeeper's homely daughter, had a sting worse than any bee. The way they knew that Bone Gap had gaps just wide enough for people to slip through, or slip away, leaving only their stories behind.

As for Finn, well, they thought he was a little weird, but that was okay with them. "Yeah, that boy's nuttier than a honey cluster," they might say. "But he's a fine-looking nut. A sharp nut. *Our* nut." Finn, they were sure, had his heart in the right place. Just the way they did.

Eventually, though, they found out that there was a good reason for Finn's odd expressions, his strange distraction, that annoying way he had of creeping up on a person. A good reason he never looked anyone in the eye.

But by then it was too late, and the girl they loved most—and knew least of all—was gone.

May
Milk Moon

Finn

Roadkill

The corn was talking to him again.

It had been a warm winter and a balmy spring in Bone Gap, so everyone with a field and a taste for corn had plowed and planted earlier than they'd ever dared before. On the last day of his junior year, exactly two months after his life had burst like a thunderhead, Finn walked home from the bus stop past plants already up to his waist. It was his favorite part of the afternoon, or should have been: the sun bright and hot in the sky, the plants twitching their green fingers. Corn can add inches in a single day; if you listened, you could hear it grow. Finn caught the familiar whisper—*here, here, here*—and wished it would shut up.

His friend Miguel would have agreed. Miguel hated

the corn, said the plants seemed . . . alive. When Finn reminded him that, duh, of course the corn was alive, all plants were alive, Miguel replied that the corn sounded *alive* alive. As if it wasn't just growing, it was ripping itself out of the ground and sneaking around on skinny white roots. Scarecrows weren't made to scare the crows, they were made to scare the corn. It was enough to give a person nightmares. Otherwise, why would so many horror movies have cornfields in them?

Finn had nightmares enough, but not about cornfields. His dreams used to be filled with the typical stuff: getting naked with this girl or that one. Evading psychos with hatchets and roller skates. Showing up in class wearing nothing but a snorkel and a single plaid sock. Flying so high that not even the clouds could keep up.

Now? He couldn't close his eyes without seeing Roza's slim hands slapping at fogged glass, the gleaming black SUV swallowed up by the gathering dark.

He didn't sleep if he could help it. And he didn't listen to the corn anymore. Why should he, when it wouldn't stop lying?

Sweat prickled on his scalp, and he stopped to switch his backpack from one shoulder to the other. The cornfield stretched out for miles, but standing here, on a hazy back road in Illinois, you wouldn't know it. The pavement in front of Finn ended in a wall of sky, as if it had been sliced off by the swing of a scythe.

He might have stood there for a while, considering the cutaway road and the perfect metaphor it was, if a murder of black crows hadn't shown up, cawing their stupid heads off.

Finn wasn't impressed. "What are you guys supposed to be? Set decoration?"

They'll pluck out your eyes before they peck you to death, Miguel would have told him. *Haven't you ever seen Hitchcock?* But Finn didn't like movies, and he thought the crows were nothing but jokers and thieves.

Which is what he called them. "Jokers."

The crows said, "Coward!" They cackled and flapped, the sun shining blue on their glossy wings, beaks sharp as hay hooks.

So maybe Miguel had a point.

Finn kept walking, feet heavy in the heat. His temples throbbed, sandy eyelids scratching his corneas. When he spoke, his voice creaked like an old door the same way Charlie Valentine's did as he yammered on about his granddad's granddad's horse farm, or how the railroad used to have a stop right in the middle of town, or the time he trapped an eight-foot-long beaver, as if the giants hadn't been extinct since the last ice age. Like Old Charlie Valentine, Finn wished he could turn back the days as easily as a farmer turning a page in an almanac. He wished that the people of Bone Gap could forgive, and that he could forget.

He hiked up his backpack, worked on forgetting. *Think of something else, anything else.* Like his chores, which his brother would want finished by dinner. Like studying for the college entrance exams, exams he would need to ace if he had any hope of going away, getting away, though the thought of going made his stomach clench. Like the Rude boys, all five of them as mean as yellow jackets, boys who liked to hurt people who got in their way, and people who didn't.

The very same Rude boys who appeared on the road in front of him.

Finn froze up like a monument to cowards everywhere. Was it them? Was he sure? Of course he was. Finn could always tell, even from this far away. All five of them were short and bowlegged, making them look like a chorus line of wishbones. The Rude boys walked as if they were permanently saddle sore.

The boys hadn't been on the bus, they hadn't bothered to come to class. Finn had no idea where they'd come from or how he could have missed them. He was always missing things. Luckily for him, the Rudes were walking in the same direction and hadn't noticed him yet. He could turn the other way. Or, if the corn were higher, he could vanish into it, go missing himself.

But then, there was no use running, no use hiding, and he had nothing left to be scared of. He dragged his heels, and pebbles rocketed across the pavement.

One of the Rude boys turned around. "Hey, look. It's Moonface. Trying to sneak up on us again."

"Whatcha doing, Moonface?"

"Mooning at the moon?"

Mean as yellow jackets, dumb as dirt. He sighed, the sharp exhale like the hiss of the plants all around.

"Who you laughing at?"

And easy, too. "I'm not laughing."

"Yes, you are."

"Okay, I'm laughing."

"Not at us," said one.

"Not if you're smart," said another.

"Haven't you heard?" Finn said. "I'm not so smart."

Easy and easily confused, eyebrows scrunching like inchworms. The Rudes didn't know what he was going on about. Neither did he.

"Never mind," Finn said. "Just talking to myself."

"Yeah, well, you just keep talking to yourself, because we got stuff to do."

"Later, Moonface."

Later, Finn thought.

And then, *Nothing will be different later.*

He hadn't been laughing, but the crows? *They* were laughing. The corn kept whispering. The sun was a yellow eye scorched in a blanket of blue. He looked at it too long, and it ate holes in his head. Just that morning, he'd gone to Roza's apartment and found all her stuff gone, the air a fog of Pine-Sol. Sometime in the night, God knew when, Finn's brother had cleaned things out, scrubbed things down, as if a girl could be washed from memory just by washing the floors.

More pebbles shot across the road, more words shot out of his mouth. "Now that you mention it, I was chatting with the crows earlier. They were wondering why you guys walk like you're wearing diapers."

The Rudes had him surrounded before he could think of a way out. Not that he wanted one. They circled him, old names and new ones dropping like crab apples.

"Spaceman! We're talking to you!"

Finn said, "What?"

"Whatcha got in the bag?" They ripped the backpack off him, searched it. The pack went flying into the field.

He could still turn this around.

"Hey! Shithead! Are you listening?"

He could dive into the corn—backtrack, sidetrack.

"Why do you have so many books when you can't read?"

Finn said, "Funny coming from guys who can't tell the difference between their cows and their girlfriends."

The first blow knocked the air from his lungs.

He bent at the waist, trying to catch his breath. He didn't even know which one had hit him—Derek, Erik, Frank, Jake, or Spike. None were more than eighteen months apart in age, all blond and freckled and sunburned, and who could tell one from the other?

Finn took a couple of rabbit punches to the kidneys before one of them grabbed a handful of his hair and yanked him upright. Finn blinked at the boy in front of him, his eyes zeroing in on that famous Rude underbite.

They weren't even trying.

He said, "Listen, Derek, if you thought that—"

"Are you messing with me?"

"No, I'm—"

"He's Derek," the boy said, pointing to another boy. "I'm Frank. And you're Roadkill."

The Rude boys suddenly forgot about the stuff they had to do, because they took their time and gave it their all, their knuckles almost as hard as their boots. And though Finn was tall, his arms and legs ropey with farm muscle, the Rudes were wider and stronger, and there were about four and a half too many of them.

When they were done, the boys gathered around and peered down at Finn, sprawled on the cracked asphalt. "You know," said one of them, "anytime Sean wants some real brothers, we could make room for him."

If Finn's teeth hadn't felt so loose in his head, he

might have laughed again. Everybody loved Sean, even the Rudes. When someone needed help, Sean was the guy who showed up, sirens blaring, arms pumping, black bag swinging in his big capable hands, sharp eyes taking it all in. And though Sean sometimes had to ask questions, he never asked too many, and never the wrong ones.

But it was more than that. The people of Bone Gap loved Sean because of Roza. Because Sean loved Roza.

Above Finn, somebody muttered something about being hungry. Somebody else said, "Shut it." Somebody's cell phone pinged. Somebody nudged Finn with his foot as if Finn were a possum. Only pretending to be dead.

He wanted to shout so that everyone could hear: *I loved her, too.* And it was true. But it had done none of them any good.

Finn spat the blood from his mouth. "I'll tell my brother you said hello."

The boys left and Finn was alone. After a bit, he decided that he should get up, just in case Old Charlie Valentine picked today to take his ancient Cadillac for a spin. He hauled himself up and off the road, fished his backpack from the field. He wouldn't leave his test prep books behind; even used, they cost a fortune. Sean would kill him.

No, that wasn't right. His brother would drive Finn back to where he'd lost the books. He might even help Finn buy new ones and put them in a brand-new backpack they couldn't afford. And somehow, that would be worse.

He hobbled the rest of the way home. Finn and his brother didn't have as much as some, but they had more than others, including a peeling white house, a matching garage, and a red barn permanently slanted to the left. Finn let himself into the house and dumped his backpack on his bed. Then he rinsed his face and inspected his wounds. (Split eyebrow and split lip. Mangled nose.) He pulled a small box off the bathroom shelf and rooted around for a bandage. The box, which had belonged to his mother, was gilded, jeweled, and far too fancy for bandages and swabs, but Sean said the jewels were fake and the box not worth a damn anyway, so they might as well use it for something. Finn shoved the box back on the shelf and slapped a bandage on the split eyebrow, which was stubbornly weeping blood. Then he went outside to the garden.

Calamity Jane, Finn's tiny striped cat, slunk under the fence and twirled around his legs. Her belly was swollen with the kittens she'd have in just a few days.

"Don't look now," he said to her, "but there's a mouse behind you and he's got a crossbow."

She mewled and made another run around his

ankles. Her name wasn't a compliment so much as a joke; as a mouser, she was a calamity. Sean said they would let her have one litter and see if her kittens could earn their keep even if she couldn't.

Calamity followed Finn as he weeded and watered their puny half acre of new vegetables—asparagus, kale, onion, beans, carrots, spinach, beets, broccoli, tomatoes. Sean and Finn were raised in a farm town; they were no strangers to growing food. But Roza, Roza had magic in her fingers. Because of what Roza had taught them, Finn and his brother could eat what they grew and still have some to sell at the farmers' market. With all the warm weather, the plants should have been thriving. Yet the vegetables seemed sad, strangely wilted. He pulled limp leaves and filled the holes left by squirrels and rabbits. As he did, he told Calamity, "You know, you could help with the squirrels and rabbits." In response, Calamity head-butted his leg, turned toward the house, and meowed.

"What?" he said, brushing the dirt from his hands. She head-butted him again and stuffed herself under the gate, which couldn't have been easy considering the load she was carrying. She looked back to see if Finn was behind her.

"All right, I'm coming." He got to his feet, stopping only to clutch at his bruised ribs, and then trailed the cat to the back of the house. She trotted right by the door to the kitchen and kept going until she sat in front of another door. The door to the apartment. Roza's rooms.

Finn said, "She's not here. Nothing is here."

Calamity meowed again, twirling in frantic circles in front of the door. While his brother was on shift, Finn would sometimes get the spare key from the kitchen, unlock the door, and sit in Roza's tidy apartment, inhaling the faint scents of mint and vanilla, leafing through the books, admiring the framed sketch of a pair of clasped hands on the nightstand, lifting the little flowerpots on the sill—all the things she'd left behind. He would imagine that she was coming back any minute, and would be surprised or maybe even annoyed to find him sitting in her old flowered chair by the window. He would say to her, "Where have you been?" And she would say in her deep, accented voice, "It matters why?" Finn would speak for himself and for Sean: "If you're back, it doesn't matter at all."

Now the door was unlocked. Though he knew what he would find, or what he wouldn't, Finn once again pushed open the door. Calamity shot past him into the empty apartment, sniffed. She let out a howl like the wail of a coyote, the sound more of a punch than anything the Rudes could ever manage.

It was too much. The whole day, the whole sleepless spring. Finn left the door open to the breeze and the dirt and the frantic, inconsolable cat and stomp-limped to the ramshackle blue house across the street. He had just raised his hand to knock when the front door flew wide. The man standing in the doorway had long gray hair. A long gray beard. He looked like the wizard from the Lord of the Rings, except for the T-shirt that said BORN TO BE WILD.

"So, what ran you down?" Charlie Valentine said. "A herd of cattle?"

"You could say that."

Charlie pointed at the jeans ripped in both knees, the white shirt so stained with blood and dirt it would have to be tossed. "If I know what's what, you're going to be pissing red. Better get Sean to look you over."

"Sean isn't home. He's never home."

"I'm not either," said Charlie. "I was on my way to a date."

"Sorry," said Finn, not sorry.

"Eh, no need. She's already mad at me anyway. Women are always mad about something. Did I ever tell you about the time I was traveling alone across this beautiful country of ours and met a beautiful woman with flaming hair? Her name was Esmeralda. Empira. Empusa. Something with an *E*. I thought we'd had a fine time of it, the two of us, until I woke up and found her trying to gnaw off my arm. Had teeth as sharp as a shark's, that one."

"Sure," said Finn, following Charlie into the house. He had no idea why he kept coming here when the old man was so full of shit.

"It's the dairy farming, you know," said Charlie over his shoulder.

"What?" said Finn. "What is?"

"The Rudes. They have all those cows. Cows will kick the crap out of you if you don't get up to milk 'em early enough. And that awful smell alone would make anyone itch for a fight."

Finn didn't mention how cows were okay if you knew how to handle them and how Charlie's living room stank with all the chickens wandering around inside. Maybe the old man noticed it, too, because he opened a window and pointed to a nearby pasture.

"There's a fine-looking horse right there. Did I ever tell you that I spent some time on a horse farm?"

"You mentioned it," said Finn, though Charlie had told him a million times, and would tell him a million more. Charlie Valentine's grandfather or granduncle or whoever once had a stableful of huge draft horses called Belgians. The horses were used to drag ice that was cut from the lake in winter. People put the ice in deep pits and covered it with sawdust. Then, in the summer, the ice was sold to the iceman. In the fall, the horses were leased out to loggers. Everyone had heard these stories, because Charlie Valentine had been in Bone Gap longer than anyone else could remember, before Bone Gap was Bone Gap, as Charlie would say.

"Now they're doing that again," said Charlie Valentine. "Using horses instead of trucks to move the lumber. Saw it on the TV. Calling it 'green logging.' Can you believe that?"

Finn folded his arms across his chest, then winced as a bolt of pain rocketed around his torso. "Sounds like a good idea."

"Of course it's a good idea!" said Charlie Valentine. "That's why they should never have stopped doing it! People forget everything that's important. Like how you have to talk to your animals. They'll listen if you just talk to them. We used to ride bareback. Didn't need any fancy saddles or anything." He eyed Finn with suspicion. "You're not taking riding lessons, are you?"

"No."

"Good," said Charlie. "The way you learn to ride is by riding."

"I know how to ride."

"You don't have a saddle, do you?"

"I don't have a *horse*."

Charlie Valentine thrust his top dentures from his mouth and sucked them back in again, his favorite gesture of disapproval. "So, how many eggs, then?"

"A dozen."

"Any particular color?"

"Surprise me."

Charlie Valentine had ordered his chickens thinking they were a special breed that laid blue eggs. The chickens *had* laid blue eggs, but they also laid pink and green and brown eggs, too, like every day was Easter. He was going to ask for his money back until he discovered that people driving through town on their way back up to the city would pay a fortune for a dozen Easter-colored eggs. But Charlie charged the locals a fair price, and charged the brothers even less. He said Finn and Sean were his favorites. And they had been, Finn guessed, until Roza.

Finn said, "Sean cleaned out Roza's apartment. It's like she was never there at all."

Charlie scooped up the nearest chicken and sat in the only chair in the room. "Valentine's not my real name."

"I know," said Finn.

"I'm not going to tell you my real name, so don't even ask."

Finn tried not to show his impatience. "I won't."

Charlie stroked the golden chicken into a trance. "Do you know how I got the name Valentine?"

"Your great love for mankind."

"Who told you?"

"Everybody."

"Who told you *first*?"

"Sean."

"Sean is a smart young man." Charlie leaned sideways and rooted around in a large basket sitting by his chair. He counted out a dozen eggs, which he set gently in a cardboard carton. "A good man. Gave up a lot when your mom left."

"I *know*."

"Not so easy to please, though," said Charlie Valentine.

Finn sighed loudly enough to reinjure his ribs. This was not what he came for. But then, he didn't know what he'd come for. What could Charlie say that he hadn't already said? What could anyone say? Two months ago, Roza had been kidnapped. Finn was the only witness. Nobody believed his story. Not Charlie. Not Jonas Apple, the part-time police chief. Not even his own brother, who found it easier to pretend Roza had never existed.

Charlie Valentine said, "My old man was a bit like Sean. When I was young, I used to try to figure out the one thing that would make him proud of me. Or at least make him smile once in a while."

Finn said, "I figured out that much."

"They all looked for her. Your brother, Jonas, everyone. They hung those sketches in every town from here to Saint Louis. They called up to the cops in

Chicago. There was no man matching the description you gave."

Finn knew what Charlie meant. He meant that Finn hadn't seen what he thought he'd seen. "Roza wouldn't have left us."

Even a man named Valentine had his limits. "Sean's right. She was a fine girl, but now she's gone. It's time to stop mooning."

Charlie Valentine handed Finn the carton of Easter eggs. "Go out and find a chick of your own."

Finn went back to his house and stood under a hot shower, even though it stung the cuts on his face and washed off his bandage. He dried off, pulled on fresh clothes—or the freshest ones he could find in the pile on his floor—and headed for the kitchen. He put up a pot of water to boil and rummaged in the cabinet for a box of spaghetti and a jar of sauce. Since Roza, they'd been back to eating a lot of things that came in boxes and jars.

Sean got home just as the water was beginning to boil. He stood in the doorway, nearly filling it to the top. Then he stepped inside, moved to the sink to wash his hands. He didn't even look at Finn when he said, "Rudes?"

Finn cracked the spaghetti in half and jammed it into the pot with a wooden spoon. "They say hi."

Sean said, "You're going to need stitches in that eyebrow."

"I don't want stitches," said Finn.

"Didn't ask you what you wanted," said Sean. "I'll fix you up after we eat."

Finn said the only thing he could: "Okay." He got a couple of pops out of the fridge and plunked them on the table. Ten minutes later, the pasta was cooked and the sauce hot in the pan. Five minutes after that, they were done eating. Finn washed the dishes, Sean dried. Then Sean motioned him to sit back down while he got his bag.

Sean had been an EMT since he was eighteen. At twenty-one, he was an emergency room tech on his way to medical school when their mother, Didi, took up with an orthodontist she'd met over the internet and announced she was moving to Oregon. The orthodontist didn't like kids, especially boys who would surely run around getting drunk and high, knocking off convenience stores and knocking up girls, or worse, sitting around the house and getting in the way. Didi told her boys that they were old enough to look after themselves. Hadn't she given up so much already? Didn't she deserve to be happy, too? Since Finn was only fifteen at the time, Sean opted to stay with his brother until Finn finished high school.

That was two years ago. Sean hadn't mentioned becoming a doctor in a long, long while.

Now Sean cleaned out the wound, numbed Finn's face with a shot, and sewed it up with a vicious curved needle clamped in what looked like a pair of scissors. Sean wasn't even supposed to have these things; EMTs didn't suture in the field. But Finn knew not to flinch.

Sean leaned back and inspected his handiwork. "You still might have a scar."

"Whatever."

"Did you at least hit back?"

"There are five of them," said Finn.

"You want me to make a call?"

That was the last thing Finn needed, his big brother to rescue him. His sad and disappointed big brother, with his stupid faith in the power of Pine-Sol. "No, I don't want you to call."

"I'll call."

"No."

A tiny muscle in Sean's neck twitched, the only visible sign that he was angry. "You haven't been beaten up since you were a kid. This is the second time in a few weeks. You can't let them get to you."

"I'm not letting anyone do anything," Finn said.

"You're walking into it, then. What's that about?"

"You cleaned out her room. What's *that* about?"

Sean didn't answer. Finn hated it when Sean didn't answer.

"It's been two months today," said Finn. "Why aren't you out there looking for her?"

Sean trashed the used bandages, then closed the black case with a snap. "If you care so much, why aren't you?"

Roza

Run

I'll be back.

Roza stood at the large picture window in the quiet suburban house and mouthed the words over and over, as if giving them form could make them true. But that was foolish. Also foolish: waiting at the window, hoping to see the yard teeming with police officers. Staring at the ceiling, listening for the sound of helicopters and the pounding of combat boots on the roof.

No one had come. No one was coming.

Except for him. He would come, as he came every day, to ask the same question: *Are you in love with me yet?*

At first, she'd answered his questions with questions:

Who are you? Who are you really? What do you want? What is this place? What's wrong with you?

But he would smile that bland, pleasant smile—the smile of an uncle, a teacher, a clerk, all those men with all those teeth—a smile that just made him all the more terrifying. "You'll love me soon. You'll see."

This was not the first place he'd brought her. The first place was a cavernous room so cold and empty and dark that she could not find the boundaries of it—it was the size of a cornfield, it was the size of a country—and all she could do was wander screaming through the blackness. Then, one morning, she woke up and found herself in a giant bed in a sunny room with plush blue armchairs and a cherry armoire. He was sitting in one of the armchairs, looking pleased with himself. "I was wondering how long you'd sleep."

She gathered the sheets up to her neck and scrambled backward so fast that her shoulder blades hit the headboard with a crack.

"Don't worry. I won't touch you until you want me to," he said, as if he should be congratulated for such scruples. "Come, let me show you the house."

She must have been drugged, because she couldn't imagine how she'd gotten there, and because she *did* let him show her the house. It was a large frame house, with miles of slippery wood floor, a kitchen clad in stainless steel so shiny it burned, a living room with a fireplace and giant TV. A picture window faced the street, where other houses—identical except for their color—sat in a line like chastised children.

"Do you like it?" he asked. "I built it for you."

Built it for her? Full-grown trees hunkered alongside the house, birds perching in the limbs as if posed. Had the trees been here first and the house built next to them? Or had he paid to have them transported and planted?

How long did it take to build a house?

"There are clothes in the closet upstairs. A very nice saleslady helped me select them, but if you don't like them, we can always get more. And the TV has every show, every movie. Watch anything you want." Again, the pleasant smile in that pleasant, even handsome, visage. "The kitchen is stocked. You're looking a little thin. You should eat something."

A long time ago, back in Poland, a horse had kicked a boy in the head, rendering him senseless and strange. This man had the same expression. Cheerful. Empty.

He gestured to a painting hanging over the fireplace. It took her a moment to understand that it was a portrait of her. She was standing in the middle of a verdant field, one blossom threaded through her fingers, another threaded in her long, coiling hair. A ring of girls danced around her. In the picture, an invisible wind pulled at her white gown, outlining her body so vividly that she didn't seem to be wearing any clothes at all. Roza edged away from the fireplace, from the horrible painting over it, like an animal sidesteps a snake.

He didn't notice, or if he did, he didn't care. He peered down at her from his great height, those icy eyes on fire. She fought for breath, as if that stare was incinerating all the oxygen in the room, as if she would be consumed along with it.

He said, "You're very beautiful."

Roza had heard this many times before, but it had never scared her so much.

"I want to marry you."

Her lips worked. When she finally spoke, she didn't say, "No one is so beautiful." She didn't say, "You're a kidnapper and a criminal and madman." She didn't say, "I'm in love with someone else." She didn't say, "Please don't hurt me."

What fell from her numb lips was what she'd said to a foolish boy she'd left in Poland. "I am only nineteen. I am too young to get married."

"Oh," he said, head tilted, considering this new bit of information. "Well, I guess we'll have to wait till you're not too young." He turned and swept from the room. He opened the door to the garage, stepped through the doorway, and shut the door behind him.

She heard the clicking of the lock, so loud that it could have been a cannon. The garage door opening. A car engine whirring to life. She ran to the front door, to the pane of glass in its center, and watched as a black SUV turned out of the driveway and drove past the house, disappearing from view.

Roza was Halina Solkolkowski's granddaughter, not easily cowed by anyone—hadn't her babcia once chased a bear from the kitchen using only a broom? Roza tried the door to the garage. It didn't budge. She aimed a kick before she remembered she wasn't wearing any shoes. She walked around the entire house, patting down every window frame for latches that weren't there. She grasped the neck of a floor lamp with the intention of swinging it at the picture window, but the lamp was somehow stuck to the floor, and she couldn't lift it, or any of the others.

She circled back to the front door, heavy wood painted white. She jiggled the knob. Yanked at it. Braced a foot against the jamb and pulled so hard her hands slid off the knob and she went sprawling. Like a cat, she launched herself at the offending wood. For a few wild minutes, she flailed at the door, pounding it with her fists, scratching at it until her fingernails were bloody. Then she stood, panting, staring at her wrecked hands until the sun set and the stars winked slyly in the purpling sky.

That had been weeks ago. Or what felt like weeks ago. Time moved so slowly here, or was it quickly? She had become unmoored from the present, loose and untethered, her mind rolling back into her memories, rolling forward into the future, anticipating, and then dropping again into this torturous, unbearable present. Here, there, everywhere. She still hovered in the window every day, mouthing the words *I'll be back,* her prayer, her incantation, but her prayers weren't working. She saw no police cars. She found no phones or computers in the house. Once, she had tried to light the kitchen curtains on fire, hoping that the flames would spread, engulf the house, and bring the trucks and the firefighters, but a hidden sprinkler system doused the flames before they even had a chance to catch. The curtains were barely scorched, and the man had replaced them without comment. Sometimes, she saw vans driving up to the other houses, sometimes mothers and fathers and children spilled from the vans, like now. She pinwheeled her arms and jumped up and down, stopping only as they vanished inside their house. No matter how much Roza shouted and waved, no one ever seemed to hear her. No one so much as glanced at the house on the other side of the street, at the girl trapped like a mannequin behind the glass.

Roza was tired of standing, of flailing, of praying. She moved away from the window and slumped on the couch, putting her bare feet up on the coffee table. He'd left piles of clothes in the closet and the armoire, but no shoes anywhere. He preferred her barefoot, he said. She had such lovely feet.

Roza didn't agree. What was lovely about feet that could not take you anywhere?

What was lovely about feet that could not run?

Finn

Showdown

The horn and hoof showdown was less a showdown than a show: steers and heifers, sheep and goats, even dogs and cats displayed and judged in tents around the fairgrounds. A few days after the Rude boys left him smeared on the road, Finn wandered among the tents, stopping to look at this sheep, that pig, this dog, that rabbit. And if the owners of the animals used the dumb nicknames, if they asked about his split eyebrow and split lip with a weird mixture of pity and satisfaction, Finn didn't much care. First, because the lack of sleep was making him delirious, and second, because a crazy goat had chewed free from his tether and was following Finn around, trying to gnaw off his back pockets.

"Will you knock it off?" he said.

"Meh!" said the goat.

Finn kept walking. The question Sean had asked him rattled around his brain. Why aren't *you* looking for Roza? But the truth was, Finn had never stopped. Right after she disappeared, he got Charlie Valentine to drive him out to the muddy fields where it had had happened, and made Charlie wait for hours as he scoured the ground for footprints and tire tracks, cigarette butts or fast-food wrappers—any evidence that the police had missed. He'd endured all of Jonas Apple's endless, repetitive questions: "Now, I have to ask you if you can describe him one more time. You said he was tall. Tall like you? Tall like your brother? Are we talking six foot two or three or four? You said he was wearing a dark coat. Was that a black coat? Could the coat have been dark blue? Could it have been dark *green*? Did he have a beard or a mustache? Did he have a beard *and* a mustache? Never mind how he moved, Finn, I have here that she didn't scream. Why do you think she wouldn't scream? Why do you think she wouldn't kick or run? You think maybe she knew this guy? You think maybe she *wanted* to go with him? Are you sure? How can you be so sure?" And Finn had borne the weight of his brother's clenched fists, his long silences, his unspoken blame.

Even now—after the people of Bone Gap had decided

that Roza left the same mysterious way she had come, as if she were some shining gift that no one could claim, and that they would never have the privilege of understanding her past or being a part of her future—Finn was scanning the crowd for Roza's glossy coiling hair, the lively bounce of her step, the smile so sunny that it seemed to blaze with a light of its own. But the people here didn't bounce or blaze, they only pointed and whispered.

"Meh!" said the goat.

"Don't you have a bridge to cross or something?"

The funny thing was, the people of Bone Gap shouldn't have taken to Roza at all. She was a stranger who had appeared out of nowhere and wouldn't say where she'd been, a *girl* stranger taking advantage of those "poor motherless boys." Sean told Finn and Roza not to be surprised if the people judged, as the people always did. And the indignant hum erupted as soon as they'd entered the grounds of last year's fair. Then the three of them had stopped at the 4-H tents so Roza could admire the calves and the lambs. Old Charlie Valentine leaned down low and whispered something that made her smile. He asked her which lamb was her favorite. When she pointed at the finest one in the bunch, Charlie declared, "Knows her critters." When she asked *him* in halting English about the acidity of soil and how it affected the corn crop, Charlie said, "Knows her dirt." He nodded as if he were making the call for the whole town, which he was. "We got ourselves a farm girl, folks. Make no mistake."

And nobody had. Except for one.

Finn smelled cake and apple pie, and his stomach turned him in the direction of the refreshment stand, the goat trailing behind. "Mr. O'Sullivan!" said the woman manning—womanning?—the stand.

"Hi, Mrs. L." Mrs. Lonogan, who had been the principal of Bone Gap Elementary since people first walked upright, wore her gray hair curled and woven in an elaborate updo that made her look like she had a dusty basket on her head. She cut him a brownie the size of a barge before he had a chance to refuse.

She handed Finn the brownie on a napkin. "How's that big strapping brother of yours? Still saving lives?"

He bit into the brownie. He thought maybe somebody had mistaken salt for sugar. "What? Oh, right. Still saving lives."

"And your mom? That orthodontist must be coming around to the idea of having sons by now. Your mother has always been able to wrap men around her little finger!"

Finn resisted the urge to spit. "Not this time, I guess."

"That's a shame."

"Is it?" said Finn.

Mrs. Lonogan raised a brow that looked as if it had

been scrawled with crayon. "So, school's done. Are you and Miguel ready to start fixing that fence of mine?"

"We'll be there at seven on Monday morning."

"My Lonny's got the tools you need. You can use his pickup to drive out to the fence. He would fix it himself, you know, but his back isn't what it used to be," said Mrs. Lonogan. "And I'm tired of those Rude cows wandering onto my property. The deer, too. And whatever else is creeping around." She shuddered dramatically, though her hair didn't move.

"We'll take care of it," said Finn. Repairing the miles of fencing would take him and Miguel all summer, but the Lonogans were paying well enough, and it would keep Finn out of Sean's way. Maybe Mrs. Lonogan knew this. Maybe that was why she'd asked him.

"Here's something else for you." She pulled a folded piece of paper from her pocket and slid it across the plastic tablecloth. Printed on the paper was this:

Reaching for the stars,
With hope inside our hearts,
We're growing, changing, yearning,
The fire within us burning.
To be the people we need to be,
To make the changes we need to see,
We must keep reaching for the stars,
With hope inside our hearts.

Mrs. Lonogan said, "It's a poem. About hope. I found it on the World Wide Web."

The goat said, "Meh!"

Mrs. Lonogan favored the goat with a frown, then turned back to Finn. "Moon—I mean, Mr. O'Sullivan, what inspires you?"

Was this a trick question? "I'm not sure what you—"

"When I was a girl, I wanted to raise champion show cats."

Mrs. Lonogan had a white Persian named Fabian that she liked to dress in skirts and push around in a baby carriage. "Really."

"It's true. I grew up on a dairy farm, where cats were for mousing and nothing more. My father wouldn't even let them in the house. He said it was because of the hair balls. But I was determined. I saved up all my pennies and bought my first Persian when I was eighteen. My father told me to choose between living in his house and keeping my cat. What do you think I chose?"

This was not a trick or a question, it was a speech. Finn stayed quiet.

"My point is that you have to fight for what you believe in. So what do you believe in? You must believe in something. What do you want to *do*?"

It popped out before he had a chance to think about it, before he could remind himself not to. "I want to find Roza. I want to bring her back."

Mrs. Lonogan steadied herself by gripping the table, as if Finn had just declared his intention to train unicorns for the fairy circus. "I know it's been difficult," she said, pouring him a cup of lemonade with the concentration of a scientist measuring hydrochloric acid. "Sometimes, people are not who we think they are. We didn't know anything about her."

"Yes, we did. I mean, we *do*."

"Nothing about her past," said Mrs. Lonogan. "Nothing that might help us find her."

He gave up, tossed the rest of the brownie to the goat. "I know that."

"Everybody has a story," Mrs. Lonogan said, her voice dreamy and distant. "Everybody has secrets."

Finn turned away from the refreshment table. He took a long pull of the lemonade, which, thankfully, contained sugar, when he saw the movement, or rather, the lack of movement. A peculiar pocket of stillness in the middle of all that color and bustle. And his gaze traveled upward from legs planted so firmly they might as well have been tree trunks to a torso carved of stone, immovable, ivory arms, up to a blanched face that—

A hand clamped down on his shoulder. Finn dropped his lemonade, whirled.

"Dude!" Miguel Cordero said. "You were supposed to meet me by the sheep."

Finn turned back, searched for that pocket of stillness, but it was gone. "Did you see that?"

"I see you spilled lemonade all over yourself," said Miguel.

"No, over there."

"What? What am I looking at?"

How could he describe it so he didn't sound like a lunatic? "There was a guy. Just standing there. I think I've seen him somewhere. Did you see him?"

"There are lots of guys here," Miguel said. "Way too many guys. Fewer chicks for us."

"Okay," said Finn, using a wad of napkins to blot the lemonade on his jeans.

"*Chicks*, dude. Like that one. She's checking you out."

Finn tried to scratch up some interest. "Who is?"

"Girl in the green shirt. No, don't stare! It's weird when you stare."

"People tell me I shouldn't look at them, and then they tell me I don't look at them enough," Finn said. "You need to make up your minds."

"I'm just saying that if you cooled it with the moony act, you'd get tons of play." Miguel didn't mention the cuts and bruises on Finn's face, either because he was too good a friend or because he was getting used to seeing them there.

"I don't have an act," said Finn.

"You know what Amber Hass told me?" Miguel said.

"No, what?"

"That you looked like that actor."

"Which actor?"

"Who cares, dude! Amber Hass says you look like an actor, you go find Amber Hass."

"Amber Hass chews on her own hair."

"Speaking of chewing, what's with the goat?"

"He started following me a while ago."

"He's wrecking your game. Doesn't he belong to somebody?"

Finn didn't have an act, he didn't have a game. "Probably."

"Meh!"

They started walking toward the livestock tents. Miguel was on the shorter side, but his shoulders were broad as barn beams, and his arms long and muscular. He was so self-conscious about them that he almost always had his hands jammed in his pockets (which caused his elbows to stick out at strange angles and only made his arms look that much bigger).

"Saw you over by Mrs. L," Miguel said. "She find something on the World Wide Web again?"

"She gave me a poem. She said she wanted to inspire me."

"Mrs. Lonogan has been inhaling kitty litter for centuries."

"There's that. You started studying for the tests yet?"

"You sound like my mother. I want to enjoy my summer, okay? Oh, look at her. No, don't *look* look."

"And you won't believe the essays they want us to write."

"That stuff isn't due for months."

"The test is in June and September. I might have to take it a few times."

Miguel said, "Who the hell wants to take a test more than once?"

"I thought maybe you'd help me with my essays. Some of the tests make you write them."

"I don't do essays in the summer," Miguel said. "If you had a geography problem, I might help you with that." Miguel and his family were into a practice they called "orienteering." They entered contests in which they were dropped in a strange forest or field or even a city with only a compass and a few landmarks. Finn had no idea why anyone would want to get lost on purpose.

"There are only three real roads in Bone Gap," said Finn. "What kind of geography problem would I have?"

"Well, if you planned to go somewhere else."

Finn imagined Roza sitting on a bus or perched in the window seat of a plane, blue sky behind her. "Go where?"

"I don't know. Saint Louis. Cincinnati. Chicago."

Finn grunted.

"What have you got against Chicago?"

"Too big."

"Since when?"

"Too many people."

"What have you got against people?"

Finn hated crowds. Thousands of people bumping and churning. "Too many opinions."

"I went to my grandma's yesterday. She won one of those exercise video game systems at bingo last weekend. My dad set it up for her and we all played with it."

"Okay."

"It said I was obese. When I stepped on the console, the little guy that was supposed to be me on the screen blew up like a tick."

Miguel was as solid as a fireplug. "That's dumb," Finn said.

"Point is, even games have opinions. But I can't even put on weight when I want to. The ghost is eating all the cookies."

The Corderos lived in an enormous, sprawling farmhouse, with an attic so packed with junk that Miguel's little brother had once gotten lost for a whole afternoon. (No compass.) Sometimes, at night, you could hear strange noises coming from that attic, and other times, food went missing. The people of Bone Gap said it was the ghost of the old lady who'd died there fifty years before. Miguel thought it was a poltergeist, a sort of mischievous spirit that liked to play tricks on the living. That, or corn on the loose.

Finn didn't believe in ghosts, and though the corn wouldn't stop yapping at him, he was pretty sure it stayed put. "I think your little brother is eating all the cookies."

"He says he's not."

"He also said that he didn't shave your dog."

"True," said Miguel.

They kept walking. The smells of hot dogs and cotton candy mixed with the ripe scent of the animals. Miguel kept up his steady chatter about girls, but none of them stood out much. A pink face, a brown face, yellow hair, red hair, cutoffs everywhere. Well, Finn did like the cutoffs.

"That one has nice knees," Finn said, finally.

"Knees?" Miguel threw up his hands.

Someone standing by the live tents said, "Hey! What are you two doing with my goat?"

Miguel said, "What's your goat doing with us?"

A dry coughing noise made them all turn. A rusty moped put-putted past them, a red wagon bouncing behind it, streaming smoke. The driver was dressed in white coveralls and a mesh face mask. Like a fencer. Or a villain in a slasher movie. There was only one person in Bone Gap who drove a moped while dressed like a serial killer.

"Come on," Finn said, pointing in the direction of the moped.

"There are all these hot girls here, and you want to follow *her*?" said Miguel. "Don't you know when to give up?"

Finn was an expert at giving up—wasn't that why Sean was barely talking to him? But by now there were a few other people chasing after the sputtering, smoking machine. The group followed the moped and its rider all the way past the fairgrounds and down the main street.

A huge mass of bees dangled like a living piñata from the weathered CHAT 'N' CHEW diner sign. The loud buzz drilled into Finn's skull and made his teeth ache. Finn couldn't imagine how many bees there were. Hundreds? Thousands? Millions? Once, at recess, one of Finn's teachers—Miguel's dad, José—had stepped into the nest of some ground bees. By the time Sean arrived in the ambulance, José Cordero had already been stung thirty-six times.

Now Priscilla Willis hopped off her moped and leaned it against the window of Hank's Hardware. She plucked a smoker from the wagon. She reached up and gave the bees a few puffs before setting the smoker on the ground. Then she grabbed a white box from the wagon bed and placed it on the curb, a couple of feet beyond the piñata of bees. She got a sheet and tucked one end underneath the box. The other end she tied around the door handle of the diner, the sheet slung between box and door like a hammock. She crouched next to the sheet, waiting.

The people of Bone Gap crowded behind Finn and Miguel, also waiting. It didn't take long for their low mutterings to give way to louder commentary. Their voices washed over Finn the way they always did. Like a strange sort of choir music, one voice blending into the next, the refrains so familiar that he could have mouthed the words along with them.

"Your mom should keep a better eye on her bugs," said one.

"Who says they're my mom's bugs?" said Priscilla, not bothering to turn toward the voice.

"Don't you keep track?" said another.

"Sure," said Priscilla. "We beekeepers tag every bee. See that one?" she said, pointing. "She's number five thousand six hundred sixty-two."

"Really?"

"Each bee also gets a tiny T-shirt with our logo."

"No need to get sarcastic."

"We own all the bees in Illinois," Priscilla continued. "Billions and billions. That's a lot of T-shirts." A bee alighted on the girl's hand. She didn't brush it away.

"What's that box, Priscilla?"

"Don't call me Priscilla."

"It's the name your mother gave you."

Priscilla didn't answer.

"Fine, fine. What's in the box, Petey?"

"It's a hive body with a few frames of comb in it," Priscilla said, in a tone that said it was the dumbest question in the history of questions.

"Her mom isn't as cranky," a woman informed the crowd. "She probably gets that from her daddy's side."

"Oh, that one! He was a good-for-nothing, and that's the truth. Ran off with one of those jugglers from the state fair. I remember because she had that red hair."

"Stop telling tales. He didn't run off with anybody. He started walking one day and kept right on going."

"She's better off without him, aren't you Pris-I-mean-Petey?"

The girl ignored the comments and let another bee march up her arm.

Someone sniffed. "You're going to get stung if you're not more careful. My niece over in Benton? She got stung on the nose. Yeah. They almost had to cut it off."

"You're full of it. Nobody had to cut nobody's nose off."

"I said *almost*, didn't I? And you should watch

yourself, Priscilla Willis. I don't think you would be happy if you didn't have a nose."

"She's not so happy anyway. Likes those bees better than she likes anyone."

"What's the big deal? I bet those bees probably don't even have stingers." Finn recognized that voice. One of the Rude boys. Derek.

With her bee-free hand, Priscilla swept off the mesh face mask. Long honey waves streaked with ropes of pink spilled down her back. "Why don't you come over here and hold these bees for me? Then you can tell me if they have stingers."

"I don't need to do nothing for you," Derek spat. "And your hair is dumb."

"Don't distract her," said one of the adults. "I've been waiting to get into the Chat for a cup of coffee for fifteen minutes already. If I don't get some caffeine soon, I might drop into one of those whaddyacallits. Comas."

"And that would be bad *how*?" said someone else, and the crowd cracked up. Only Priscilla Willis's "SHHHHHH!" hushed them.

"Before bees swarm, they stuff themselves with honey, so they're usually too full to sting," she said. A single bee finally inched out on the sheet and used it as a walking bridge to the box. Another bee followed.

"Are they going to *walk* over to that hive you put there?"

"Why would you walk if you had wings?"

"Bees have tiny little brains."

"I only got out of bed because I thought this would be more exciting."

Finn blurted, "Why is the hive white?"

Priscilla Willis turned her dark, wide-set eyes on him. The people of Bone Gap said it made sense that Priscilla Willis was born into a beekeeping family, because she resembled nothing so much as a bee. But Finn didn't want to hear what they had to say about Priscilla, because the weight of her gaze felt like a hand on his shoulder.

Or a slap across the face.

He said, "Why is the hive white? Why not red or purple or whatever?"

She said, "It isn't white. It's blue."

"It's white."

"Not to the bees. Bees see the white as blue. Bees like blue best."

Derek Rude laughed. "Bees like blue. Right. She's crazy. What kind of girl spends all her time with bugs?"

"Says the guy who dates farm animals," Priscilla said.

Derek's mouth worked as if he were chewing bark. "We all know who you date." Snickers from the crowd.

"I'll date anyone except you."

"I wouldn't go out with you, you look like a bug."

"And you're an idiot. In thirty years, which do you think will matter more?"

Derek stepped forward, his face so red he put tomatoes to shame. "Ugly ass—" he said, biting off the words when the man standing next to him smacked him upside the head.

Priscilla stood. She took the glove off one hand, flexing her fingers as if testing their strength. The people of Bone Gap whispered, *No, don't, please*, as she slipped the bare hand inside the writhing mass of bees. The buzzing deepened, sending sparks along Finn's nerves. The crowd held its collective breath. When Petey pulled her hand free, she wore a brown sleeve of insects. She held both palms up to face the sky, one gloved, one sleeved in bees, like a shaman performing some ancient ritual. A breeze made her hair dance. All around her, dozens of honeybees whirled like tiny moons in orbit, anchored only by her gravity.

Finn thought, *I don't know what that is, but it's not ugly.*

"Big deal," said Derek, but his voice was as high as if he'd sucked on a helium balloon.

"Shut up, Derek," said Finn.

"I'm not Derek. I'm Spike."

"Shut up anyway," Finn said. Let them surround him here. Let them start punching now. That would be okay. That would be just fine.

One of Priscilla's hands twitched, and Finn knew she had been stung. She glared at him. "What are *you* looking at, Spaceman?"

Roza

Jump

Roza dug around in a box of Ritz, pulled out a cracker, nibbled. If she wanted, she could go to the kitchen and pick a piece of fruit from the bowl piled high with apples and pears, peaches and plums. But the fruit in the kitchen looked too perfect; she was afraid of it. Afraid that the man had tainted it somehow, ruined it, that she would bite into the soft cheek of a peach and fall away dead.

Like the prisoner she was, she lived on bread and water, though she was sure the water must be drugged.

"Zijem na chlebie i wodzie, jestem niewolnikem tutaj," she said. Even terrible things sounded better in Polish. She had tried to teach Sean and Finn. Easy words—cat, dog, table, washing machine. In Polish, nouns were gendered; sometimes there were two ways to say the same thing—kot or kotek for cat—and sometimes just one. *That makes no sense,* Sean had said. *Why are tables masculine? Why is a washing machine a girl? What kind of crazy language is this? Not so crazy as English,* she'd told him. *Little words everywhere. "A" and "the" and "this" and "that." Useless! Like dirt under fingernails!* He'd laughed and said, *You have point.*

"I have no point," she told him, though Sean was not here, though no one was. She examined her hands, the useless, boneless things dangling off the ends of her wrists. Not so long ago, they'd been lean and strong, able to crack a nut with a pinch, able to press a seed deep into the earth with one stab of a finger. But they were not used to such idleness and had gone limp with despair. She fumbled with the cracker box, and crumbs rained down over the coffee table and the carpet. Anywhere else, that would be something to do, a necessary task, cleaning up after herself. But she didn't even need to do that much. She could go to bed, and in the morning, every crumb would be gone, as if the man had a flock of birds or a parade of biddable ants on staff.

She might as well be that picture over the fireplace.

She shoved the cracker box away and turned on the TV. She scrolled through chat shows, cooking shows, home decorating shows, cop shows, movies. She tossed the remote to the couch. She never really watched the TV, but sometimes liked to leave it on, liked to hear the voices so she didn't feel so alone. She had never been alone before. Though she'd had her own apartment at the O'Sullivan place, someone was always home. Sean. Finn. The little barn cat that hated the barn and always found a way to sneak inside. Even Charlie Valentine, who would come over looking for one of his wandering chickens, or for a game of cards. His favorite was a type of poker where the players held a single card to their own foreheads so that everyone could see what you had but you. They bet pennies and sometimes cookies. Seeing Sean—enormous, serious Sean—with a card stuck to his forehead always struck her as so funny that she made absurd bets, pushing whole stacks of pennies to the center of the table, eating the cookies before they made it into the pot. Sean's mouth would twitch, a smile, and he would warn her that if she didn't watch it, she would lose.

"Watch what?" she'd said.

"Watch yourself," he said.

"How? I roll eyes back in head?"

She didn't care about losing, because Charlie always won. And she didn't understand the saying, she didn't understand how a person watched themselves in the first place. The game they played just proved her point.

So she had stopped watching herself, or maybe

she'd never quite begun, and here she was, trapped in a coma, trapped in a nightmare, trapped in a suburban house in a pile of cracker crumbs, boneless hands as useless as her naked feet. The man hadn't come, but he would, and just the thought of that same question—do you love me yet?—that bland smile, those stony eyes scraping up and down her body made her shiver. She turned up the volume on the TV. On the screen, a man was pacing in a bedroom, running his hands through his hair and muttering to himself, reminding her of, well, her. Suddenly, he flipped the mattress off the bed, uncovering the bars that held the mattress in place. He wrenched one of the bars free and turned toward the camera, brandishing the bar like a sword.

Bars. Bars under the mattress.

She flew from the couch, ran up the stairs. Her own bed was king-size, and a platform, so that wouldn't do her any good, but in the spare bedroom, there was a smaller bed. For a child, he had told her, when the time was right. It was disgusting, that a man at least twice her age would want . . .

"The time will never be right," she said out loud, then heaved the mattress and box spring off the bed. Wooden bars extended from one edge of the frame to the other. They were not screwed down. She hefted one. It was about as long as a baseball bat, and nearly as heavy. She almost cried.

She ran back down the steps, new tool in hand. She shoved the love seat away from the picture window, took a deep breath, reached back, and swung the bar as hard as she could. Instead of a satisfying crash, the bar thumped against the glass. Frowning, she ran her fingers over the surface, found that she had barely scratched it. She brought the end of the bar to the glass again and again, the bar thumping instead of crashing. She tried the back windows with the same results. *Thump, thump, thump.* Some kind of special glass, then. To keep people out, to keep people in.

You have no point.

But she would not give up, not yet. The glass down here was too thick, but what about the glass upstairs? Maybe he thought she wouldn't be stupid enough to try to jump out of an upstairs window. And she wasn't. But there was a tree outside her bedroom. A tree—drzewo, neither male nor female. The tree was big and strong, the nearest branch a few feet from the house. If she could break the window, she might be able to reach far enough to grab it. Maybe.

She ran upstairs again and paused in front of the window. She said her silent prayer, and then swung the bar with everything she had. The first blow cracked the glass, sent the birds outside scattering. The second sent a web of smaller cracks throughout the pane. The third shattered it completely. She smashed the remaining bits of glass from the edges of the window. Then she ran to the closet and pulled all those fine dresses from the hangers. She lined the bottom of the window with the clothes so that she wouldn't get cut.

She leaned out the window and immediately felt dizzy. But she had no other choice. She wouldn't wait here for him to return. For all she knew, he was out buying her a wedding gown. The thought almost made her laugh out loud. If she hadn't been so scared, she might have.

She patted the clothes that she had piled on the window ledge. Nothing poked through. Good. She leaned her body over the ledge and stretched for the tree branch, but she couldn't reach it. Before she had time to think better of it, she'd stepped up onto the ledge, holding both sides of the sash. There she hadn't been as careful to knock out the glass, and a sliver sliced one palm. She gasped and almost pulled her hand away but forced herself to hold on so that she didn't go tumbling out the window. She was only two stories up, but a fall could still mean broken legs, and broken legs would mean that she was just as trapped as she'd been before. Even more than trapped. Completely helpless. So she held on, taking huge gulps of air, tensing her muscles, priming them for flight.

—Ready.

—Set.

—Jump.

She sprang from the window, extending her arms as far as she could. Her forearms thudded against the branch, the bark scraping her skin as she scrambled to get a firm grip. She hung from the tree, feet dangling, sliced palm stinging. She barely had a second to congratulate herself for making it before the branch creaked and then cracked. She fell, hitting first one branch, then another, then another before thudding to the ground.

She sprawled there, lungs gasping for the breath that had been so violently knocked from them.

Which was when she saw the beast. Because of course there was a beast.

A beast for the beast.

It growled, showing her its graveyard teeth.

Finn

The Night Mare

Miguel was waiting on the steps of the Lonogan house, work gloves in his lap, a little sheepdog frantically bulldozing his knee.

"This dog has mental problems," Miguel said. "Doesn't he get that I'm sitting down?"

"That's what happens when a sheepdog lives with show cats."

The dog, a mottled thing named Mustard, ran over to Finn and jackhammered his calf. Finn allowed himself to be herded over to the steps. A posthole digger, shovels, a few bags of quick-set concrete, large buckets with lids, a role of fencing wire, pliers, and a couple of hammers were piled on the ground near the bushes.

Miguel stood next to Finn while Mustard danced around their legs. "You just missed the Lonogans. They left the truck and said we should start in the southwest corner, where the fence is the worst."

The new posts were already stacked in the bed of the pickup, so they loaded the rest of the equipment and filled the buckets with water for the concrete—jobs made more difficult with Mustard's determination to keep them together. When Finn opened the door to the cab, Mustard leaped inside.

"Let's hope he can dig," said Miguel.

The southwest corner of the fence abutted the main road but also separated the Lonogan property from the Rude farm. Finn knew the fence was in sorry shape, but it was even worse up close. The wire between the posts was rusted and torn, bowed up along the bottom by animals snuffling underneath it and down on the top by animals leaning or climbing over it. The corner post leaned toward the road, and large black ants covered its surface. Finn pulled a chunk from the post, exposing the smooth tunnels made by the insects.

"That one has to go," said Finn.

"I don't know," said Miguel. "Maybe this is where the Lonogans store their larvae."

With the pliers, they plucked the staples holding the wire to the post. They dug around the base of the post to loosen it, then kicked the post over. Hundreds of ants spilled from the lacy wood. Immediately, the dog tried to herd the insects with his nose. When that didn't work, he ate them.

"That'll teach you," said Finn.

"I hope you're not talking to the bugs," Miguel said.

The new posts were thicker and longer than the old ones, so Finn and Miguel took turns with the posthole digger to widen and deepen the hole. When it was deep enough, they inserted the post into the hole, checking with a level to make sure it was straight. Then Miguel held the post while Finn poured a little water into the hole. After that, a layer of concrete mix, then more water, more mix, until the hole was full.

Miguel said, "One down, eleventy million to go."

They moved on to the next post, Mustard on their heels, muzzle littered with ant parts.

"What the hell happened to this one?" Miguel said. The post was splintered and gouged, gnawed in places.

Finn fingered the gouges. "Horses will sometimes chew the wood."

"Horses don't have fangs. And the Rudes don't have horses."

"Well, it wasn't the corn."

"How do you know?" said Miguel. He squinted at the field across the street. "Anything could be in there."

For a second, Finn almost saw her, Roza, crouched

in the plants, laughing at him. Then he shook the sun out of his eyes and started removing the staples that held the wires in place on the chewed-up post.

"Did you see her?"

Finn fumbled with the pliers. "What?"

"Amber Hass. She just rode by on her bike."

Finn let out a breath. "No, I didn't."

"I might have told her you'd be here today."

"Okay."

"Maybe you should take your shirt off."

"What? Why?"

"Then she'll come over here."

"Cut it out."

"Don't you want to talk to her?"

"Not really."

"She's unbelievable, man."

She can't do that thing with the bees. "She's okay."

"Okay? You're not a normal human."

"That's what everyone keeps telling me."

"There she is again, riding the other way."

"Maybe she's here for you," said Finn. "Maybe you should take your shirt off. Isn't that why you work out so much?"

"She's not here for me."

"How do you know?"

"Her dad once asked my dad if he knew any gangsters in Mexico."

"Isn't your dad from Venezuela?"

"Do I really have to explain this to you?"

"The hell with her dad," said Finn. "Maybe Amber likes Mexicans."

"Which might help if I were Mexican. To her dad, I'm just another brown kid."

"What's wrong with that?" Finn said, though he knew what Miguel was talking about. Roza was the sort of color that older ladies first called "dark" and then later called "olive," as if being green was somehow nicer. "Maybe Amber would like you even if you were—"

"Do not tell me you were going to say green. Or purple."

"I definitely wasn't going to say purple."

Miguel pointed at Finn's face. "Well, you're red already. That shit's going to hurt tomorrow. And it serves you right for all this 'We Are the World' crap."

"You're changing the subject."

"My arms are too long."

"That's good. Amber will always be able to spot you in a crowd."

Miguel ripped a staple from the wood. "I see why you get beat up all the time."

"Twice isn't all the time," said Finn.

"What's Sean say about it?"

"About what?"

"About subsidies for corn farmers," Miguel said. "About your face being smashed in, dumbass."

Finn stabbed the ground with his shovel, stamped down on the edge to bury it deeper. "What should he say about it?"

"Nothing, I guess," Miguel said.

They dug for a while, the only sound the scrape of the shovels against the rock and the dirt. Then Miguel started to laugh.

"What?" Finn said.

"Your brother. Remember that Halloween when we were around seven or eight and those big-city kids came down to the corn maze dressed like skeletons?"

"They were chasing us," Finn said. "They wanted our candy."

"And your brother jumped on Amber's pink bicycle?"

Finn smiled. "The one with the white basket. And the flowers."

"He caught up with them, took a flying leap off the bicycle, and cracked their heads together? Knocked them out cold. *That's* gangster."

"He got in trouble for that."

"Not too much," said Miguel. "Jonas Apple hates city people."

Finn leaned on the handle of his shovel and pointed past the fence. "Maybe you should go ask Amber what happened to that pink bicycle."

"Yeah? Maybe you should ask your brother to teach you how to fight."

If he were talking to me, maybe I would.

Suddenly, Mustard went rigid, rearing and barking at the cornfields.

"See? He's barking at the corn," said Miguel. "You can't say I didn't tell you."

"What is it, boy?" Finn said. They stood there, scanning the fields, the dog barking, the corn waving.

Just like that, Mustard stopped barking. He leaned his weight against Finn to move him closer to Miguel, as if that would keep the flock safe.

Late that night, Finn sat at the kitchen table, test prep books spread in front of him, steam curling from his fourth cup of tea. Calamity Jane, also spread out on the kitchen table in a nest of papers, watched as Finn poured nearly half a jar of Hippie Queen Honey into the cup.

"I know," Finn said. "I should just skip the tea and drink the honey instead."

But he drank the tea anyway, frying the taste buds off his tongue, because he didn't drink coffee and because he wanted to stay awake. The clock read two in the morning, and his body begged for sleep, but Finn was having none of that. Even if he got in bed, there would only be twisted sheets and damp pillows as he thrashed and sweated out all the hours of the dark. Maybe other guys would watch TV all night, but TV was just a bunch of noise, and when Sean came home, if he ever came home, he would tell Finn to turn it off.

So he rubbed his eyes and leafed through the prep books that he would have to study for the next four months. It did not help that he was bad with tests. It did not help that he kept mixing up the test and the scholarship and the application deadlines—June? September? October? November? It did not help that even the tests had essay questions. It did not help that all the questions were stupid. *Do you think that cities have the right to limit the number of pets per household? Do you think that high school should be extended another year? Do you believe that previous failures always lead to later successes?*

He tapped the pencil on the paper, searching his brain for answers. Through the open window came the sound of a horse snorting.

"I could do without the commentary," said Finn.

Calamity yawned.

"From you, too."

The cat blinked, once, twice, three times.

"I don't speak blink."

Instead of limiting the number of animals, cities could make ordinances to keep people from hoarding chickens in living rooms. High school can be extended five or even ten more years, but only for people named Rude. Previous failures will mean that your brother will work extra shifts and come home at dawn so that he doesn't have to see you anymore. They mean that your brother will hate you and the town will hate you and you will hate you and you will never sleep.

Somewhere, the horse snorted again. "Shut up, already."

The man was tall. And he was so still. I've never seen anyone that still. But when he finally moved, he moved like a cornstalk twitching in the wind.

A sharp whinny. Calamity swiveled her head toward the window.

"It's just a horse," Finn said.

Another whinny.

"A loud one. Possibly with fangs."

A thud. Like hooves against a barn door.

"Is that *our* barn door?" Which it couldn't be, because the only things that lived in the barn were the mice and the birds. Except . . .

Finn pushed back his chair and went to the window. He squinted, trying to make out the barn in the dark. He was about to sit down again when he heard the second thud and saw the barn doors shake. He left Calamity to guard the books and the honey and raced outside, skidding to a stop right in front of the slanted structure. The horse—he hoped it was a horse and not, say, a bull—was kicking hard enough to take the doors down.

"Hey, horse," he said.

The kicking ceased.

"If I open the barn, do you promise not to charge me?"

There was a hushed whinny, as if the horse understood what he was saying. Except he couldn't speak horse either, and for all he knew the horse had just promised to eat him. His hands fell on the latch. Should he open it now or wait until morning?

The horse gave the doors a hard kick, the force nearly knocking Finn over.

"Fine," he said. He stood as far to the side as he could while still keeping his hand on the latch, flipped it open. He leaped around the side of the barn, expecting that the horse would explode from the building, galloping off to wherever loud, furious horses went. But no, though the latch was open, the doors stayed closed. Finn took a deep breath, grabbed a handle, and walked one door back. He waited for the horse to show itself. No horse. Maybe Finn had had too much tea. Maybe he'd had too much honey.

A soft nicker from inside the barn.

Finn stepped inside. He felt along the dusty shelves on the wall where he knew Sean kept an old flashlight.

He flicked it on, and a wan yellow glow illuminated the barn. He swung the flashlight around. And there it was. Gleaming. Enormous. At least eighteen hands high, but not thick in the way of shire or draft horses. Lean and elegant as a racer. So black that it almost blended into the shadows pooling in the corners. Warily, he walked all the way around the horse. It was a she.

"Whoa," said Finn. "Where did you come from?"

The horse shook her head, stepped forward, and nudged his chest with her nose. She wore a bitless bridle made of leather nearly as black as her coat, but no saddle. "Hey there," he murmured, stroking the long face, the silky mane. It was then, when he was petting the horse's nose, he noticed the smell of fresh hay. A dozen bales were stacked by the door. So someone had put the horse in the barn along with some feed. He'd heard that sometimes families who had hit hard times would leave beloved animals with people they thought could afford them. But Finn didn't know any local people who had owned a horse as special as this one; he would have remembered. Besides, Finn and Sean couldn't afford to take care of a horse. They could barely afford the cat.

And *when* had this mythical family left the horse and unloaded the hay? Sean was on shift, but Finn had been sitting at the kitchen table all night. Even if he had been too preoccupied to hear the sounds of trucks or voices, Calamity would have, so quick to startle now that her kittens were close.

The horse gave him another nudge. She seemed young and healthy, groomed and clean. She allowed him to pick up one hoof at a time and check the shoes. They looked new.

A horse. What the hell was he supposed to do with a horse?

The mare threw him three times before he managed to stay on her back. He'd ridden a million times before, but not a horse this big, not a horse this strong and fast and fierce, and never at night. He'd barely gotten his hands wrapped in the reins when she was off, tearing a furious path through the darkness as if something wicked was nipping at her heels. He tried using his knees to guide her, he tried to stop her from jumping fences and crashing through streams, he tried to keep her from running all the way to Idaho, but the horse had her own ideas, which boiled down to galloping as fast as she possibly could. After a while, it was all he could do to hold on and hope they wouldn't die.

Finally, the horse's hooves slowed and Finn's heartbeat slowed and they wandered together past farms and houses, all of them so quiet that Finn almost believed that he and the mare were the only living creatures left in a muted, dormant world.

The horse slipped between the Bone Gap cemetery and the Corderos' stone farmhouse, winding her way through the grasses at the edge of the Willises' beeyard. Mel Willis was the owner of Hippie Queen Honey, and she lived on a shaggy, overgrown patch of berry bushes and brambles and flowers with her hives and with Priscilla. But the beeyard was not dark the way that the other yards were; a small fire glowed in the center of the circle of hives. A figure was silhouetted in front of the fire.

Finn heard Miguel's voice in his head—*Don't you know when to give up?*—but he wasn't ready to go home yet. And besides, if he was looking for punishment, he'd rather take it from Priscilla Willis than from anyone else.

Finn urged the horse toward the figure, and this time, the mare was in the mood to comply. Priscilla Willis glanced up from the flames as Finn and the mare stepped close. She tented her hand over her eyes, trying to make him out in the dark.

"Who is that?"

"Finn," he said. "Finn O'Sullivan."

"Okay, Finn O'Sullivan. What are you doing here?"

"I thought I'd stop by."

"You thought you'd stop by for what?" she said, voice sharp.

Priscilla never made anything easy. "To talk to you."

She gazed at him for a few moments longer, then dropped her hand. "Isn't it dangerous to go riding at night?"

"More dangerous than hanging out with a bazillion bees?"

She gestured to the fire. "The smoke calms them. Besides, they won't sting unless you piss them off."

"How do I know what pisses off a bee?"

"Forget the bees. I saw the bruises on your face the other day. Looks like you pissed off someone a whole lot bigger. Did the horse do it?"

"She has a mean right hook."

"Where'd you get her?"

"She showed up in my barn."

"She showed up in your barn," Priscilla repeated. She picked up a stick and poked at the flames. "What kind of barn is that, anyway? A magical barn?"

Maybe Priscilla was thinking of other things that had just shown up in Finn's barn, but he wasn't going to talk about that. He touched the mare's neck, and the horse took a few more steps closer. "I was sitting at my kitchen table, reading, when I heard a noise from the barn. And there she was."

"I've heard of people doing stuff like that, leaving horses with other people. But regular horses. Not that kind of horse. That's some sort of fancy show horse."

"Maybe. But she was in my not-very-fancy barn

with ten bales of hay, so I guess someone wanted us to have her."

Priscilla frowned, the firelight etching angry lines in her skin. People said Mel Willis was a pretty woman, but Finn thought that even mad, Priscilla was a whole lot prettier. Not that he could tell her that. He had known her forever, but something had happened in the last year. She was just *there* all of a sudden, there in a way she hadn't been before. Spiky as she'd always been, but leaner and lusher at the same time. In class, he would stare at her. He didn't know he was doing it until she threatened to cut him with a corn knife.

Other kids stared, too. Some of them said Priscilla Willis was smokin', as long as you didn't look at her face. But Finn didn't see what was wrong with her face. That was what he should have told Miguel: Priscilla Willis didn't look like anybody else.

Priscilla said, "I bet she's worth, like, a million dollars or something. People don't leave million-dollar horses in barns. That's crazy."

"It is crazy. But now I have a horse."

"Are you going to keep her?"

Finn shrugged. It was odd to be sitting on a million-dollar horse, talking to Priscilla Willis in the middle of the night, but then it was a relief to be talking to someone besides the cat.

"Mind if I sit with you, Priscilla?"

"Petey. I hate the name Priscilla. What if I called you Finnegan?"

"That would be weird, because my name isn't Finnegan."

"Well, my name isn't Priscilla."

"Okay," he said. *This is going well.*

"What did you say?"

He shut his mouth and shook his head for fear she'd whip out that corn knife. He slid off the horse's back and patted her flank. He didn't bother to tether her to a tree. Someone might have put her in his barn, but for some reason, it seemed as if she was her own horse and would decide where and when she wanted to stay, and where and when she wanted to go.

"You're not using a saddle? Are you nuts?"

"I don't have a saddle. And it didn't seem right."

"So, you are nuts."

"She has a bridle and reins."

"Great. So, she could have dragged you behind her."

"Not by the bridle, she wouldn't have. Even though it doesn't have a bit, it would have hurt her, wrenched her in circles." Finn dropped to the ground on the other side of the fire. "Though I guess she still could have thrown and trampled me."

"Awesome." Petey watched the horse cropping the grass by one of the hives. "What's her name?"

"I just met her."

"Still."

"I'll think about it."

"Come up with a good one. One that she'd like. No one wants to be saddled with a name they don't like."

"Saddled, I get it."

"It wasn't a joke."

"Okay."

"My jokes are *funny*."

"Okay."

The fire lit Petey's face from below, making her eyes appear even larger, blacker, angrier against the honey skin. Finn had trouble keeping them both in his field of vision, so he looked from one eye to the other and back.

Petey gave the fire a sharp stab, sending sparks spiraling into the air. "You're staring again."

"Sorry," he said. But he didn't stop staring.

She dropped the stick and met his gaze. "I thought they said you never look anyone in the eye."

No one else had such interesting eyes. Another thing he wouldn't tell her. "Do you always pay attention to what they say?"

"If I did, I'd have to walk around wearing a paper bag over my head."

"I wouldn't want you to do that," said Finn.

Petey blinked so rapidly it was like watching the beating of wings. Finn cursed himself for his big, stupid mouth.

Then she said, "Your horse needs some water. I'll be right back." Despite the fire and the half-moon overhead, she snatched up a flashlight long enough to double as a club and jogged toward the house. Petey ran on the track team, and her stride was long and graceful. At the spigot, she filled a bucket with water and brought it back to the beeyard. It must have been heavy, but you wouldn't have been able to tell from watching Petey. She was used to hauling buckets and hives and boxes filled with honey jars.

She set the water in front of the horse, and the horse lapped at it. She murmured to the mare. The mare exhaled and nuzzled Petey's ear.

"She likes you," said Finn.

"She's a good horse," Petey said. "You really should keep her."

"Maybe I will."

Petey stood for a while, hugging the horse, which probably should have seemed strange but didn't. The mare was huggable when not kicking things or careening across the prairie at a hundred miles an hour.

Petey said, "You hungry?" She didn't wait for him to answer. She dug around in a bag by the fire, pulled out a marshmallow, and speared it. She handed the stick to Finn, who held the marshmallow over the flames. Petey did the same. When their marshmallows were burned the right degree of delicious, Petey gave Finn two crackers and a piece of chocolate. He pressed the marshmallow between the crackers and chocolate and took a bite.

"No, no," said Petey. "Dip it in this first." She held out a large jar of Hippie Queen Honey. The mouth of the jar was just wide enough to fit the edge of his s'more. He took another bite.

"Even better, right?"

"Even better." He managed to cram the rest of the s'more into his mouth. Then he had to lick his fingers to get the rest of the honey. Petey, on the other hand, took delicate nibbles, like a bee sipping at a flower.

"You never told me why you were out here in the middle of the night," said Finn.

"You didn't ask."

"I'm asking."

She shrugged. "Can't sleep."

"Why's that?"

"I don't know. Just restless. End of school does that to me. Keeps me awake. My brain won't stop talking."

"My brain does that, too, sometimes." *All the time. Every night.*

"It's worse now. Maybe because I'm thinking about what I'm doing after graduation next year."

"College?"

Priscilla—Petey—nodded. "You, too?"

"Yeah. Everyone says it's early, but . . ."

"I've been thinking about this since I was ten years old."

"Thinking about college?"

"Thinking about getting out of Bone Gap."

"Oh," he said.

"I was looking at the applications online. It's like a bunch of guys got together, got drunk, and tried to see how many essay questions they could think up. You know that one of them wants us to write a five-hundred-word essay on the color red? And that's not even the craziest one. There's one that asks you to write a poem or essay or play, but you have to mention a new pair of loafers, the Washington Monument, and a spork. What's that about?"

"Which college is that?"

Petey waved a hand. "Who cares? Someplace I can't afford to go to anyway." She sighed and examined her fingernails in the dim light of the fire. "Most I can hope for is the state university."

"Me, too. You don't sound that excited about it."

"It's big. Forty thousand people or something."

Finn swallowed back the knot that immediately rose in his throat. Forty thousand people, forty thousand people, *forty thousand people.*

"And people . . .," said Petey. "Well, I don't particularly like people. But they have a bee research facility there. I would like that. But it's hard to get into.

And it's really expensive, too. My mom won't be able to help much."

"My brother, either," Finn said. "I'm on my own. Scholarships if I can get any, and loans, if I can get those."

"What about your mom?"

"My mom calls once a month to tell us how happy she is to be away from boring old Illinois. For my birthday, she sent me ten bucks."

"Isn't she with some rich guy now?"

"Yeah. Some *cheap* rich guy. Maybe that's how rich guys stay rich."

"Doesn't that make you mad?"

He didn't know what to say to that. Getting mad at his mom seemed about as logical as getting mad at a thunderstorm.

Petey said, "I guess ten bucks doesn't cover much tuition."

"But it almost buys a whole pizza."

One corner of Petey's bow mouth curved upward, her version of a grin. She tucked her long, wavy hair behind her ear. In the dark, the pink streaks looked black.

"You could sell the horse, skip college, and buy a hundred thousand pizzas."

They turned to the horse, which suddenly stopped munching on the grass to regard them with deep, fathomless eyes. "I don't think she'd like that."

"How do you know what she'd like?"

"I know animals. I'm good with them."

"Or maybe they're good with you?"

"Either way. I want to work with animals. Study them. Be a vet or scientist or—"

"A rodeo clown?"

"That's exactly what I was going to say. A rodeo clown."

Petey stretched her long legs. "I told you why I'm up. Why are you two wandering around in the middle of the night?"

"I guess I can't sleep either."

"Roza?"

When he didn't respond, her expression changed. Not a frown, exactly, but a slight tightening of the features, a twitch and a tic. She bent one knee and dug the toe of a ragged gym shoe into the dirt. "Lots of people miss her. She was beautiful. I mean, she is beautiful."

That might be why other people missed Roza, but it wasn't why Finn did.

Petey said, "She was nice, too. For a second I thought you were her."

"What?"

"I know, it's weird. She never rode a horse or anything. But she used to come and visit sometimes."

"She did?"

"Yeah. She liked the bees. And we would talk. I made her s'mores with extra chocolate. She liked chocolate. But she liked honey more. She would drink it right out of the jar."

Finn rubbed his fingers together, feeling the tug of the honey drying on his skin. "What did you guys talk about?"

"Stuff," Petey said. "None of your—"

"Beeswax, I hear you." But Finn was surprised. Not that Roza would want to visit Petey and talk about *stuff*, but that he didn't know about her coming here.

"People say the word 'nice' and they mean 'boring.' A lot of times nice *is* boring. But that's not what I mean. Roza was nice and not boring at all."

"Yeah," said Finn. Finn wondered if Sean knew that Roza and Priscilla Willis were friends. Maybe he did. Maybe Sean knew about all of Roza's friends. Maybe Sean knew Roza so well that he would have told Petey himself: make sure she gets extra honey before Roza ever had to ask. Maybe he'd give up his own honey so she could have more. Sean had done it for Finn. When their mother was still around, she would buy them ice cream bars from the freezer at the grocery—an almond bar for Sean, a Bomb Pop for Finn. But Finn hated the Bomb Pops; they stained his lips so red that people asked him if he was wearing his mother's lipstick, and the Rude boys would follow him around, making kissing noises. Sean told their mother, "Finn doesn't like Bomb Pops, I like Bomb Pops," and he would trade his almond bar for the Bomb Pop, even though almond bars were his favorite, even though his lips got red, too.

But thinking about Roza and about Sean and about Bomb Pops and the Rude boys made Finn's ribs ache. He said, "Got any more marshmallows?"

Petey tossed him a marshmallow and he caught it out of the air. He stuck it on the end of his stick and put the stick in the fire.

"So, I guess you haven't heard anything new about her," Petey said. "Roza, I mean."

"Not sure they'd tell me, considering they blame me."

"They'd tell you," Petey said. "Everyone knows how you felt—feel—about her."

"I don't think so."

"It's not a secret."

Finn wiped his forehead where the sweat was beginning to bead and only managed to wipe honey all over himself—sticky everywhere. "Okay, how do I feel?"

"What?"

"If it's not a secret, if everyone knows, why don't you tell me how I feel about Roza?"

Petey jerked slightly, as if he'd poked her, and her hair fell like a curtain over half her face. "Never mind."

"You want to talk about it, let's talk about it."

"I'm sorry I brought it up."

"No, really." He was tired of everyone believing they knew everything there was to know about him, as if a person never grew, a person never changed, a person was born a weird and dreamy little kid with too-red lips and stayed that way forever just to keep things simple for everyone else.

"Forget it," she said.

"Go ahead, tell me."

Petey's breath came out in an exasperated huff. "Fine. You're crazy about her. You and your brother both."

Finn's marshmallow flamed blue, skin blackening, crackling. It was perfect, and now he didn't want it. He dropped it into the fire. "Well, who am I to argue with all of Bone Gap?" He stood and moved to the horse. He tangled his fingers in her soft mane, then dragged himself over her back. He angled the mare away from the fire, away from Petey, but only had to lift the reins and the mare knew to pause. "You're right. All of you. I am crazy about Roza. Just not the way you think."

Finn

The Promise Ring

Nearly a year before, a fierce spring storm had woken Finn in the early hours of the morning. After the rain let up, he pulled on some clothes and went into the slanted red barn to see the swallows. A pair of birds had built a small nest of mud and grass in the highest beams, had themselves a family. Finn liked listening to their hysterical cheeping. He liked to watch as the birds swooped back and forth, scooping up crickets and dropping them into the gaping mouths of their chicks.

But when he swung the creaky door wide, he didn't hear the hysterical cheeping. He didn't see the swooping and dropping. He saw what he first thought was a bale of hay in the corner of the barn. But Sean hadn't bought any hay. And hay didn't have feet.

Finn crept over to the "hay." It was a girl, curled into a ball. She was wearing a ratty beige sweatshirt streaked with mud. A red flip-flop hung sadly off one big toe. The other foot was bare. Her hair was a spill of black liquid curls. Finn didn't know anyone in Bone Gap with that kind of hair. And he didn't know anyone from Bone Gap who would want to sleep in the barn, except maybe Charlie Valentine's chickens.

Right then, a swallow dived past the open door, twittering and squeaking loud enough to wake even strange girls sleeping in other people's old barns. The girl sat up. Saw Finn. Screamed. Or at least she tried to scream—her mouth opened nearly as wide as a chick's—but nothing came out. She slapped a hand over her mouth and scrabbled backward till she was pressed against the planks. Her chest was heaving as if she just couldn't get enough air. There was a bruise purpling one cheek.

"Are you okay?" Finn said.

She didn't answer. Just stared, her eyes as wide as her mouth had been, and so bright against her skin that it was painful to look at her. Then she seemed to gather herself. The heaving in her chest slowed. Her hand dropped away from her face. She struggled to her feet, wincing as she did, clutching the wall.

"Are you hurt?" Finn asked.

Again, she said nothing. She straightened as best she

could and limped past Finn toward the open door. He reached out to stop her, to tell her that it was okay, that he only wanted to help. But when he touched the skin of her elbow, she lurched from him, stumbled.

He reached for her again, but then thought better of it. He turned and ran to the house. He threw open the back door. Sean was standing at the counter by the coffeepot, willing it to brew faster. He was already dressed for work.

"What did I tell you about slamming that door?" he said.

"There's some girl in the barn. I think she's hurt."

Sean didn't ask any questions. Both he and Finn ran back to the barn. The girl was gone.

At the time, Sean was only four inches taller than Finn, but to Finn, it felt more like a foot. Sean stared down his nose at his brother. "Is this your idea of a joke?"

"No!" said Finn. "She was here." He pointed down. All around the barn, the storm had churned the dirt near to mud. In the wet earth, strange footprints tracked from the front door. A print of a bare foot alternating with the flat print of a flip-flop.

They followed the odd prints to the back of the barn. They followed them around the side of the barn. The girl was barely hidden in the green bushes. When she saw Sean, she screwed her eyes shut as if pretending he wasn't there.

Sean crouched next to her. "Hello."

She didn't answer.

"Can you tell me what happened? Are you injured?" Sean put out his hand. She knocked it aside.

"Okay," Sean said to Finn. "You stay with her. I'm going to go inside the house and call an ambulance. She should go to the hospital."

At the word "hospital" the girl shook her head violently.

"Yes," said Sean.

She shook her head again.

"Will you let me help you?"

She shook her head.

"I'm calling an ambulance."

He moved to stand, but she grabbed his hand, then dropped it as if it had been dipped in acid. But she swallowed. Nodded.

"Good," Sean said. "Now, I'm going to help you walk to the house."

More shaking.

Sean said, "Listen, I can't—"

The girl pointed at Finn.

"You want him to help you up?"

She nodded.

"Okay," said Sean. "Finn, lean down next to her. Try to lift her by putting your hand around her back and underneath her arm. But don't press too hard."

Finn shuffled close to the girl. He wasn't sure how old she was. Nineteen? Twenty? Hard to tell. Her breath was coming out in pants. He held out his hand, sure she was going to punch or bite him. But she let him put his arm around her back. She let him lift her from the ground. And she leaned on him as they walked slowly to the house. She was so small, he thought about trying to carry her instead, but decided that would not only terrify her, it would probably make him seem like the world's biggest tool.

When they got inside, Finn walked her into the front room and lowered her to the couch. She groaned a little as she stretched out, but her big eyes were wide and wary and tracked both Finn and Sean around the room. Sean got his black case and brought it over to her.

"Let's make sure you're not hurt," he said.

She shook her head wildly. Her black hair, silvered by dust on one side, stood out in a halo around her head. Again, she pointed at Finn.

"He's not a doctor. And he's only sixteen."

She jabbed her finger at Finn again and again, like someone tapping out a beat.

Sean sighed and motioned Finn over. "Help her sit up, will you?" Sean pulled a stethoscope from the bag. "Can you take off that sweatshirt?"

She gripped the top of the zipper.

"I can't listen to your heart very well through the sweatshirt."

She sank into the couch, shaking her head *no no no*.

"You could have broken ribs."

This time the girl didn't bother shaking her head. She glared hard enough to barbecue the nearest mammal; even Finn took a step back.

"Fine," said Sean, stuffing the scope back into the bag. "What about that wrist?"

The girl crossed her arms.

"Now, how is that going to help?" said Sean, almost to himself.

But the girl seemed to understand. She made a clucking sound with her tongue—sounding a lot like Charlie Valentine as she did it—and held out her wrist. It was badly bruised. Some of her fingernails were broken off and bloodied, as if she'd tried to scratch herself out of a box. Sean inspected them without touching them, and without comment.

"Can you flex your wrist?" said Sean. "Like this?" He held out his own arm and flipped his hand up, like a policeman telling someone to halt.

The girl flexed her wrist. She winced, but she could do it.

"Now, can you do this?" Sean dropped his hand limply, as if the hand itself had no bones in it.

The girl complied, still wincing.

"How about twirling it around?" Sean demonstrated this.

The girl could do this, too.

"Okay," said Sean. "Do you have pain anywhere else? What about those feet?"

The girl shook her head.

"No?" said Sean. "You've got at least two toes on your left foot that are probably broken, or at the very least probably hurt like hell. Maybe some on the right, too. Can't set toes, though. You should have some X-rays."

The girl said nothing.

Sean said, "I'll be able to scare up some crutches for you when I get to work. But it will hurt to use them if you've got bruised ribs, which I'm guessing you do. You'll have to rest for a while."

The girl pressed her bloody fingers to her temples, rubbed. Finn didn't want to say it, but he wondered if someone had beaten her up. A husband or a boyfriend or a random perv. Some asshole who Sean would have to—

"Are you sure I can't convince you to go to the hospital?" said Sean.

Again, a head shake.

Sean examined his own large hands. "Anyone we can call for you? Anywhere you want to go?"

The girl stared past Sean, lips pursing, as if there were a place, but she didn't know what to call it.

"I suppose," he began, flexing one hand, then the other, "I suppose you can go back to the barn, if you want. We're not using it. But we have an apartment." He pointed toward the back of the house. "It's nothing fancy, pretty much just a room and a bathroom, but it's clean, and it's vacant."

It had always been vacant. Their mother wanted to rent it, but she always asked for too much. And Sean never wanted to let strangers in the house before.

"Anyway," Sean said, "you could stay for a couple of days."

The girl sat frozen, squinting at Sean as if she could see into his mind, see his intentions. Finn, who often found himself frozen at the worst possible moments, felt bad for her. "We won't dive-bomb you."

She turned a quizzical gaze on Finn as if he were some creature that had yet to be identified by science.

The hot flush spread over him. "I mean, we won't dive-bomb you like the barn swallows will. That's what they do. To protect their chicks. So."

"Unless you have somewhere else to go," Sean said. "We can drive you wherever you want."

Finn thought of something else. "It's got its own entrance. The apartment, I mean. It's private. We won't bother you."

"Right," said Sean. He went to the kitchen, came back with a key. "We don't normally lock up. But you can." He held out the key, but then thought better of it. He gave the key to Finn.

A tear cleared a path down the girl's dirty cheek. She swiped it away. Then she reached out her hand, so that Finn could place the key in it.

"Okay, then," Sean said. "I'm Sean O'Sullivan. That's my brother, Finn."

The girl took a deep breath. "Roza," she said gravely, in an accented voice much deeper than Finn would have expected.

Sean sat back on his heels, the barest hint of a smile on his face, one palm pressed over his heart. "Nice to meet you, Roza."

At first, Roza hardly left the apartment, and only nibbled on the food that Sean would bring her in the mornings and evenings. Then, barely a week later, she limped into the kitchen as Finn was scratching around in the cabinet for boxes and jars. She took one look at the box in Finn's hand and frowned. She put it back in the cabinet. She rummaged in the fridge and pulled out some ground beef, an onion, and some cabbage. That night, they had stuffed cabbage with sweet-and-sour tomato sauce. The night after, pierogi, which was some type of dumpling. Every night, she cooked, making enough for a whole crew of poor motherless boys. When Sean reminded her she was supposed to be off her feet, she grunted and dumped more goulash onto his plate.

He said, "You don't have to cook for us."

Roza laughed, a loud, happy sound too big for her body. "I cook for me. You get what's left."

Finn remembered what Charlie Valentine said, that he might never figure out what made his brother happy. But already Finn knew. When Roza laughed, Sean grinned, too, like a kid getting a birthday present.

Eight months after Roza arrived, Sean showed Finn the tiny ring he bought—not an engagement as much as a promise—a ring that he tucked in a box in a dresser drawer. He was waiting for the perfect time to give it to her.

But he never had the chance. By the time he'd gathered the courage, Roza was stolen by a man who looked like everyone and no one at all.

Roza

Storming the Castle

Roza awoke, not in the bedroom with the blue chairs, the armoire, and the smashed bedroom window, but in some sort of museum.

At least, that's what it looked like. A roped-off room in a castle somewhere, a room made entirely of blocks of stone, icy and cold, even though a fire burned low in the hearth. A room where doomed queens went to die.

She sat up. She was wearing an elaborate gown of silk and brocade, so heavy that it felt like armor. Her wounded arms, arms she had cut on the window glass when she'd leaped to the tree, were wrapped in bandages. The bed in which she lay was canopied in red velvet with golden accents. The elaborately carved furniture and drapes matched the bed. On the walls hung portraits of dukes and kings and strange goddesses cavorting with goat-legged men.

The door creaked open. A maid carrying a pitcher curtsied, moved toward a washbasin in the corner of the room. She poured the basin full of water, then set the pitcher next to the basin. She curtsied again and pulled the covers away from Roza. Deft fingers untied the gown knotted at Roza's throat. When Roza brushed the maid's hands away, the maid barely seemed to notice. She curtsied a third time and took a few steps back.

"What is this place?" said Roza.

"Your home," replied the maid.

"This isn't my home."

The maid said nothing, merely bowed her head. She gestured to the basin.

Roza said, "There are drugs in the water. That's why I'm seeing things. I'm probably in a coma right now."

The maid frowned. "Drugs?" she said, as if she didn't understand the word.

Roza stood and walked over to the basin. She unwound the bandages and rinsed her raw hands and arms, splashed some water on her face. The maid brought her a length of cloth, which Roza pressed against her damp cheeks. More cloth to rewrap the wounds.

"Can we open a window?" said Roza.

The maid curtsied once more, went to the heavy drapes, threw them open to reveal a large square window cut into the stone. Sunlight flooded the dark chamber. Roza moved to stand by the maid.

"We are in the tower," said the maid. "Very far from the ground." She did not say this with any particular emphasis, but Roza knew she was being warned against jumping. As if she needed a warning.

Roza pressed her face against the wavy, uneven glass. This was, indeed, a place where queens were doomed to die. A castle. Complete with a moat and drawbridge. Guards on horseback patrolled grassy fields outside the moat and the woods beyond.

"What's in the moat?" said Roza.

The maid smiled. "Monsters."

Just as she had at the suburban house, Roza had the run of the castle. There was a throne room, a vast hall with a banquet table so long it could seat thirty, a library, a portrait gallery. Unlike the suburban house, however, the castle bustled with people. Maids, cooks, groundskeepers, guards. Cats prowled the kitchens, catching rats. Hooded birds darted and dived outside the windows at the behest of falconers perched on the ground. Here, at least, there were people to talk to, people who said, "Good morning," and asked what would please her for dinner. And though she never ate what they served, except for a few slices of bread and a goblet of water, she always thanked them; she was always grateful for the questions.

Except for this one: "Are you in love with me yet?"

She did not meet his eyes, instead watching a mouse scurry along the floor. It was a little scrap of a thing, this mouse, perhaps still a baby, on its first foray into the world. The mouse found a shred of cheese and turned it in its tiny paws as if attempting to discern its edibility.

"You'll love me one day," said the man. He was sitting on one of the thrones, the one decked out in black velvet, the one with the elaborate carvings of people screaming—in fear or in pain, Roza did not know.

"You like the castle," he said. This was not a question.

She slouched at the foot of the throne meant for her. "I could do without the crown," she said, touching the golden circlet on her head, weighty as the anvil on which the blacksmith hammered the horseshoes.

"You don't have to wear it. You don't have to wear anything you don't want to wear."

"Hmmm," said Roza. She had to be drugged. She had to be unconscious or dreaming. She was in a hospital right now, eyeballs darting beneath papery lids. She wondered if she would ever wake up, and if Sean would be waiting for her when she did.

The tiny mouse ate the shred of cheese, sniffed for

more. Roza kept an eye out for the castle cats. She adored the cats, but . . .

He said, "I could crush that mouse by just thinking about it."

"I'd rather you didn't."

"I know. Which is why I won't."

So stoic was his expression, so even his tone, so bland his smile that his moods were difficult to discern, but Roza was learning them. Today, he was happy. The servants were abuzz about a wager with some stranger who had come to the kingdom and bet he could defeat one of the most fearsome dogs with his bare hands. He did, and claimed the dog for his prize, only to return it later. "This dog is too much trouble! He tried to eat my mother. And he stinks," said the stranger. The icy-eyed man smiled and said he'd known all along the dog would best the stranger eventually. He had never lost a wager, he said, and he never would. How could he, when he could read people as easily as reading a story?

The mouse rose up on its hind legs, sniffing, then ran to the wall, disappearing into a nearly invisible hole in the mortar between the stones.

She said, "Why do you want me?"

"Why? Because you are beautiful."

"There are a lot of beautiful women."

"You are the *most* beautiful."

If she hadn't been drugged or dreaming or in a coma, she would have cried. She would have cried if any of this was real, or if she hadn't already cried herself out.

She didn't cry. She said, "That's not who I am."

He continued to stare and stare and stare, waiting for her to say more, perhaps, or perhaps nothing that came out of her mouth was as interesting to him as the mouth itself. She pretended he wasn't staring. She pretended his eyes weren't scouring her up and down, steel wool scraping her skin raw. Her vision blurred, time stretched and knotted, memories looping, bringing her back to where she had begun.

Roza grew up in Poland in a town so small it had no name. The inhabitants called it "here." They called everywhere else "there," as in "Why would anyone want to leave *here* and go *there*?"

Here, cows and horses roamed freely down streets indifferently paved with cobblestones. Along the main thoroughfare, the houses were built right at the edge of the road, as if huddling for warmth during the cold Polish winters, and hoping for company in summer. Neighbors would call to one another through their windows, exchanging news or insults or both.

Roza loved it. Roza's grandmother, on the other hand, said it was like living in a beehive, but with a lot less privacy. The grandmother—Babcia

Halina—always encouraged Roza to travel when she got old enough.

"Don't you want to see the world?" she'd say, rolling out the dough for pierogi and then spanking it with her palm.

"I see enough of the world," said Roza.

"You take after your father," said Babcia. "He never wanted to go anywhere either. Always sitting under that elm on the hill, playing that concertina and dreaming the days away. And what happened?"

Roza plucked a knuckle of raw dough and popped it into her mouth. "Lightning struck the elm."

"And it fell on him," Babcia said "If your father had left this place like I told him to, he'd still be here."

"Except my father wouldn't be *here*," said Roza. "He'd be *there*."

"He'd be somewhere."

"And where would I be?" said Roza.

"Right where you are now, stealing my food," Babcia said, slapping Roza's hands away. Babcia spooned some potato filling onto a circle of dough and pinched the edges into a neat purse. Later, she would fry the pierogi with onions right from the garden, and the very air would taste good enough to eat.

Roza said, "Why would I ever want to leave you?"

"I'm old. I'm cranky. You need young people."

Roza smiled. "There are young people right here."

"I hope you're not talking about that Otto Drazek again."

"Why shouldn't I talk about him? He's handsome, he's strong, he's—"

"A meathead," finished Babcia. "A golobki."

"He's not a golobki!" said Roza. "When there's a puddle in my way, he picks me up and carries me over it."

"So, he's not such a golobki," said Babcia. "You, I think, are the golobki."

"Babcia!"

"What?" said Babcia. "This pierogi has more to say than Otto Drazek." She held the pierogi to her ear and nodded knowingly. "In comparison to Otto Drazek," she announced, "this pierogi is a philosopher."

Roza looked down at her bare feet. "Otto carries me—"

"Over the puddles, yes, I heard you the first nine hundred times you told me. Don't you know that he hauls you around like a sack of cabbages to prove to his meathead friends how strong he is?"

"I like that he's strong," Roza said.

Babcia spooned more filling, pinched the edges of the dough. "Lots of boys are strong. *You* are strong."

"Are you going to make cookies today?"

"There will be boys who will tell you you're beautiful, but only a few will see you."

"You're not making sense, Babcia."

"How about finding yourself a smart boy? Or better yet, a kind boy, a boy who listens to what you have to say?"

Roza shrugged. She didn't know any boys like that.

"You need to have an adventure. Do something different. And maybe then you will meet a boy who listens. Who sees."

"I'm already doing different things," Roza said. And she was. She commuted two hours a day, three days a week, to her first year of university classes. She moldered in humid rooms with droning biology and composition professors. At night, she fell asleep on top of her books and woke up with the pages sticking to her cheeks. She loved it.

Babcia grunted. "You need to do *different* different things."

Roza smiled and hugged her grandmother, believing that university was enough of an adventure. And so was Otto Drazek. Until the day he was carrying her over a puddle and asked her to quit school and marry him.

She laughed. "Otto, we're too young."

"We're eighteen. Not too young," he said.

"I *like* school," she said.

"What can you learn in school that you don't already know?"

"A million things."

"Why do you need school when you already have me?"

"One has nothing to do with the other," she said.

"Who do you think you are?"

"What do you mean?"

"Is there someone else?"

"No!"

"What then?"

"You're squeezing me too tight."

"Sorry," he said, and dropped her in the puddle. When she would not quit school, he dropped her completely.

She didn't have time to be sad about it. After Otto, there was Aleksy, Gerek, Ludo. "Beautiful," they said. "So beautiful."

"Don't be too proud," said Babcia.

"But it's nice!" Roza said.

"It is nice. But a pretty face is just a lucky accident. Pretty can't feed you. And you'll never be pretty enough for some people."

But Roza was pretty. And lucky. Everyone told her so. She liked Ludo best because, though he told her she was pretty, he didn't try to carry her over puddles, because he was delicate and smart and beautiful, and he gazed at her with soft gray eyes like twin pools in which she could lose herself. It took months before she noticed that they only talked about the books he'd read and the movies he liked, that he never asked her a question, that he chided her for everything from her love of raucous polkas to how loud she laughed and how much she liked to eat. *Don't you worry you'll look silly? Don't you worry you'll get fat?* He poked her in the sides to show her where she was soft.

And when she found herself getting a little too quiet, a little too worried about how much she liked to eat, she told Ludo that they should take a break. Because he was so delicate, he sobbed like a baby. Because he was so delicate, he shook her hard enough to rattle her teeth. *Who do you think you are?*

She didn't tell her babcia. She didn't talk about how she'd cried, how she'd kissed him just so he would stop shaking her. How he'd touched her after. How she didn't want to kiss anyone else ever again, how the thought of kissing made her skin itch, made her bite the insides of her cheeks till they were bloody.

What she did tell her babcia: that she had applied and been accepted to an exchange program with an American university. Three months over the summer, living in a dorm in Chicago, far away from Otto, Aleksy, Gerek, Ludo, far away from everything and everyone she knew.

Babcia said, "America is like El Dorado! Mrs. Gorski's son told her that women go to the market wearing dresses made of fifty-dollar bills."

"Mrs. Gorski's son is a golobki," said Roza.

"True," said Babcia. "But I still like imagining dresses made of money."

Roza already regretted the decision. "I don't know why I signed up. I can't afford the airfare." And what would it change?

Babcia had held up a finger, disappeared into her bedroom. She returned with a cigar box. When Roza opened it, it was stuffed with zlotys.

"Babcia, where—"

"I save," she said simply. "I saved it all for you."

"But—"

"You will see the world. You will have love affairs with boys who see past a pretty face. You will be strong. You will call and tell me all about it. And then I will crow to the neighbors and make them all jealous."

Even as Roza packed her bag, she missed the smell of frying pierogi. She missed the rolling hills and the woolly sheep and the feel of brook water running cold over her feet. She missed the familiar drafty classrooms, the textbook pages sticking to her cheeks. And, as far as love affairs went, she would be happy if no boy ever looked at her again. She snarled her hair in a bird's nest and zipped her sweatshirts all the way up.

But Babcia sounded so sure, the way Babcia always did. Maybe it would be good for her to do a *different* different thing.

"Okay," said Roza. "But I'll be back soon. I promise, I'll be back."

The man gazed at her. "You don't need to go back. You have everything here."

Roza blinked, remembered where she was. Could the man hear her thoughts? No, he'd never given any hint of that. She must have spoken aloud.

She hadn't intended to tell him this story, or any story, but maybe she had. Maybe the loneliness was getting to her. Maybe *he* was getting to her somehow, wearing her out, wearing her down, gazing upon her with that indulgent smile, ice-chip eyes twinkling—twinkling! Was she so pathetic that she would ramble on, offering bits of her own story, bits of *herself*, like some second-rate Scheherazade?

Who do you think you are?

She turned away, training her eyes on a stained-glass window. But his stony fingers found her chin, brought her gaze back to his. She hated to look at him, hated him looking at her, the way his eyes mentally unbuttoned her clothes, mentally unzipped her skin. Her throat constricted as those fingers, cold, so cold, traced the length of her jaw, the curve of her ear, the hollows of her neck, where a pulse fluttered like a dying moth.

He'd said he wouldn't touch her, and she had

believed him. Now his fingers dragged across her flesh, and his icy eyes burned with a strange fire. Soon, she would be sitting on the throne next to him, that stupid crown on her head, stuffing her face with turkey legs, in the sad hope he wouldn't hurt her, as if he hadn't already.

The gown lay against her skin like a dress made of lead, pinning her to her seat. Her voice was barely a whisper when she said, "You told me you wouldn't touch me."

The fingers curved around her neck, strumming the delicate cords there. "Until you want it."

"I don't want it."

He released her neck, slid his hand down to spread his palm over her heart, pressing into the soft flesh. "You do."

She fought the bile that begged to choke her, begged to end this before it went any further. "Where is the beast?"

His hand stopped its downward slide. "Excuse me?"

"The beast. The one in the yard. The one at the other house. The hideous one that almost ripped out my throat."

"He was just doing his job. But I'm sure you don't want to see him again."

"Bring him to me. If you want to please me, that would please me."

"And why would that please you?"

"Because," she said. She leaned back in the chair as far as she could go, leaving his hand frozen in the empty space. *Because he's just as pretty as I feel.*

Finn

Sees the Fire

Sean stood in front of the open barn door. His large form casting a long shadow. "Since when do we have a horse?"

"Since four nights ago. Which you would know if you'd been home."

"Uh-huh," said Sean. "And how do you expect to feed her?"

"There are ten bales against the wall."

"And how do you expect to feed her after those are gone?"

"I'll figure something out."

"Right," said Sean. "And what's that?"

"This? This is a goat."

"A goat."

"Yes, for the horse. The Hasses gave him to me for twenty bucks because he won't stop eating the pants off the line."

"Great," said Sean. "I'll start saving up for new pants. Dinner in fifteen." He turned on his heel, stalked toward the kitchen door, then disappeared into the house.

Finn led the goat into the barn. "Goat, this is Horse. Horse, this is Goat. I'm still working on your names, but that's all I got for now."

"Meh!" said the goat, peering up at the horse. Suddenly, the goat leaped straight up till he was eye level with the horse. He did this three times. The horse's whinny sounded like a laugh.

"I can see you guys are going to be friends." Finn took a carrot out of his pocket, giving half to the horse and half to the goat. Then he searched for the cat. Calamity Jane wasn't in the yard. She wasn't in the hayloft, or under the bushes, or perched in the crook of her favorite tree. Her food, sitting in a bowl by the kitchen door, was untouched. It wasn't like her, and a nail of anxiety pierced his gut.

The nail turned into a screw when Charlie Valentine charged across the street toward Finn's yard. Charlie's long gray hair was rattier than usual, and he had forgotten to put in his teeth. He marched right by Finn and pounded on the back door till Sean came out again.

"Runaround Sue got out," Charlie said.

Sean said, "Maybe it's time for a coop, Charlie."

"The chickens don't like the coop."

"They don't seem to like the living room either."

"Are you going to help me find her or not?" said Charlie.

"Get your great-grandchildren to help you," said Sean. "There's a lot more of them. You'll cover more ground."

"Is that your idea of a joke?" Charlie said.

"I don't joke," said Sean.

"You used to," Charlie said. "When Roza was around. You used to joke and smile and play games. Now you're just a boring old pain in the ass. You need a new—"

Sean gestured to his uniform. "Let me get out of this first."

"I'll be in my yard," said Charlie. "Sometimes she likes to roost in the marigolds."

"Charlie!" Finn called after him.

"What?"

"How long do you need me to keep the horse?"

Charlie sucked his lips into his face. "What horse?"

"You gave us a horse."

"Now why would I do a stupid thing like that?" said Charlie, stomping across the grass toward his house.

Finn followed Sean into the kitchen. "I'll help you look for the chicken."

"It's getting late," said Sean. "Why don't you feed and water that horse? And check on Calamity Jane while you're at it. She's almost ready to have those kittens."

Finn didn't bother mentioning how long he'd been looking for Calamity already. "Okay."

"Got to work you while I can," Sean said. He peeled off his thin jacket. "You'll be going to college soon. Then I'll have to do everything myself."

Finn stood there, blinking in surprise. He had more than a year left before college, but Sean was ushering him out the door, like he couldn't wait for Finn to go. And then what would happen? Would he sell the house and the barn and puny parcel of land? Would he finally go back to school to become a doctor? Would he call Finn once a month, and send ten-dollar checks on his birthday? Would he talk about what a relief it was to be out of Illinois?

Finn opened his mouth to ask, but then Sean wound the jacket around his hand like a boxer protecting his knuckles. "What?"

Finn remembered sitting at the kitchen table with Sean, both of them trying to say the word "table" in Polish. Roza had said, "You have tongue like cow!" and laughed and laughed.

"What?" Sean said again.

He had tongue like cow, he had mind like cow. Dull, wordless.

Finn said, "I'm going for a ride."

But he didn't. Not right away. With Sean searching for Charlie's chicken, Finn took care of dinner: a box of macaroni mixed with a pound of ground beef and some peas. By the time Sean got back to eat, it was cold, but he didn't complain.

"Did you find Charlie's chicken?"

"No," said Sean.

"Charlie needs a coop."

"Hmmm," said Sean. He put a forkful of food into his mouth, chewed. Finn tried to think of something else to talk about. Their mother, Didi? No, talking about Didi made Sean seize up like a busted transmission. Their father? No, Sean would mutter something about their father being dead for years, about Finn being too young to remember, and what was the use of bringing it up? But Roza had asked about their parents once, and Sean hadn't seized up. He'd gone to his room and come back with a photograph, let her look from the photograph to Sean's face back to the photograph. To Finn, the photo looked like every other photo of every other family: two parents, two little kids, all the people smiling like nothing could ever go wrong. But Roza seemed to see something in the picture. When she offered it back to Sean and he grasped the edge, she didn't let go—for a moment, both of them holding on.

Finn took a deep breath, banished thoughts of family, thoughts of Roza. Chickens. Back to the chickens.

He said, "I guess a coyote could have gotten her."

Sean's fork stopped midway between his plate and his mouth. "Gotten who?"

"The chicken," Finn said.

Sean put the fork down. "Or maybe she just ran away. Her name was Runaround Sue. Maybe she was living up to it."

"Then maybe she'll come back," said Finn.

Sean got up from the table, scraped the remnants of his dinner into the sink. "If she ran, she'll keep on running."

Sean went to bed, which meant that he went to his room so as not to have to look at or talk to Finn anymore, and Finn set up shop at the kitchen table with his books and his tea and his Hippie Queen Honey, too knotted up inside to write essays about his biggest accomplishments, about his worst disappointments, about what his room would say about him if his room could talk.

At ten o'clock, when the jittery sky had finally settled itself into a streaky blue night, Finn checked the yard again. And the barn, and all the rooms of the house.

No Calamity.

He was sorry he'd ever said the word "coyote." He was sorry that Bone Gap seemed to be cursed somehow, big losses salted with tiny tragedies almost too insulting to bear. Years ago, the police chief's wife stuck a Post-it on the fridge to tell him she was leaving and that she was taking the dog. After Jonas had one too many ciders, he'd talk about how that dog visited him in dreams and told Jonas that he lived in the desert now, that the sand was hot on his feet, and it was getting harder to remember the smell of the rain.

Here was an essay: *You cannot keep chickens, you cannot keep cats, your dog lives in a trailer park in Tucson, Arizona, and has a new name.*

Finn went to the barn and climbed up on the horse, and though the goat was unhappy to be left behind so soon after making his new friend, Finn and the horse took off, charging past houses and fields, through streams and down roads. He'd ridden every night, but he hadn't been to Petey's for a week, not since she'd tried to tell him what he felt about Roza. Maybe he'd been wrong to argue, to insist that his own reasons were the things that mattered most. Maybe it didn't matter *how* he was crazy, only the fact that he was, the fact that he wanted someone to be crazy with him.

The horse allowed herself to be led behind the Corderos' farmhouse, and then into Petey Willis's beeyard. There was no fire by the hives; the yard was dark. Finn and the mare stood in the circle of hives, listening to the deep hum of the bees, feeling that hum in their skin. Instead of moving past the house, beyond the house, instead of charging around Illinois by way of South Dakota, the mare walked toward the house, toward the gray windows like closed lids. The horse sniffed and snorted, lingering by one of the windows. She tossed her head, mane shimmering in the moonlight.

"This one?" whispered Finn.

The horse snorted again. Finn leaned over and rapped on the window. When there was no answer, he did it again.

Thin hands shoved the curtains aside, and Petey's wide, angry eyes were framed in the window. She reached down and yanked up the sash. "What's going on? What are you doing?"

He didn't know what he was going to say until he said it.

"I can't find my cat."

She was wearing only a thin T-shirt and the kind of cutoffs that melted his brain, but she pulled on some boots and climbed out of the window as if she'd been doing this sort of thing for years, and maybe she had. He'd heard about the things that Petey did. And maybe, if he was honest with himself, it was one of the reasons he was here. But it wasn't the most important one. He was too happy to see her. Too interested in what she might say, no matter how much it stung.

She scrunched up her face, her fingers idly stroking the horse's nose. Then her face relaxed.

"Okay," she said, looking up at him. "Where to?"

"I thought maybe we'd go for a ride," Finn said, something else he hadn't known he was going to say.

"Does the horse know where the cat is?"

"She seems to know a lot of other things."

Petey gathered her hair and tied it into a knot at the nape of her neck. "You still don't have a saddle. How am I supposed to get up there?"

He glanced around the yard, spied a large rock at the corner of the house. He pointed to it. She nodded and took a few quick strides and a leap to land on top of it, smooth and graceful. He walked the horse alongside the rock, holding the reins in one hand. Petey looked at the space behind Finn and the space in front of him. Then she turned her face away, focusing on some star in the distance, as if looking at him directly was a little too hard.

She blew out her breath just like the mare. "Listen.

I'm sorry about the other day. Sometimes I'm … I should…"

The words tumbled out. "You should wear those shorts more often?"

Startled, she glanced down at herself. At first he thought it had been the wrong thing to say, the kind of thing one of the Rude boys would have said right before they told her she had a rockin' body but a butterface, but then Petey looked up and smiled with half her mouth.

She smiled with both sides when he said, "Here's a college essay idea: Describe the shorts that changed your life in the form of a poem."

"I like it." She put her hands on her hips. "So?"

"So, what?"

"Where's my poem?"

"Maybe someday I'll write you one."

She grabbed ahold of the horse's mane and swung one leg over the horse's neck, faltering only for a moment till Finn steadied her with a hand on her hip. She settled against him, her back to his chest. She didn't say anything more as he put one arm on each side of her and urged the horse forward.

The mare walked quietly from the yard, as if she was trying very hard to be sneaky, and began a gentle trot as they passed the Corderos' farmhouse. Each step of the mare brought Petey closer, until she was fitted to

Finn like a puzzle piece, her head under his chin. He hadn't realized how much of her height was in her legs, smooth bare legs that glowed gold in the moonlight.

The mare splashed through the stream, peppering her riders with droplets of cool water, then headed for the cemetery, which was clouded over with a strange silvery mist. Older than Bone Gap itself, the cemetery had a couple of stones dating back to the early 1800s. Once, Miguel had surveyed the rows and rows of stones and said, "Everyone looks the same when they're dead." But Finn didn't think that was true. Each stone was different. Some of the older ones canted crazily, like crooked teeth, the names and dates eroded from decades of sun, wind, and snow. The more recent stones were polished granite in various colors. Dark gray, black, and, in the case of Mrs. Philander "Muffin" Gould (1903–1982), Pepto-Bismol pink.

But now the silvery mist muted all the colors of the grave markers, the uneven ground dancing with strange shadows. The mare stopped, letting them survey the stones, the willow tree dangling its fingers over the rooftops of the two small mausoleums, the dusky grove of poplars beyond.

"Spooky," murmured Petey.

"Hmmm," said Finn, who had discovered that if he turned his face a little bit, his lips would brush her hair.

"Look!" breathed Petey, and he glanced up and

saw one of the shadows flickering, gathering scraps of moonlight and cloud to assemble itself into a vague shape that drifted over the tops of the stones.

"Are you seeing this?" Petey said.

"Yes."

They watched the shape glide through the still air, passing so closely that Petey shivered. The shape slipped out of the cemetery and into the darkness beyond.

"Was that a ghost?" said Petey.

"A cloud, probably. Fog," said Finn.

"I think it was a ghost."

"Maybe it's going to Miguel's house. Maybe it's hungry."

And maybe it was a ghost, maybe it was hungry, but if it was, the mare wasn't troubled. She ambled past the cemetery to the unclaimed land beyond. The field should have had rich green grass springing up around the horse's knees, it should have been wild with bluebells and violets and larkspur, bayberry and lily and clover, but the field burned gold in the thin light of the moon, and Finn wondered why the grass and the flowers seemed to be dying. Surely that was a trick of the eye or the mind or the fact that Petey Willis was warm against him and smelled like a million things you'd want to eat and this was jumbling his thoughts, confusing him, making it hard to pay attention to anything but her.

The mare trotted across the golden field and into a deep still forest, a forest that Finn didn't remember. Crickets whirred and owls hooted and the ground crunched under the horse's feet. They seemed to be at the mouth of a very long path through the dark wood, a path through a wood that he had never seen before.

"What is this place?" Petey said.

"I don't know."

And he didn't. But the mare seemed to know, as she seemed to know so, so many things, too many things for a horse to know, and she moved from a walk to a trot, a trot to a gallop. Finn drew his forearms in tighter so that they brushed against Petey's waist. If she thought he was getting too close, she didn't say. She didn't say anything about his lips in her hair, or the fact that his breathing had gone ever so slightly ragged.

And then the trees blurred as the mare ran faster and faster. At first Finn tried to keep an eye on the path in front of him, but it was too dark and the horse was running too fast. He tried to keep his eyes on the moon, but it blazed too hot and too whitely bright, and it etched its image across his vision. He looked around, but what he saw made no sense—trees bleeding into clouds, and the clouds parting for winged lions carved from stone, and the stone lions charging down a staircase made of glass, and the glass shattering into fire.

The mare ran all the way through the forest and out the other side, and suddenly the sounds of the forest were replaced by the crashing of horseshoes on rock. The mare thundered across a flat gray plain that Finn saw too late, too late, was the edge of a mountain, and then the mare was leaping into the air, and they were falling over the cliff, until they felt the wind catch them, carry them in its soft, dark hand as if the horse and two riders were nothing but a feather that wended its way down the mountainside.

And since none of this could be real, Finn closed his eyes and held on to Petey and wondered if she could feel his heart beating against her back, if she noticed his arms wrapped around her waist, if the moon had etched itself upon her otherworldly eyes, if the moon could ever be full enough to fill them.

Hours later, days or weeks or months later, the mare's hooves again found the ground, and they were no longer falling off a mountain or flying through the forest, they were trotting back across the golden field, through the now pitch-black cemetery, past the Corderos' dozing stone house, and into the beeyard, the only sounds the sounds of Finn's breathing, Petey's breathing, the mare breathing.

When they reached Petey's window, Finn released the reins and slid from the horse's back, knees loose and watery, hands trembling. Petey put her own hands on Finn's shoulders as he helped her down. They stood there in the hushed dark of the yard, struggling for words.

Finally, Petey said, "I'm sorry we didn't find your cat."

Finn decided not to press his luck, not to do anything but say *Thank you*, say *Good night*, say *Maybe tomorrow*, say *Did you see the fire?* say *Did that just happen?* but when her fingertips traced down his arms to his wrists, when she turned her face up to his, lips parted, breath sweet, there didn't seem to be anything to say, anything to do, but kiss her.

And so he did.

Somehow, Finn got home, stabled and watered the mare, patted the goat, stumbled into the house. Instead of sitting vigil at the kitchen table, as he had done sixty-whatever gray and troubled nights, he dropped into his bed and careened into sleep, his feet jerking as if he were still riding with Petey through a forest that existed only in dreams. But only a few hours later, thin cries woke him.

Finn threw back the sheets, disoriented. He lurched toward the open window, not sure whose name to call out.

Another sharp cry.

Finn glanced around. Then he dropped to his knees and peeked under the bed.

Calamity.

And six tiny kittens, not much bigger than the mice Calamity was such a calamity at catching.

"It's all right," he whispered to the squeaking, squirming pile of them, nosing their mother's belly. "I'll look after her, she'll look after you. You'll see."

He crawled back into bed. *You'll see, you'll see, you'll see.*

Roza

Just Like the Rest of Us

The beast that had prevented Roza from escaping the yard of that horrible suburban house was the largest, ugliest, most miserable dog that Roza had ever seen. His teeth were long and yellow, his tail a spiked lash, his eyes the color of tombs. He growled every time she moved, erupted into furious snarls if she dared walk from one end of the room to the other, barked till he was hoarse if she lingered too long by the doors or windows.

The castle maids and guards kept their distance from Roza and her ferocious new companion. But that night, when the cook asked if she would like some eel pie for dinner, Roza said, "Yes. Thank you very much."

The cook was so delighted to have someone to cook for, she prepared *two* eel pies. Roza took the dog and the pies to her chambers in the tower, broke the pies into pieces, and offered them to the dog. The dog turned his bloodshot eyes up at her, confused by the offer, by the kindness.

"It's okay," she said.

He took one bite, gulped, looked up at her again.

"Go on. It's all for you."

He ate one pie, then the other, and belched contentedly. She sat in a chair by the fire, and the animal laid his head across her ankles and drooled on her bare feet. The darkness came, and he sprawled out at the foot of the huge bed, taking up more than half of it with his mangy, flea-bitten form. And though she might have to have these sheets burned in the morning, and possibly have to bathe in lye herself, it was nice to have a friend.

Because of his matted, reddish coat, Roza decided to call him Rus.

She didn't mind talking to Rus, as the dog didn't gaze upon her with that horrible, indulgent smile, the dog didn't touch her with cold fingers, the dog didn't trace the lace on the bodice of her gown and chuckle when she shivered and jerked away, the dog didn't the dog didn't the dog didn't the dog didn't.

Roza had the cook make eel pies every night. After the dog had devoured them and put his great shaggy head across her ankles or in her lap, she would tell him a story. She would say, "I grew up in a village so small that it didn't have a name." Or, "Before the day I boarded the flight to America, I had never been on a plane. Never been so far from home. Never been so close to the sun."

On the plane, there were other students in the program giggling and turning around in their seats in the rows in front of her, but Roza's eardrums felt like overblown balloons, her heart hammered in her chest, and her tongue was heavy as stone in her mouth. Was she sick? Was she scared? If someone had asked, she wouldn't have been able to answer. All around the plane, the vast blue sky shimmered in the sunlight. Far below, the gray ocean defined the word "forever." Everything felt both huge and small, as if the plane were hanging from a string held by the hands of gods.

Roza was grateful when they finally landed. On stiff and frozen legs, she followed the other students off the plane and into customs, trying to keep her eye on them as they were split into different lines. Why hadn't she talked to one of these people on the plane? Maybe they knew where they could find their bags. Maybe they knew where the buses were. Maybe they didn't feel so sick or so scared, as if they'd already handed their fates over to someone else without even realizing it.

Her line was slow, and then the customs officer stared at her passport for a long, long time, and at her face even longer. She knew some English, though her accent was heavy. She said, "Yes? Is okay?"

"You're Polish."

"Yes."

"You don't look Polish."

"Sorry?"

"Polish girls are blond."

She didn't know what to say to that. She bit her lip.

The man smiled in a secret way, as if he had not meant the smile for anyone else, not even for her. He said, "Are you a model?"

Heat crept up her neck into her cheeks. Was he joking? "No, no. I come for study."

"Who needs school when you could be a model?" He held the flat of his hand over her papers, trapping them there, trapping *her* there. She glanced back at the line of people behind her, but nobody was watching. The last of the other students was disappearing through the doorways in front of her. She wanted to peel back the man's fingers till he yelled. She wanted to punch him. She wanted to cry. But this was a grown man and some sort of official, and she didn't dare say a word. Instead, she waited with her burning cheeks and her own dumb smile until he slid her papers back to her, rough fingertips briefly brushing her wrist.

She grabbed the papers and ran, rubbing her arm on her jeans hard enough to start a fire. But she needn't have worried about losing the other students. They were too boisterous to miss, loitering around one of the baggage carousels, laughing and talking as if they'd known one another for years. Roza scooped her ancient flowered bag off the belt and trailed the students to a man who held a placard with the name of the university written on it. He gathered them, counted them—there were a dozen from Poland, another dozen from other places in Europe—and took them out the door into the surprisingly wet and chilly May air. He pointed to a waiting bus. Roza dropped into a seat next to a girl wearing a sad puppy expression on her face.

"Isn't it horrible?" said the girl.

"What?"

"This place."

Roza rubbed her arm where the official had touched her. "I don't think I've been here long enough to decide."

"I have," said the girl. Her name was Karolina, her horrible parents had made her come, she'd had to leave her boyfriend behind, she hadn't had lunch, she was starving, it was *cold*, she said, eyes welling, and it was all too horrible for words. Horrible, horrible, horrible.

Roza dug around in her backpack and pulled out a paper bag. She opened the bag and found the babka she'd bought two airports ago in Poland. Not too stale. She offered it to Karolina.

Karolina sniffled and took the bread studded with fruit. "I haven't had this in ages."

Behind them, the English words rang out, so exaggerated that they managed to make the speaker sound that much more Polish: "Omigod, you're eating *carbs*?"

Karolina dropped the bread into her lap as if she'd just been caught with heroin.

Roza turned around. Behind them, a pretty but brutally skinny girl blinked heavily lined eyes. "What? Carbs will make you fat."

"She's hungry," Roza said.

"So?" said the girl.

Roza turned back to Karolina. "You didn't have lunch."

Karolina shook her head and held the babka out to Roza. "It's okay. You eat it."

Roza shrugged, took a bite. The girl behind her sang, "Fat!"

Roza thought being fat was better than looking like an angry chicken carcass boiled for angry soup, but said nothing more. Which was lucky, because the brutally skinny chicken carcass turned out to be her new roommate.

Her name was Honorata. Honorata's parents didn't make her come to America, she'd demanded to come. And now that she was here, she had twelve weeks to find a rich boyfriend who would buy her lots of jewelry. If Roza wanted a boyfriend, Honorata said, she better start wearing some makeup. And buy a decent pair of jeans. And get rid of the ratty sweatshirt. And stay out of the sun; she already looked like some kind of Egyptian.

"I like these jeans," Roza said.

"Don't tell me you're here to study," said Honorata.

"I am. Botany."

"Botany? As in *plants*? What are you going to be, a potato farmer?" Honorata threw open their door. "Hey, guys! My roommate wants to be a potato farmer!"

Roza pushed past her into the hallway.

"Where are you going?" Honorata said.

Roza said, "I'm going to see if Karolina wants some potatoes."

She found Karolina's room, four doors down. Karolina was sitting on her unmade bed, texting her boyfriend, and crying.

"I'm going to get us some food," Roza said. "You'll feel better after you eat something."

"What *kind* of food?" Karolina said. "Who knows what they have here? Bugs? Bats? Snails? *Carbs*?"

Roza rolled her eyes but forced her voice to remain cheerful. "Don't be silly," she said. "They have McDonald's, just like in Kraków."

Outside, it was nothing like Kraków. The buildings were squat and boxy. Trash cans overflowed with fast-food wrappers and soda bottles. She'd thought all of Chicago was going to be made of marble and metal and glass, like something out of a sci-fi movie. Where were the sleek new skyscrapers? Where were the women in dresses made of fifty-dollar bills?

Never mind that. Where were the trees? Where was the grass? She thought of the rolling hills of her village, the chocolate-eyed cows, the woolly sheep, the chatter of her neighbors, the smell of Babcia's cooking, and felt a wave of loneliness so strong it almost knocked her down.

The smell of Babcia's cooking. She found herself in front of a small grocery from which came the odors of garlic and sauerkraut. Roza almost burst into tears herself when she saw the sign in the window: mówimy po polsku tutaj. We speak Polish here.

She bought a large container of beet soup, a green salad, sauerkraut, roasted potatoes, and Polish sausages warm from the pan. Roza brought the bundle back to Karolina. "Look!" Roza said. "No carbs!"

"Potatoes have carbs."

"Yes, but only delicious ones."

Karolina wiped her eyes and put away her phone. They spread the food out on the desk. The smell of garlic and beets drew in the other exchange students, who couldn't keep themselves away from something that smelled so much like home.

Classes began. Roza's took place in the biology department's greenhouse with a gray-faced professor visiting from central Illinois. She learned about the effects of carbon dioxide on different plants, the medicinal properties of hops and licorice and red clover. Not the same as being outside, hands in the earth, sun on her back, but better than being stuck in a classroom. At night, she cooked soup and sausage and pierogi on a small hot plate she'd smuggled into the dorm room. She cooked so much that the Polish girls started to call her "Mama." The boys did, too, some of them sweetly and shyly, some of them smacking it with their lips. Which drove Honorata crazy. "What's so special about *her*?"

One of the boys, Balthazar—"Bob," as he introduced himself—was a big golden boy with big blue eyes. Most of the girls could barely keep from drooling in his presence. Didn't matter that he couldn't keep those blue eyes off everyone's breasts. Didn't seem to matter that all he did was brag about his part-time job with his cousin, who had been in the country for five years. "Big money.

All the rich Americans want us to fix their houses. They can't do it themselves. Too stupid."

With his big money, Bob bought a rusty old car that looked as if it had been painted with brown house paint and invited Roza, Karolina, and Honorata for a ride. She didn't want to go, she didn't like Bob, Bob was a golobki, but Honorata said Roza sounded like someone's cranky grandmother, and she should shut up and stop ruining things for everyone else. Inside the old car, it smelled of old goat and moldy sausage (or moldy goat and old sausage, Roza couldn't be sure). Or maybe it wasn't the car at all. Maybe it was Bob. He'd made sure that she had the front seat, but Roza curled away from him like a flower seeking the sun as everyone else rattled away in Polish.

"I have second cousins here, too," Karolina said.

"Yeah?" said Bob. "Where do they work?"

"I think one of them works at a meat company. He said he could get me a job if I want to stay longer."

"A meat company? What, like making kielbasa?"

"I guess," said Karolina. "I don't know what they make. I'd work in the office. I'm going to be an accountant."

Bob laughed. "Girls aren't so good at math."

Roza clucked her tongue. "Who told you *that*?"

Bob laughed again. "Are you going to be an accountant, too?"

Honorata leaned forward, breathed in Bob's ear. "Roza likes to play in the mud."

Bob waved his hand by his head as if shooing gnats. "That could be fun."

"I study plants," Roza said.

Honorata said, "She's taking a class in magic."

"Don't be stupid," said Karolina. "She's studying herbal remedies."

Honorata laughed. "Yeah. Remedies for hot flashes. She's going to help all the dried-up old ladies."

"Is that what you're doing?" Bob said.

Roza wondered what she was doing in this car with these people. She and Karolina could have gone to a movie. She could be back in the greenhouse listening to the gray-faced professor drone on about his plants. "Aspirin came from the bark of a tree," she said, "so why not other medicines?"

"It's nice you're helping the old ladies," said Bob. "They're not much good for anything."

While they idled at a red light, a sad man with a dirty beard and a cup limped to the driver's side. Bob rolled down the window and spat: "Get a job!"

Roza rubbed her head, wished she had some willow bark, decided there wasn't enough willow bark in the world. "Why did you yell at him?"

"Because he's a bum," Bob said in Polish. "This is America. You work for your money."

"What if he was sick?" she said.

"He looked healthy enough to me," Bob said.

"He looked sad."

"You're kidding me."

Roza was about to say that no, she wasn't kidding, the man really did look sad to her, but she realized that Bob wasn't interested in what she had to say.

He said, "I work hard. I bought this car myself."

"It's a very nice car," she said.

"It's a piece-of-garbage car, but it's *my* car, and that's the point. And don't think I won't get a better one soon, because I will."

"Absolutely," said Roza. "Probably a Mercedes."

He stared at her, wondering if she was playing with him. He must have decided that she was sincere, because he said, "This is America." He stepped on the gas, and the old tires squealed in protest. "I want a Mustang."

He asked Roza out for dinner. She said, "I'm sorry, I have a late class." He asked her out to the movies; she said, "I have homework." He asked her to go dancing; she said, "No, thank you, I have to call my grandmother." It was too hot for sweatshirts, but she wore hers anyway, zipped to her neck.

He caught her in the dorm hallway, backed her against the wall. The meaty goat smell came off him in sickening waves. Up close, his eyes looked watery and gray like Ludo's.

"What's wrong with you?" he said. "Why don't you wear a dress or something?"

"I wear what I want."

"You think you're too good for us?"

"Who is *us*?" she said.

"Me. You think you're too good for me?"

"No!" she said.

"Then prove it."

She shoved at him. She was strong, but he was stronger. "I don't have to prove anything!"

He loomed over her, stinking, staring. She turned her face away, chewing the inside of her cheek so hard, her mouth filled with blood. The professor had told her about doll's eyes, another name for the white baneberry that could cause cardiac arrest. She wished she had a handful to stuff down his throat.

"Bitch," he said. "You're nothing but a stuck-up bitch."

The next time Roza tried to get into her dorm room, she found the door chained from the inside. She waited in the lounge for an hour before trying the door again. This time, the door flew open and Bob charged past her, bumping her hard enough to knock her off balance.

Honorata sat on her bed, eyes dark and unreadable, lipstick smeared like a wound.

"I told you he was horrible," Roza said, only recognizing the cruelty of her words as she said them.

Honorata whipped a pillow across the room. "Go to hell!"

"Did he hurt you?"

"What do you care?"

Roza picked up the pillow, laid it on Honorata's bed. She opened her books on her desk, pretended to study.

Much later, after she'd shut off the light, Honorata whispered, "You're no better than the rest of us," voice so thin and tight Roza thought it might snap. "Someday, someone will show you."

Roza was better. *They* were better, even angry Honorata. Roza could have been any of them, every one of them. The story hadn't changed. Only the costumes. Only the players.

One of the benefits of the costume: concealment. At dinner in the castle, when the icy-eyed man stopped staring at her long enough to take a sip of wine from his jeweled goblet, Roza slid a knife from the table, tucked it in the folds of her gown.

June
Strawberry Moon

Finn

Lost

Since they'd started the job, Finn and Miguel had replaced more than a dozen fence posts, spliced hundreds of yards of wire, and still it was as if they'd barely begun. Each day, the sun grew hotter and more punishing, too hot for June, and the fence seemed to get longer and longer, like a living thing snaking out across the prairie. Now they did strip off their shirts, for no other reason than to stay cool; their backs and ribs were marked where the fencing wire had whipped and stung them. They were extra careful with the barbed wire that they installed on the top and bottom of the fence, wire that could easily tear them open.

After only two hours of work, Finn took a break to pour a bottle of water over his head.

"Hey," said Miguel. "You're not going to faint on me, are you?"

"Sorry. Not getting much sleep."

"I heard."

"What did you hear?"

Miguel knotted off a section of fencing wire, tossed the clamps and pliers to the ground. "I heard you weren't getting much sleep."

"Come on," said Finn.

Miguel took a drink of water. "It's Bone Gap. People talk."

"Which people?"

"All of them," said Miguel. "You might be wandering around in the dark, but we can all hear the hoofbeats."

"I like to ride."

"No shit. Where do you go?"

"Nowhere."

"Nowhere?"

"Wherever the horse wants."

"Awesome."

"Seriously, we just ride around. It's not a big deal."

Miguel nodded. He looked at the ground, at the shovel, at Finn, everywhere but the road.

Finn said, "Is she here today?"

"Who?"

"Mrs. Lonogan," said Finn dryly. "Amber? Pink bicycle? Chews her own hair?"

"Oh, her," Miguel said.

Finn laughed.

Miguel grabbed his shovel and resumed digging. "Fuck you."

"Fuck *you*."

Miguel tossed a shovelful of dirt at Finn's feet. "I wouldn't want to make your horse jealous."

"Maybe I should bring the horse tomorrow. She can take you to see Amber, since you don't have the balls to go on your own."

"Don't rush me, dude. I'm waiting for the perfect time."

"Is that what you're doing?"

That was the one thing Finn couldn't do: wait. Every evening, when the darkness had settled over Bone Gap, Finn sneaked out to the barn. And every evening, the night mare took him to Petey's house. Sometimes Petey was waiting in the beeyard, a fire lit, the bees humming soft and low. Sometimes the beeyard was still, and he would ride up to the house and rap on her window. She would emerge like a butterfly from a chrysalis.

When she met him in the beeyard, they would roast marshmallows, dip the s'mores in a jar of Hippie Queen Honey, and talk about the grind of high school and how they'd survive their last year; Calamity Jane's six kittens; Finn's fickle mom; Petey's deadbeat dad; silent, angry Sean; Charlie Valentine and all his alleged dates with mystery women no one had met; the Rude boys; the weirdest college essays they could think of: *Describe someone who has had the biggest impact on your life using only adverbs. Explain a moment that changed your worldview, written in recipe format. Tell us how you feel about Thursday—is it better or worse than Tuesday?* And if Petey's words and moods occasionally stung, her lips were always soft.

When Petey wasn't waiting in the beeyard, when he knocked upon her window and she climbed from the house, they would ride the mare past the stream, across the giant meadow, through the forest that wasn't there, over the cliff with the wind that caught them in its soft, plush hands. Hours later, they would return, breathless and weak-kneed and trembling, not understanding where they'd been, but knowing they'd been somewhere too impossible to exist. Finn would pull Petey into his arms, and he would kiss her until they were both so dazed they could barely walk.

Finn was still dazed. A perpetual daze.

To Miguel, he said, "Petey Willis."

"What?"

"Where I've been going."

Miguel nodded.

"You're not surprised."

"Surprised that she's into you maybe," said Miguel. "Petey, huh?"

"Petey," Finn said.

"You didn't give up."

"I guess not."

"Well, she's not boring, I'll give you that. Hot in her own way. I can see it. So, what do you guys do?"

"We hang out."

"You hang out. And what else?"

"We talk."

"Okay. About what?"

"Stuff. I don't know. College essays. It's like a running joke. We talk about the strangest possible essay questions and—"

Miguel rested his forehead on the handle of his shovel. "Dude, I haven't had a girlfriend in months. And when was the last time you had one? You have to get enough play for both of us. And you can't get any play if you're talking about *essays.*"

"Petey and Amber are friends, maybe I could—"

"Amber likes *you*. A lot of girls like you."

"No, they don't."

"There are a bunch of them sitting on the side of the road watching us right now."

"Watching isn't the same as . . ." Finn trailed off. "I thought you didn't know who was sitting on the side of the road right now."

"There are *nine* of them."

"Why are there nine girls sitting on the side

of the road? Provide your answer in the form of a question."

"Huh?"

"Never mind."

"You need to lay off the books. We have to get through our last year of high school first. We have to get through the summer."

Finn didn't want to get through the summer. He wanted to fall into it, hunker down and stay for a while. He'd already laid off the books, already missed the first of the college entrance tests, already didn't care. More and more, Finn could manage neither the s'mores nor the horse rides, because there was Petey, bee-eyed and lush and way too much to take in at once, and he couldn't wait until a quiet moment over the fire or the end of a wild and impossible ride—he had to kiss her right away, and keep kissing her to prove to himself she wouldn't disappear like so many other things had.

"Come out with me," he asked her one night, as she pressed him down into the grass, small fingers tracing his ribs through his T-shirt, breath warm on his neck.

"Out where?" she said.

"Anywhere. The diner, the movies, *out* out. Where people can see us. Where I can see you."

"You can't see me now?"

"Yes, but . . ."

"But what? Who cares if anyone else sees us?"

He couldn't explain what he was scared of, it sounded too strange—that he worried she wasn't real either. But if they were seen somewhere, the talk of the people of Bone Gap, the chatter, the opinions, the endless considerations, would make it so he could believe. He wanted to believe in her.

But that was nothing he could say. So he said, "I just want to spend more time with you, that's all."

She laughed. "If you spend any more time here, you'll have to move in. My mom is cool, but she's not that cool."

It was precisely because he didn't want Petey to vanish that Finn thought he should make an appearance at her house while there was still daylight, maybe say hello to her mother, be a man, rather than sneaking around like some dumb horny teenager (even though he was a dumb horny teenager). He left the mare in the barn and took the main road to Petey's house, keeping out of the way of cars and trucks, stopping traffic to allow a duck with a parade of ducklings cross the street, ignoring the impatient drivers leaning on their horns.

He turned down the lane toward Petey's house, set some ways back from the main thoroughfare. One of the Willises' dogs lay sleeping in the middle of the pavement. He had a name, but no one used it. Everyone called this dog the Dog That Sleeps in the Lane. No impatient driver could impress this dog; he moved for no one and nothing. You drove around him or you turned back to wherever it was you came from.

"Hello, Dog," Finn said.

The Dog That Sleeps in the Lane lifted his head, eyed Finn as if he was nothing but a dumb horny teenager, and went back to sleep.

Finn approached the house, thinking too late that he should have brought something for Petey's mom—flowers? candy? a signed declaration of only slightly dishonorable intentions?— when he saw the smoke curling over the roof of the house. Strange that Petey would have a fire burning in the daytime and in June, but then Petey had used a smoker to calm the swarm at the café. He made his way around the side of the house, hoping he wasn't walking right into another swarm. But instead of a swarm, Finn walked into a massacre. Or rather, an autopsy. Mel Willis had one of her hives partially dismantled. From a nearby crab apple tree, a small ball of confused bees hung like a ragged skein of yarn. Both Mel and Petey were wearing white bee suits and hats with nets. The air smelled of ashes and honey.

Mel, recognizable in her gear only because she was even taller than her daughter, said, "Hey, Finn! Not too close, okay? We've got some disoriented bees here."

"I'll stay back here if you want," Finn said. He remembered Miguel's dad after he'd been stung dozens of times, red and swollen all over, Sean scraping the stingers out of his skin with a credit card.

"You can come closer than that. Priscilla's got the smoker," she said. "But move very slowly, okay? Bees are myopic. Anything large and still looks blurred to them; anything quick or jerky gets their attention."

Finn slowed his movements and stopped some feet away from the beehive and keepers. From where he stood, he could see at least one of the problems with the hive. Large black bugs had burrowed through some of the combs.

"Roaches," Mel said.

As if on cue, a roach fell to the grass. It was big enough to tow a tractor. "Cool," said Finn.

"What's cool about it?" Petey snapped. So maybe Petey was a little spikier during the day. Or when her bees were pissed.

Mel sighed. "Don't yell, Priscilla. You'll upset the bees."

"They're already upset!"

"Thank you for the update," said Mel. "Now keep your voice down, please."

Petey folded her arms across her chest, the smoker puffing huffily for her.

"Did the roaches attack the bees?" Finn asked.

"Roaches can find a way into any beehive, but a strong colony can deal with them. I don't know what happened to this one, and so fast, too. It's one of my best hives. Or it was."

"So why did they swarm?" Finn said.

"Lack of space or an aging queen."

"Or because the bees feel like it," muttered Petey.

"If there's no space in the hive, the old queen lays some eggs, which are then fed something called royal jelly so that they grow into new queens," Mel said. "Before those new queens emerge, the old queen flies off with some of the workers to form a second hive."

"Maybe it wasn't too crowded. Maybe something disturbed the bees," Petey said, in a softer voice this time.

Mel said, "Like what?"

"I don't know," said Petey. She tilted her masked face at the sky, as if the clouds could tell her. "In any case, if they planned to swarm, or even if the bees planned to replace a sick queen, the hive would have a new one. We've got empty queen cups—new queen cells—but no queens."

Finn squinted at the exposed comb, a few bees buzzing and crawling on it. "Is that bad?"

"A queenless colony can't survive," said Mel. Like Petey, she tilted her face at the sky. "Let's hope a new queen is on her mating flight and that she'll be back soon. In the meantime, we'll clean out the roaches, replace a couple of the frames, hope for the best. After that, we'll try to get those bees into a new home." She nodded at the bee ball hanging from the tree branch.

Finn helped Mel and Petey knock the roaches from the old frames. Mel replaced two of the frames with fresh ones that still smelled of wood sap. A single bee alighted on Finn's arm. He was too fascinated to be nervous. "I can feel her feet."

Petey snorted. "Her? That's a he."

"How can you tell?"

"The ginormous eyes that practically take up his whole head. The girls don't have those kind."

"But most bees are girls, right?"

"They keep a few drones around for fun," said Mel, grinning behind her mesh. Petey aimed the smoker at her, and Mel put her hands up.

"I know, I know, stop embarrassing you," said Mel. To Finn, she said, "She's so squeamish."

"Mom," Petey said.

Mel said, "Fine. Let's get that swarm in a box. Finn, you have to back up a bit in case Priscilla needs to use that smoker."

"Don't call me Priscilla," said Petey.

Mel said, "Don't smoke them unless you have to."

"I know!"

Mel took a spray bottle and misted the bee ball. The

bees hummed and buzzed. "Sugar water," she said. "They can't fly so well if they're wet. And licking the sugar water calms them. I keep telling Priscilla that it's better than smoking them, but my daughter doesn't like to be told what to do." Mel tied a sheet around the tree branch right under the bees. She stretched the sheet from the tree branch to the hive in the same way Petey had done back at the Chat 'n' Chew.

"Now," said Mel, "we wait for the queen. It's easier to see her against the white sheet."

Finn and Petey and Petey's mom knelt in the grass as one bee after another marched back to the hive. When the bees started to move in clusters, walking and flying, something occurred to Finn.

"How do you know which one's the queen?"

"She's bigger than the others," said Mel.

"That doesn't always help," Petey said. "I can't always find her."

"Because she's not that much bigger," said Mel. "You don't rely on her size as much as you try to use the way she moves. It's hard to describe. It's as if she walks in a more determined way." She pulled off her hat and smoothed her long, straight hair. "She's got a big job. Babies to bear. Workers to inspire. A colony to manage. She moves like that. Like she's a woman with a plan. The best way to see her is to let your eyes lose their focus, let things get a bit fuzzy on you. See the bees as a whole rather than individuals. When you do that, you understand the entire pattern. The queen's movements will stick out because they're so different from everyone else's."

"You mean, you try to see like a bee," Finn said.

Mel laughed. "Exactly. That's exactly right."

Finn did as Mel suggested, letting his vision go slack and blurry. It didn't take long. "There," he said, pointing to a long bee in the midst of all the others making their way across the sheet.

Mel leaned in to look. "That's her!"

"You've got to be kidding," said Petey.

"Finn, it looks like you have a talent for finding the pretty ladies." Mel jerked a thumb at Petey. Petey ripped a daisy from the ground and popped the head off, but it only made her mother laugh again.

Even though Finn knew Mel was talking about Petey, he suddenly couldn't help thinking of Roza, and how he had *not* found her, how he had almost forgotten about finding her since his brain and his dreams and his nights were so filled with Petey. And he thought about Sean, if Sean had been kissing Roza the way Finn had been kissing Petey, which he must have been. What it would feel like if Petey were suddenly taken, if Sean had been there to witness it, and Sean had done nothing to stop it, and had made no sense when he talked about it later? Finn's stomach crawled up into his throat.

"Finn? Are you all right?" Mel asked.

"What? Oh, yeah. I'm fine."

"Always in your own world, aren't you?" said Mel, but not unkindly. Mel didn't call him Spaceman or Moonface or Sidetrack or Dude or anything else—she called him by his name. She didn't seem to blame him for Roza the way so many others did, and that just made it worse.

"Let's go inside and have some tea and honey clusters," she said. "I just made them this morning."

Mel Willis's honey clusters were almost as famous as her Hippie Queen Honey, and nobody would refuse, not even a dumb horny teenager torn between paralyzing guilt and an insane urge to carry a bee-eyed girl to the nearest bed to show her all those things he couldn't say, all the ways he didn't want to lose her.

Instead, the three of them filed into the kitchen, Finn keeping his eyes on the ground as Petey stripped off the white coveralls. They sat around the Willises' kitchen table, dunking the honey clusters into lemony-sweet tea. And after Finn had eaten more honey clusters than was lawful in the state of Illinois, Mel packed an extra tin for Sean, along with a large jar of honey, in a brown shopping bag.

"Oh!" Mel said. "Before you go, you should sign Petey's yearbook." She held out a slim maroon hardcover.

Petey made a strangled sound, as if she were choking on her own tongue. "Uh, Finn doesn't need to *sign my yearbook*."

"Why not? Everyone wants people to sign their yearbooks."

"I'm not everyone. And I didn't even want a yearbook. You ordered that book for yourself."

"So, I'll have Finn sign it for me, then."

Petey rolled her eyes, but when her mother's back was turned, Petey reached out and gave Finn's pinkie a squeeze.

Finn flipped pages, reading the lists of names until he came to his own, three names down from the top of the page. Then he went to the row of pictures, counted three photos over. He took the pen and scrawled something over it.

Petey watched him do this, frowning. Mel, on the other hand, was delighted, the way she seemed to be delighted by most things. "Thank you, Finn. Even though Priscilla thinks this is silly, five years from now, she'll be happy to read your message."

"I won't even open that yearbook," Petey said.

"Yes, you will!" sang her mother.

"No, I won't!" Petey sang back. "And I'm walking Finn out now!"

"Don't get lost," said Mel.

Petey slammed the kitchen door shut and stalked

into the backyard. She waited until they were around the side of the house before she said, "Okay, seriously? *I hope you never change*?"

Finn flushed to his hairline. "I was going to write something about my dishonorable intentions toward you, but I didn't think your mom would approve."

"Oh, yes, she would. She likes to think that she's hip about all that stuff. Which she is, I guess, but it's sort of weird to listen to a thirty-six-year-old woman reminiscing about all the boys she made out with under the bleachers when she was in high school. Who wants to hear about that? Even if it's not illegal to say out loud, it's got to be illegal-*ish*."

"We never made out under any bleachers."

"Who needs bleachers?" Petey threaded her fingers through his and pulled him into a patch of wildflowers, more weeds than flowers, a patch that came up almost to their elbows. "So, about these intentions of yours. How dishonorable are we talking?"

He was going to make a joke—*Write about the moment of your most dishonorable intentions in the form of a fortune cookie*—but her flashing eyes, the curve of her shoulders in the tight T-shirt, the secret wink of her collarbones under her skin, the sweet smell of strawberries thick in the air, sent his thoughts scattering like fish at the splash of a rock. He dropped the shopping bag, not caring what broke. Twining his hands in her hair, he kissed her as if possessed, and they tumbled into the flowers, their bodies hidden in the tall grass. She wrapped her arms around his neck and her legs around his hips and they moved together, losing themselves in each other. And though there were layers of clothes between them, he could imagine himself inside her.

He didn't have a coherent thought for a long, long while.

Finn took the same route back home, passing the Dog That Sleeps in the Lane, who didn't even lift his head to yawn when Finn said, "Later, Dog." As day drifted into night, the sky shucked its oranges and purples for black and blue. A sickle moon threaded itself into the silk. Finn walked in the ditch on the side of the road so that the passing cars wouldn't mow him down. Or so he wouldn't stagger into oncoming traffic, he wasn't sure which.

He trudged along, the night air filled with the song of crickets and the calls of frogs and the *Who? Who?* of the occasional owl. The sour-milk-and-manure smell of the cows came and went with the breeze. Pollen tickled his nose. The grass crunched beneath his feet. The plants could use some rain. The frogs, too. The whole town. He'd like to be outside with Petey in the rain, one of those warm summer rains that was just hard enough to drench you, but not hard enough to chase you indoors.

Behind him, the rumble of an engine, the whir of tires, a voice yelling, "MOOOOOOOON-FAAAAAAAAACE!" He ducked just in time to avoid a rotten green tomato to the head as the Rudes drove by in their old pickup, their cackles wafting behind.

Then the Rudes were gone, and their cackling with them, and Finn had the road to himself. He was so busy listening to the crickets and the frogs and the crunch of his own boots and imagining Petey in a rain shower, skin slick and sparkling with raindrops, he didn't notice the footsteps behind him until they were *right* behind him. He spun around, fists up. But the road was dark and empty. No one was there.

He shook his head and kept walking. Again, the crickets and frogs lulled him and his mind drifted into another storm and burst of Petey, and again, only the sound of strange footsteps kicked him out of his dreams. He stopped, head cocked. Even the frogs and the owls held their breath.

Nothing.

The houses were set far back from the road, cars dark and silent in the lanes. The fields stretched for miles in either direction. He couldn't see anything moving on the road or in the fields, but still, the skin on the back of his neck prickled.

Miguel's voice boomed in his head. *Any minute now, a cat will jump out in front of you and you're going to feel like a dumbass. And just when you relax, the ax murderer will chop off your head. Surprise cat, then head chop. Always in that order.*

"Shut up," Finn said.

He picked up the pace. He wished Miguel hadn't seen so many horror movies. He wished Miguel didn't *talk* about the movies so much. He wished—

A white ball of feathers exploded from the weeds and hit him right in the stomach. He lurched sideways, almost crushing the dazed chicken flapping at his feet.

Dumbass. On cue.

He scooped up the chicken with his free arm. Runaround Sue coming full circle, he guessed. Charlie would be happy to see her, anyway.

He started walking again, the paper bag in one arm and the chicken in the other. He thought the chicken would calm as he carried her—Charlie carried all his chickens around—but her frantic clucks added to the chorus of crickets and the crescendo of the owls: *Who? Who? WHO?*

He slowed when he finally got to Charlie Valentine's house, but the lights were out; maybe Charlie was off on yet another "date." He circled around to the back of the house. If the door was unlocked, he could tuck the chicken inside. But the chicken flapped her wings, erupted from Finn's grasp, and half ran, half flew across the yard.

"Great," said Finn. "That's just great."

A voice like the echo in a sewer said, "I see that you found a chick of your own."

Finn's skin went cold and pebbled all over.

Slowly, he turned. A tall man stood in front of him, taller than Finn, taller than Sean, a total stranger yet so familiar at the same time.

Finn asked the owl's question. "Who are you?"

The man held up both palms and tipped his stone head. And then Finn knew. He knew.

Finn could hardly breathe, could hardly believe he would get this chance, but he once again dropped the bag he was carrying, forced the words out: *"Where's Roza?"*

"How is *your* young lady?"

"What?" Finn said, as he tried to match that icy stare, memorize features as bland as a scarecrow's. "You've been following me."

"I was . . . curious. She's quite striking, though I imagine not everyone agrees."

"How do you know who I visit? If you go near her, I'll—"

"Please," said the man, cutting him off. "I'm interested in only one woman. Unlike some people." He pointed at Charlie Valentine's house.

So the freak had been following Charlie, too. Finn planted his feet more firmly. "Where's Roza?"

"Think of Priscilla now. Think of what everyone else will think."

All the wrong questions exploded from him. "Think about what? What do you mean?"

"Strange boy, ugly girl, maybe he's taking advantage of her, maybe she'll do anything to—"

"Shut up!"

"He's so strange, that boy. Too strange. Maybe he had something to do with what happened to that other girl . . . you never know. Even your own brother believes this."

"Where's Roza, you creepy piece of shit!"

"She'll love me yet," the man said. He twitched like a cornstalk in the wind and slipped right through Finn's furious, outstretched hands, as if he'd never been there at all. Finn heard a car engine and raced to catch the plate, but the black SUV was halfway down the road before he got to the end of Charlie's lane.

Like a brainless terrier, Finn chased the car down the road until it vanished in the darkness. He bent under the disappointed moon, hands braced on his knees, panting into the warm summery air, wanting to give himself a beating for letting the man get away. But he took off again, this time in the other direction, not stopping until he reached Jonas Apple's house more than a mile away. He pounded on the door, begging for Jonas to open it, until Jonas did, his hair standing on end like the comb of a rooster. Jonas listened to Finn's story, nodding and sighing.

"Okay," he said. "Well, what did Charlie have to say about it?"

Finn stopped talking. "I don't think he was home."

"You didn't check?"

Finn closed his eyes. "No, I ran right here."

Jonas smoothed his hair, which promptly sprang up again. "Listen, son, have you been sniffing something?"

"No!"

"Don't be afraid to admit you have a problem. Sean would help you. I would help you. All of Bone Gap would help you."

"I'm not sniffing anything!"

"Jeez Louise, it's not meth, is it? That stuff will eat holes in your brains."

"I don't have holes in my brains!" But he sounded as if he did, and Jonas was eyeing him as if he did, even as he pulled on some shoes to go with Finn back to Charlie's. It didn't help that Charlie was home, that apparently, he'd been there the whole evening.

"Nope," said Charlie, "didn't hear anything. Wasn't expecting any guests either. Especially no one who twitched like a wheat stalk."

"A cornstalk," said Finn.

"Listen, kid, you're obsessed. You have to let it go," said Charlie.

"I can't! He was here! He was spying on you, too! He was spying on me! He knows me. He knows Sean. He . . . he knows things he can't know."

Both Jonas and Charlie stared at Finn as if he weren't just high, he was completely barking mad, and any minute he'd take to sleeping in the middle of the lane, and Finn thought maybe that was an excellent idea, because then a car might hit him, and the people of Bone Gap could tell one another that they'd always known he'd come to such an end. Poor Sidetrack, poor Spaceman, poor motherless boy.

"I'm sorry," Finn mumbled, a global apology for everything he was, and everything he was not, and all the ways he couldn't let it go. Instead, they let *him* go, watching as he gathered up his paper bag full of honey and stumbled like a drunk toward home, to the brother he hoped might believe him.

Sean

Good for You

Sean sat in the dim light of the kitchen, a sketch smoothed out on the surface of the table. He was five when he learned he could draw. *Really* draw. His horses looked like horses, his cows like cows, his cats like cats. But people were his best subjects, looking like people and not stick figures or scarecrows. When he brought a drawing home from preschool, the paper decorated with gold stars and happy faces, his mother, Didi, would take the drawing and exclaim, "A star! Good for you!" She would gather him up and squeeze him tight, enveloping him in a cloud of perfume and cigarette smoke, and tell him what a wonderful boy he was, and how he'd be a great artist one day, and how she was so proud. Sean was her big boy, and he would grow up to be a great man.

The drawings papered the front of the refrigerator, waiting for the next time his father would come home. Hugh O'Sullivan drove a truck and had only a few weekends a month to spend with his wife and his son. But the first thing he did when he limped into the house—the army had left him with a bum leg, trucking had given him a bad back—was stand in front of that refrigerator, examining all the drawings Sean had made since the last time his father was home. Hugh would put one large hand on the top of Sean's head and cup his own chin with the other, scratching at the growth of dark beard. After a good five minutes had passed, he would choose his favorite. It was almost always a picture of Sean's mother. Sean drew his mother a lot because, well, she was his mother, because she was prettier than anyone in Bone Gap, and because his father loved those drawings best and would fold them up and put them in his wallet, already fat with pictures.

Sean's father would then pour a glass of water from the tap, drink the whole thing down, and do it twice more. He would set the glass next to the sink and call for his wife. Didi would come running the way she always did, leaping into his arms like a child. Hugh would catch her—no matter how sore his leg, no matter how sore his back—and he would call her his Dark Horse, his lovely Dark Horse, and wouldn't ask her what she'd been doing while he was away.

Sean was six when Finn was born. If Sean was his mother's big boy, Finn was his mother's beautiful boy. Both had inherited their father's thick black hair and espresso eyes, but Finn also inherited his mother's delicate features, her dreamy distractibility. You couldn't leave Finn alone in the yard lest he follow a parade of ants right into the road. He would disappear into the cornfields for hours, because he claimed the corn was whispering to him. He had whole conversations with birds and fireflies, goats and horses. When people spoke to him, however, Finn focused on their mouths, or their hair, or their eyebrows, or their shoes, and forgot to focus on their words. "What?" Finn asked, over and over and over. "What?"

Which was exactly what he said when Didi told her boys that their father had died in a trucking accident on I-80 in Ohio. The ambulance had taken him to the hospital but hadn't gotten there fast enough. Twelve-year-old Sean had held his mother while she sobbed, and Finn had said, "What? What?"

Didi was young, and so pretty that the people of Bone Gap assumed that, after a time, a new man would step in, and that it would be good for everyone. Didi was the kind of woman who needed a man, they said, and all young boys need a dad. But Hugh O'Sullivan had been the only man who had ever held Didi's attention for longer than a few months, and even he had never held it completely; none of the new ones were up to the task. Didi grew dreamier and more distracted, and found other things to smoke besides cigarettes. Sean bought the groceries and made sure his brother had clean clothes and notebooks for school. Finn talked to squirrels and mooned out the window.

When Sean brought home a test with a perfect score, a paper with an A-plus, a new drawing, his mother still said, "Good for you," but she didn't look at him, or hug him, or tell him she was proud. The people of Bone Gap said Sean looked so much like his father—tall and broad and so strong he could throw a car across a yard—that Didi couldn't bear it. Sean couldn't bear it either. He didn't stop getting perfect test scores or A-pluses, but he stopped bringing home the evidence.

He also stopped drawing.

He poured his energies into becoming a doctor, the kind of doctor who would be able to save anyone who needed saving. And Sean was almost there, too, close enough to feel the scalpel in his hand. Didi was flighty and flirty and half-baked on one thing or another, but she liked that her younger son was almost as nice-looking as she was, and Sean thought Finn would be all right. And though Finn occasionally got the crap kicked out of him for being moony and strange and too pretty for his own good, he was also growing tall and strong and didn't want Sean to protect him anymore.

He would do it himself, or he wouldn't. Either way, Finn told him, it wasn't Sean's problem.

So Sean filled out his applications and lined up his financial aid and packed his bags, and Didi said, "I met an orthodontist on the internet, and I'm moving to Oregon," and Finn said, "What?"

Sean unpacked his bags.

As much as he tried, Sean couldn't hate his mother. First, because he wasn't the type, and second, because he finally understood how fragile she was, how unmoored and untethered, like a shiny balloon floating through the air, no hand to steady her. And he couldn't hate Finn either, because Finn was so strange, and because who hates a fifteen-year-old kid who has lost both parents and can't look anyone in the eye and says "What?" when he means "How?" or "Why?" or "No!" or "It's not fair"?

And Sean didn't hate his work, either, because he got to drive an ambulance as fast as he wanted and he still got to save people who needed saving, and that was something he could be proud of. He dated sturdy nurses, exhausted interns, and fearless phlebotomists. He avoided anyone too pretty.

And then Roza showed up in the barn.

He had met battered women before. He had seen them huddled on porch steps, eyes blackened, teeth wadded up in bloody tissues. Roza couldn't have been more than twenty to Sean's twenty-three, but she had the same sorts of bruises as those other women, the sprained wrist, cracked ribs and broken toes, the wariness of a wounded bird. Sean half expected some enraged lunatic of an ex to come storming his front door, which didn't concern him too much, as he could knock almost anyone on his ass, and because he was friends with every police officer in a hundred-mile radius. But he was worried when she refused to go to the hospital, worried when she would allow only Finn to touch her. And he worried about Finn, too, how easily a teenage boy could fall for a wounded bird, an *absurdly beautiful* wounded bird who didn't speak much English. He didn't want to come home one day to find Finn and this girl licking each other like cats. He figured he'd let her stay a few days, then call up one of the social workers at the hospital, find a shelter.

And it might have gone that way, if Sean hadn't needed the hospital himself.

Roza had just raided the fridge and pantry, setting out ingredients for another of her Polish dishes—flour, potatoes, onions, butter. He hadn't expected all this cooking and wanted to help. Or at least communicate that this wasn't her job and that he wasn't such a useless idiot he couldn't chop some potatoes like a normal person. He made the first cut and almost chopped off his finger. He couldn't help the hiss that escaped his lips, and the blood that poured all over the counter and floor. He knew without examining the wound that it would need stitches.

Immediately, Roza wrapped his finger in a dish towel and elevated his arm. "Doctor," she said. "We go."

"No," he said. "I'm fine. I just need my bag."

"Doctor," she said, louder.

"No, it will be okay. My bag is in my room."

A hiss escaped *her* lips, and she let loose a stream of Polish that he didn't understand. At last, she muttered something that sounded like "Golobki." He was wondering if she'd just called him a meatball when she ran out of the kitchen. She returned with his bag, dropped it on the table.

He kept his one arm elevated and fumbled with the clasp. She pushed his hand away and opened the bag. First, he grabbed Betadine to clean the wound. At his awkward attempts to dampen some gauze with the solution, Roza clucked her tongue and did it for him. He unwrapped his hand and wiped down the finger, gritting his teeth against the sting. After that, anesthetic. An injection would be fastest, but he couldn't manage a bottle and needle with his wounded hand. So he found a topical anesthetic. Again, Roza took the bottle from him, dampened the gauze with solution. Sean placed the gauze on the wound. The cut was deep, and the anesthetic would take a while.

Without him having to ask or gesture, Roza found a clean towel and rewrapped his hand with the gauze underneath. She spread another towel on the table.

While he was waiting for the anesthetic to numb his finger, he did more digging and found a sterile package with a curved needle and thread, a needle holder, and forceps. Though he wasn't supposed to suture anyone, he'd practiced stitching on pigs' feet till his hands ached, till each stitch was tight and A-plus perfect. But he needed more than one hand to open the package with the needle. He was about to ask her to do it when she spoke again.

"Doctor," she said.

"No, I can do it, I just—"

Again, the musical stream of Polish spoken in her disconcerting alto. She was too delicate for that strong, scratchy voice, as if her birdlike outside was just a pretty little tale she liked to tell, and the true story was something she kept deep down inside. He searched her face—her skin rich and deep, her eyes clear and bright—and tried to find something to hold on to in the stream of sounds. She shook her head, opened the package to free the curved needle and silk thread. She set these on the towel. She ran her hands over the other things he had laid out: scissors, antibiotic ointment, bandages. She didn't seem to be upset by the sight of these things, or by the blood that had soaked through the towel or dripped onto the table and floor, and she did not seem to be afraid. Which was interesting.

More interesting was when he finally removed the towel and gauze and attempted the first stitch. He was able to pull the needle through his flesh, but he couldn't tie off the thread. He explained how to wrap the thread around the needle holder and use the forceps to make a knot. She took the needle holder and forceps, watching his face carefully to make sure the knot was both tight enough and not too tight. He did the second suture; she tied it off and cut the thread. When he was about to do the third stitch, he hesitated, held out the needle holder to her. She took it and deftly did the last stitch, the punch of the needle through his skin almost pleasant. She daubed the ointment onto the wound, picked up his hand, and examined the spidery black knots as if they were a work of art—a painting, a sculpture.

Her face burst into a grin, and it was like watching the sun rise. "Frankenhand."

"Excuse me?"

She gently tapped his hand. He tore his eyes away from her, looked down at the black stitches. He nodded. "Frankenhand."

She laughed, reached up, and—to his surprise—patted him on the top of his head. "Good for you!"

she said. She packed up his bag and returned it to his room. He put on rubber gloves to protect the stitches. Together, they wiped down the counters and floor and made potato dumplings sautéed in butter and onions, as if there was nothing in this house that could wound, and no blood had ever been spilled here.

Later that night, he'd rummaged in his closet, found an old sketchbook, some pencils. He drew a picture, the first he'd drawn in years.

A sketch of his Frankenhand in hers.

Sean heard the footsteps outside, refolded the drawing, and stuffed it back into his wallet. His tea was cold, but he sipped it anyway as Finn burst into the kitchen.

Finn dumped a grass-stained paper bag on the table. "I saw him. He was at Charlie Valentine's."

Sean felt as if he was stealing Finn's line when he said, "What?"

"Him!" said Finn. "The man! The one who took Roza! He was at Charlie Valentine's house. At his back door. He knew me. I mean, he recognized me. But then, he . . . he . . . I went to see Jonas, I went to tell him. But he didn't believe me."

"I wonder why," said Sean.

"He was following me. He was spying on Charlie."

"Which is it?"

"Sean," Finn said. "I saw him."

"Yeah, you said that. Where have you been anyway? Where do you go?"

"What does that have to do with anything?" said Finn.

"You go out every night. You think I don't know that?"

"I saw the guy who took Roza. He was at Charlie Valentine's."

"Where else would he be?"

"Sean!"

"What's in the bag?"

"Are you even listening to me?" Finn said. "Are you hearing what I'm telling you?"

Sean reached out, grabbed the bag, and yanked it toward him. He pulled out the large jar of Hippie Queen Honey, the cookie tin. He opened the tin. Something in his chest hitched, broke, as the warm scent wafted up toward him, honey and nuts and vanilla. And he knew where Finn had been going every night, night after night, and he knew why. He had tried so hard not to despise everyone—his father for dying on him, his mother for drifting from him, his brother for lying to him, Roza for leaving him—but he didn't think he could stop himself anymore. He didn't have the heart.

"Priscilla Willis, huh?"

Finn didn't answer. He didn't have to. Sean's whole

life was in the toilet, and his brother was making time with the sad girl who'd go down on any guy who would tell her she wasn't ugly.

Sean unscrewed the jar of honey, dipped a finger, tasted. "Good for you, brother," he said, voice a rusty blade. "Good for you."

Petey

Get Real

He was late.

With the crickets chirping through the open window, Priscilla "Petey" Willis sat cross-legged on her bed in the dark of her room, waiting for Finn to appear like some sort of magic trick.

This was unusual. Petey Willis wasn't the sort to wait for anyone. And if she was forced to wait, she wasn't so damned happy about it. Normally, Petey was too mad about too many things to list: her given name, her own face, that one horrible party, to name just a few.

She should have gotten over her name by now, and maybe she would have, if the people of Bone Gap remembered to call her Petey. But they didn't. They wouldn't. And her mother outright refused. Priscilla, her mother said, was too much fun to say, tripping off the tongue like a favorite song. Pris-cil-la. "And you are my all-time favorite song," her mother told her.

And as much as the people of Bone Gap forgot her name, they wouldn't stop reminding her of her face. Oh, most of them weren't mean about it, at least not outright. But she could see them looking at her when they thought she wasn't, saw how their eyes flicked from her mom to Petey back to her mom, and she knew what they were thinking: How did bright and sunny Mel Willis with her sweet smile and brown-sugar freckles produce such an unlovely daughter, more vinegar than honey? As a child, Petey would catch a glimpse of herself in a mirror or a window or the surface of a still pond and find her own outsize features interesting and unusual—unforgettable even. And how would that ever be a bad thing?

While she was growing up, Petey's mother, frank as she was, would talk to Petey about falling in love and falling in lust and everything in between, because surely someone would one day notice Petey. Petey was as curious as anyone, but her mother's explanations too often veered from the scientific to the nostalgic as she remembered what it was like to be eleven and having your first crush and thirteen and getting your first period and fifteen when Tommy Murphy tried to jam his hand down your jeans during the movie previews and actually got stuck.

Tommy Murphy was the last straw. Petey had snatched up the nearest utensil. "If you do not stop talking, I will find a way to off myself with this teaspoon." Later, her mom simply had to appear as if she might start waxing poetic about making out with this boy or that one and Petey would say, *"Teaspoon!"* and her mother would laugh and change the subject.

But Mel did not give up. When Petey was in the seventh grade, her mother gave her a book called *Get Real*. It had a hot-pink cover, strangely fascinating and explicit cartoons, and all sorts of information for girls who liked boys and girls who liked girls and girls who liked everybody and people who didn't believe in gender binaries and about birth control methods and how to prevent STDs and fun things to do with showerheads and why it's not such a good idea to text a picture of your boobs to that guy you just met at the mall.

And then her body popped like a kernel of corn, and with that came the boys who followed her down the street, making comments about it and discussing which piece of it they preferred most and what they wanted to stick where, but when she turned around, they told her she was wrecking the view.

The nice girls suggested different makeup and

She closed the book and smoothed the quilt on her bed. Unlike the girl in the novel, she hadn't made it herself, knew little about quilting or sewing or craftiness. And unlike the girl in the novel, she understood heat and wind more than ice and snow, and had no intention of breaking anyone's heart, except maybe her own. Even *Get Real* had said nothing about this, about sitting on your bed in your room, stomach and head buzzing, nerves thrumming, heart beating in your earlobes and your toes, hoping so hard that there was one boy out there who wanted you as much as you wanted him, because you wouldn't know what you would do with yourself if this were not true.

Petey got up from the bed and went to the window, listening for the hoofbeats of the mare, but all she heard was the incessant rasp of the crickets. She loved bugs, all bugs, except for crickets, sawing away no matter what was happening around them. They had been cranking on the night of the party, the one that Amber Hass had begged her to attend. Petey wouldn't have gone to that party for anyone but Amber. They had met on the first day of kindergarten. Amber had taken one look at Petey and announced, "You look like a fairy from the land of fairies!" and her opinion had never changed. When the other girls offered makeup tips or sympathy, Amber's pretty face scrunched up in bemusement. "What's wrong with the lip gloss she's wearing?" she'd say. "Why would she want to borrow your hat?"

The party was a town away, but Amber was hoping that Finn O'Sullivan would be there, because he was *so hot*, even though he was a little spacey, wasn't one to attend parties, and though a mysterious and beautiful girl named Roza had just shown up in his barn, and if you were a teenage guy and a gorgeous chick appeared in your barn like a princess out of a fairy tale, you might opt to stay home, too.

Petey's throat had gone tight at the mention of Finn's name. "I thought you said he was weird."

"Just a little weird."

"Not just a little. Remember when he was going out with Sasha Butcher? And she decided to cut her hair into a pixie? And when she saw him at school, he walked right by her as if he didn't even know her?"

Amber shrugged. "In his defense, Sasha didn't look like a pixie. She looked like a boy."

"You'd want to go out with a guy who'd dump you because of a bad haircut?" said Petey.

Amber waved her hand. "She dumped him. And anyway, he's weird, but he's *pretty*. I wish he would just stand in the corner of my room so I could look at him."

"Maybe you're the weird one," Petey told her.

"Doesn't matter," said Amber, "because Finn likes Roza."

"Finn doesn't have a chance with Roza. Roza likes his brother."

"How do you know that?" Amber said, handing Petey a paper cup full of punch.

Petey took a sip, so sweet it nearly rotted her teeth on the spot. "You can tell. When she's around Sean, Roza doesn't stop smiling."

"Maybe she just thinks he's funny," said Amber.

"Funny is the last thing Sean O'Sullivan is. He looks like Wolverine, only bigger."

"If I were as gorgeous as Roza, I'd smile all the time," Amber said, glancing at the clots of guys assembled in the dank, dim basement. "We should all be that gorgeous."

Petey swirled the red liquid in her cup, thinking about how Amber wanted to pose Finn like a doll in the corner of her room. "Being gorgeous might be more trouble than it's worth."

"I'd be okay with that kind of trouble," Amber said, as a pair of flannel-clad farm boys headed toward them. Petey braced herself for their reaction; only Amber would think that Petey would make a good wing-woman. But one of the boys asked Petey her name and where she lived, and grinned when she mentioned her mother's honey business. They talked about the bees, and how to harvest the honey, and which Batman movie was the best one. He topped off her cup with the too-sweet punch. It was spiked with something, but she wasn't worried. This boy seemed reasonably human, Amber was crammed in a corner making out with his friend, no one had said anything awful, and for Petey that was good enough. She was careful to sip at the punch rather than drinking it down, however, because she didn't believe in tempting fate. And when he wasn't looking, she dumped the rest in a potted ficus.

Maybe it was sips of the drink, maybe because it was creeping toward midnight, maybe because the party was getting loud, maybe it was the fact that the reasonable human took her hand and brushed her knuckles with his lips, that she followed him up the basement steps, that she went out to the yard with him, that she let him kiss her as they stood in the shadows under a tree. It took a lot of energy to keep your guard up all the time, and she was tired of it. Plus the kissing was okay, and she wouldn't have minded more.

Except, after a while, he put a hand on each of her shoulders and pressed down, which was annoying, and distracted her from the kissing, which was at least entertaining if not electrifying. She grabbed his wrists and pressed upward to release the tension. And then they were locked in a strange battle, him pressing down, her pressing up, a squat machine made entirely of flesh and bone, Petey unable to understand what he was trying to do until she remembered certain cartoons on the pages of *Get Real.*

Abruptly, she let go of his wrists and allowed him to push her to her knees. She looked up, waited for his smile.

And she punched him in the nuts.

If it had been a direct hit, if he hadn't managed to pivot at the last second, her dignity might have been left intact. But instead of falling to the ground and squealing like a piglet as she had hoped, he jumped back, clutching himself, and spluttered, "What the hell is wrong with you, you ugly whore!"

Suddenly, lights flooded the yard, cops swarming, gathering drunken revelers as they came. "Party's over," a voice boomed.

The not-at-all-human boy pretended to fix his fly. "Sorry, officers. We were just having a little fun out here."

A cop shone a light directly into the boy's eyes. "You been drinking?"

"No, sir!"

The cop glanced down at Petey, sitting on her heels. "What about you, miss?" the officer said, aiming the light. She blinked furiously, no way she was going to cry. The officer turned to someone behind him, jerked his thumb at Petey. "Why don't you take care of this one, O?"

The cop grabbed the farm boy by the shirt collar and marched him from the yard. Sean O'Sullivan, the least funny man in the universe, stepped forward, huge and imposing in his crisp uniform. He crouched in front of Petey. His dark eyes were solemn as he regarded her.

She said, "Since when do they call ambulances to house parties?"

"Since a bunch of kids are puking up their guts in the bushes out front and the neighbors are worried about alcohol poisoning. Are you hurt?"

"Is that a joke?"

"It's a question."

"Stupid question."

"How about this one: Are you drunk?"

"Are you?"

He shone his own smaller penlight into her eyes, sighed, stood. "Did you come here with someone?"

"Amber Hass."

"She drunk?"

"I don't know."

"Maybe you should find her. And if she's drunk, you're driving, okay?"

"Sure," said Petey. He held out his hand to help her up, but she got to her feet without his assistance, brushed the grass from her knees.

Sean said, "You should be more careful, Priscilla."

Petey laughed. "I thought I was."

Petey found Amber in the kitchen. Since Amber wasn't drunk either, or at least, not drunk enough for the cops to arrest her, they were allowed to leave. As Petey drove them home, windows open, hot wind tossing their hair, the song of the crickets seemed to reach a furious crescendo. Only male crickets could produce the sound, drawing the one wing against the other, all to attract a mate. Once she was near, the male switched to a song of courtship. Some crickets even sang a post-mating song of celebration.

Not-at-all-human boys have those songs, too, it seemed, because when Petey went to school the next day, she learned all the things she'd done with not just one, but many guys at that out-of-town party. According to the stories, Priscilla Willis might not have a face you want to look at, but she was a real sweet piece.

Petey didn't want to think about that party, didn't want to think about the crickets, didn't want that humiliating night spilling over, tainting this one or any other. But she couldn't help but hear the townspeople's whispers hissing in her head, the new judgment in them.

Where was Finn?

She whirled away from the window and marched back to her bed. She scooped up the graphic novel and opened it to any random page, determined to get her mind on something else. But of course the page she turned to was a picture of two people kissing, melting together—you could not tell where one person's face ended and the other's began.

"Petey?"

She fumbled with the book. Finn was framed in the open window, his face beautiful as always—divine—but a little sad, too.

He pressed his fingers against the screen. "Do you want to come outside?"

Petey had been called many names in her life, but coward wasn't one of them. She set the book on the bed. "Do you want to come in?"

He blinked at her, perhaps surprised himself, then murmured to the mare, jumped down. He put a hand on either side of the frame. He threaded one of his long legs through the opening, then hefted himself into the room. She always forgot how tall he was until he was standing near her, and the cramped space made him seem even taller. He glanced at the photos on the wall behind her—bees, flowers—the bookshelves stuffed with fairy tales and myths and manga, the messy desk with the laptop and the piles of papers, the poster with E. B. White's poem "Song of the Queen Bee," the rumpled bed.

"What are you reading?"

"My favorite. Well, one of them." She grabbed the

book and handed it to him. He stood, lanky and awkward and distracted, and flipped through the pages. While he was flipping, she dropped into the chair by the desk, waiting—for what, she wasn't sure. For him to kiss her in the hungry way he always did. Or for him to tell her what was wrong. Because something was definitely wrong.

He had the book open to one spread or another, but she couldn't see what it was. Then he shut the book and placed it on the desk next to her. He stared at her, and she stared back, because she was accustomed to the weight of his gaze, and because he looked at her like she used to look at herself in mirrors and windows and ponds so long ago. As if her face was interesting and unusual—unforgettable even.

A pulse ticked in her neck, and she wondered if he could see that, too. "Are you okay?" she asked.

He shook his head but didn't offer a reason. He stepped toward her dresser, where she had a random array of photographs—Petey and her mom, Petey with the hives, Petey and the Dog That Sleeps in the Lane—and picked up the nearest one, examining it. Her chest ached, and she prayed he wasn't there to ask for space, or tell her about all the commitments he wasn't ready for, or that he had found some regular-looking girl and this had all been a dream or a joke, because she would push him right back out the window, burn all her stupid fucking books in a ceremonial fire, and give herself over to her bees once and for all.

Instead, he put the photograph back on the dresser. He knelt in front of her, wrapped his arms around her waist, and laid his head in her lap.

Her arms jerked up like the limbs of a marionette, shocked by this gesture, this posture. But again, she waited. Waited for him to slide his hands up the back of her shirt or try to undo her shorts with his teeth or whatever it was that guys did when girls plucked up their courage and asked them in. Another thing her books had neglected to mention: what to do when the prettiest boy you've ever seen lays his head in your lap and seems content to camp out there for a few weeks. She dangled her fingers loosely, limply in the air over his back, wishing she could Google it.

But he breathed softly against her thigh, his long eyelashes tickling her skin, the warm soapy tang of him wafting up like steam from a cup of herbal tea. She let her hands drop. He gave a little sigh as her palms slid down the curve of his back, as she outlined the broad wings of his shoulders, as she traced his spine from his neck to the dimples peeking out from the band of his jeans.

His arms loosened, and he looked up at her, a lock of dark hair falling over his brow.

"I saw him," he said.

Again, she was surprised. "Saw who?"

"The man who took Roza."

She didn't know what to say to that, so she said nothing.

"Last night. After I saw you and your mom. He was at Charlie Valentine's house, sneaking around the yard," Finn continued. "I chased him, but he got in a black car and disappeared."

"Why didn't you tell me?"

"I'm telling you now."

"But," she said, "if he has Roza, why would he come back here?"

"I don't know!"

"Are you sure that it was—"

"I'm *positive*. He moved just the same way. I told Jonas Apple and he didn't . . . and then I tried to tell Sean, but . . ." Dark eyes, wounded eyes, searched her face. "I saw him, Petey. I swear I did."

"Okay, okay. Maybe you should go to a sketch artist or something?"

"A sketch artist can't draw the way he moves!" Finn burst out. "That's how I knew it was him. The way he moves. Not because of his coat or his hair or whatever."

"What about his face?"

He clutched at her, fingers digging into her hips. "He has a regular face! How do you describe a regular face?"

"Okay."

She knew the stories told by the people of Bone Gap, how those stories had metamorphosed from Finn being too strange and too scared to help Roza when she needed it to Roza being just another girl desperate to leave a small town and Finn a boy so infatuated with her that he covered her tracks, hiding her even from his own heartsick brother.

Yet no one knew the truth about Petey herself; they had gotten her story all wrong, and from all the wrong people. A voice echoed in her mind, Sean's voice: *You should be more careful.* But how can you be careful with a boy who comes riding on a magical horse?

Being careful hadn't helped her anyway. Hadn't protected her.

"I believe you," she said.

His breath came short and clenched, as if he'd been running a great distance. He fell back to her lap, wrapping his arms around her even more tightly than before. She took her time with every bone, every strap of muscle and thread of sinew her fingers could find, mapping the landscape of him. The twitch of her nerves was like the beating of a billion tiny wings, as if messages passed from his breath and his hands through her skin and back again, the way bees stroke one another's antennae, feeding one another by touch. Maybe this was what a new queen felt like before she launched herself into the air, the drones closing fast.

Her knees fell open, drawing him in. She buried her hands in his hair and bent to whisper in his ear, "What am I going to do with you?"

But she already knew the answer to that.

Roza

No One Is Fine

Roza hid the heavy knife under a loose stone in the floor. At night, before she interred herself in the enormous canopy bed, she hefted the knife in her palm, ran her finger along the blade until she felt the bite.

But when she slept, she dreamed of bees.

She knew she was dreaming—a dream within a dream, or rather, a dream within a nightmare—but, like everything at the castle, the sounds and smells felt real. She walked the creaking drawbridge, over the teeming, monster-filled moat, past the stone-faced falconers, under the soaring raptors, and into the woods beyond. The trees were dense, braceleted with mushrooms. Twigs snapped underfoot, birds flitted in the leaves. A red fox perched on a stump, two dusky kits peeking around the vixen's back. All around, the scent deep and rich as the darkest chocolate.

After some time, Roza broke through the wall of trees into a grassy meadow. Three girls sat in the grass.

"What are you doing here?" Roza asked.

Karolina said, "We were waiting for you."

"You took long enough. This place is so boring," said Honorata, yanking a flower from the ground and tossing it.

Priscilla Willis held up her finger, where a bee rested, baskets packed with yellow pollen. "At least there are bees."

Honorata sniffed. "Not big enough to do any damage."

"*You're* not big enough to do any damage," said Priscilla. She released the bee and pulled a jar from her pocket. "Have some of this."

She passed a honey jar to Honorata. Honorata twisted the lid, inhaled. "Smells like oranges."

"I'm starving," said Karolina. "I haven't had lunch."

"Honeybees have a better sense of smell than other insects," said Priscilla, "but a worse sense of taste."

"Too bad for them," said Honorata, tipping back the jar. She poured so much honey into her mouth that it ran down her cheek and neck.

"Don't drink it all!" Karolina said. She took the jar and sipped, then handed it to Priscilla. Priscilla drank.

"Look!" said Roza. Amber Hass ran through the grass chasing a blue butterfly.

Priscilla said, "Butterflies are pretty, but they're solitary, and they don't live long. Bees are better. They'll do anything to protect the hive." She held up the honey jar to Roza. "Here. You need this more than we do."

"Says who?" Honorata said.

Roza flopped to the grass. The bees danced from blossom to blossom and then darted away. Karolina plucked a flower, tucked it behind Roza's ear. Roza took a sip of the honey, tangy and sweet.

"So," said Honorata, picking the flower from Roza's hair and flinging it back over her shoulder. "What are *you* doing here?"

"What do you mean?" said Roza.

"What she means is," Priscilla said, "when are you going to do something with that knife?"

Roza woke in the dark chill of her castle prison, the taste of honey on her lips.

She practiced wielding the knife as a weapon rather than a tool. She sliced and stabbed at the air, prancing like a fencer. She dragged a chair away from the fire and flipped it around. She threw the knife into the back of the chair again and again, hiding the rips under a fur throw, the resulting cuts and abrasions on her hands under gloves.

"Look at me, Rus," she said, holding up the gloves. "I'm a warrior now."

Though he'd had no luck with knives either, Sean had looked like a warrior, or the closest thing she'd ever seen up close. Strange, then, that she never dreamed of Sean, but of woods and bees and honey. Strange that she would dream of *Honorata* of all people, because Honorata would have been furious to hear Roza call herself a warrior, even as a joke. Roza was nothing special, Roza was no better than anyone else, Roza was no one's mama, Roza was neither pretty nor lucky, Honorata said. Honorata kept inviting Balthazar—"Bob"—back to the room no matter how badly he treated her, no matter how many other girls he dated. Sometimes Roza was locked out all night, and she was forced to camp out on the lumpy lounge couches, a poem by Wisława Szymborska beating in her head: *Four a.m., no one feels fine.* Her schoolwork suffered, her professors wanted to know if anything was wrong, and Roza said no, everything was great, except her roommate was sleeping with a boy who hated girls, which only made her hate herself, and Roza even more.

And then Roza's money started to run out. Karolina offered to hook her up with the cousin who worked in the meat plant. Honorata said that Roza should be placed on the killing floor, or maybe given a job wrapping packages of sausage. Instead, the visiting professor, the teacher who talked about willow bark and licorice, absinthe and baneberry, gave Roza a job cleaning up the greenhouse in the evenings and on weekends, told her she would be paid under the table. Honorata said the world was an unfair place, that certain girls would always get special treatment for no good reason, as if sweeping and stacking fertilizer were something glamorous.

"You're doing a very good job, Roza," the professor told her.

"Thank you."

"It doesn't bother you, working here?"

"Work doesn't bother me," Roza said, not sure what he was getting at.

"I meant the type of work we do here."

"Type? I type," she said.

The professor gazed down at her. "Getting dirty. Some of the young ladies don't care for the dirt."

"Things grow in dirt," Roza said.

"They die there, too," said the professor. "You're not squeamish, either. I've seen you handling the worms and the insects. Fearless, some might say."

Roza gathered the collar of her sweatshirt in her fist. "I don't like the dark," she offered.

"Hmmm," he said. "The dark is something one gets used to."

After she had worked for the professor for a month, he started bringing Roza little gifts. A pop. Candy. A tiny dog carved of wood. She didn't want gifts from men, no matter how harmless the men seemed. She tried to give back the dog.

"Please keep it. My son carved it. He's eight."

"Oh!" she said.

"My wife tells me that I have to be as nice to people as I am to my plants. But between you and me, people aren't nearly as interesting." He smiled blandly and walked away. She tucked the little dog in her pocket, relieved.

On the last day of the summer session, he came to the classroom where she was changing from her work shoes to her flip-flops, zipping up her sweatshirt and gathering the rest of her things. "May I give you a ride to the train?"

Roza hesitated. He was nice, but he was still a stranger. And yet, she was so happy, so relieved to be going back to Poland, that she decided she was being stupid. He was an *older* man, a teacher, with a wife and a child. He wouldn't do anything. And there was no way she was taking a ride from Bob, not even to go back to the dorm to pack.

She followed the professor to his car. It was a very

fancy car, a black SUV so shiny that it seemed to be streaked with silver. She imagined how she would describe it to Babcia, the silvery black paint, the cream leather interior, the dashboard that looked like the cockpit of a spaceship. He offered her a bottle of water for the road and then turned the car out of the lot.

They had driven for about fifteen minutes when he said, "This is not the way I planned it."

"Hmmm?" said Roza. She was looking out the window at the lights of Chicago. Sparkling, brilliant. Funny how you notice how beautiful things are just when you're about to leave them, she thought.

"I wanted to do things differently. Take more care."

"Um-hmm," Roza said. Next to the car, a cabbie laid his hand on his horn, then gestured wildly to the driver in front of him. Even his gestures looked beautiful to Roza, like an exotic dance.

"I assumed we had more time," he said, turning the car onto the highway. "I never thought you'd want to leave here and go there."

Roza turned away from the window to look at him. "What?"

"You are the loveliest creature I've ever seen."

Creature?

"What is this road?" Her tongue caught on the stiff English words. "Where we go?"

"It's a bit out of the way, but I think you'll like it well enough."

"What I like?"

He didn't answer. The cars sped by, blurs of red, blue, gold. Her hands curled into fists. He whistled as he maneuvered easily through the rush-hour traffic, as if the vehicles parted just for him. The car gained speed, and Roza had to grip the door handle to keep from sliding in her seat. Golobki, golobki, her brain yapped, as she cataloged the gifts he had given her, the cryptic compliments, the number of exits passing by.

"Stop the car, let me out," she said, not realizing until the sentence left her mouth that she spoke in Polish.

"I'm afraid I can't do that," he said, also in Polish. His eyes cut to her. "I speak many tongues, but I like the taste of yours."

Her stomach lurched, and she pressed her face against the glass. They were moving too fast now, too fast for any kind of car on any kind of highway, and she started to believe she was dreaming, or that he had slipped absinthe into her water, because there was no other way this was happening. She remembered her cell phone in her purse, but then also remembered he had put all her things in the trunk, and she hadn't said a word, so focused on where she was going that she didn't spend a minute thinking about where she actually was.

At last, the car slowed as they reached an exit far outside the city limits. The landscape was dark and vast and empty, with few cars and even fewer houses, and she tried to swallow the guts that had climbed their way into her throat.

He turned the car onto an endless stretch of country road, cornfields along either side. "You have nothing to be scared of."

Weeks before, he'd said she was fearless, and now she wished so hard that it was true that some strange iron infused her bones, some steely calm clamped down upon the panicked chattering of her brain. Without waiting for the right moment—for when would a better moment come?—she scrabbled at the door latch. She shoved open the door and threw herself into the night, hoping that the cornfields would be kind even if the world was not.

The corn had hidden her for as long as it could, and then Sean and Finn had hidden her for a time, even if they hadn't known it. But the man found her again. They were destined, he said. It had been written, he said.

She had tucked the blade in the folds of her skirt. She pushed her food around her plate, nibbled on a slice of bread. Wine gleamed red in her goblet, blood gleamed red in her eyes. But she had no talent for knife throwing. He would have to get close.

He ate his food in tiny, fastidious bites, hideous bites, napkin pressed to carved lips after each forkful. She thought of Ludo, delicate Ludo: what he'd done when she wanted to leave him, what she'd done so he would let her go.

"Do you love me yet?"

She rubbed her mouth with the back of her hand.

He laid his fork across his plate. "Is something bothering you?"

She choked back a laugh. She didn't even know if he could be wounded. "I've been having strange dreams. Nightmares."

"Ah. And were you frightened?"

"Yes."

Icy eyes seared her skin. "Still?"

"Yes."

"The beast doesn't comfort you?"

Rus's growl rose from his place underneath the table. Roza's throat went tight. She couldn't do it, she couldn't offer herself, she couldn't.

But she did.

She said, "The beast isn't enough."

He was at her side in a fraction of a second, hands on her shoulders, lifting her from the chair, pulling her into his stony embrace. His breath was cold and musty as a mausoleum, but she endured it until he finally, finally closed his eyes, his lips an inch from her face. She pulled the knife from the folds of her brocade gown and plunged it into the white flesh under his jaw, where it sank all the way to the hilt.

Finn

Sidetracked

Finn jabbed the shovel into the earth, stamped on the footrest, tossed the dirt over his shoulder, jabbed, stamped, tossed, jabbed, stamped, tossed. Sean had not believed him, Jonas had not believed him, but Petey had believed him, had shown him how much. He'd fallen asleep with his nose in her hair, breathing her scent, holding on to her as if she were the only sure thing, the only real thing he'd ever known.

It had been this way for the last four nights. He could dig postholes for the rest of his life. He could dig his way through the planet and come out the other side. Maybe he could even find Roza. Maybe—

"Dude, we're not drilling for oil," said Miguel.

"What? Oh, sorry."

Roza liked Miguel. The first time Miguel had come over to the house after Roza arrived, she had broken out in a grin so wide that Finn and Sean thought she knew Miguel from somewhere. But Miguel said no, he'd never seen her before, because there was no way he could have forgotten a girl who looked like *that*. "Like what?" Finn wanted to know. "There's no hope for you," said Miguel.

They wrestled another gnawed and splintered post from the ground. They heaved a new one into place, set it in concrete. Then they sat in the yellowing grass to rest for a minute.

Miguel inspected the old post. "Looks like a bull went after this one."

"Don't the Rudes have a bull?"

"The Rudes *are* bulls. Maybe they're the ones who have been charging the fence."

"Wouldn't surprise me," said Finn. "Where's Mustard?"

"Went down by the road to herd the girls again."

Finn tented a hand over his eyes. "Amber with them?"

Miguel shrugged.

"You don't want to talk to her?"

Miguel plucked up a handful of grass, sifted through it as if looking for something he'd dropped. "You don't want to talk to me?"

"Huh? We talk every day."

Miguel threw the grass, brushed off his hands. "When you think about it, building this fence is crazy. Animals will keep climbing over it, or under it, or chewing their way through it. All kinds of animals. Maybe even ones we didn't know existed."

"Okay," said Finn.

"So, you're really not going to tell me?"

"Tell you what?"

"That you saw him. The guy who took Roza."

Finn opened his mouth, shut it. Said, "How did you know?"

"This is Bone Gap. Everybody knows."

"Do you believe me?"

"You're a dumbshit." Miguel hauled himself to his feet, brushed the dirt off the seat of his jeans. He moved to the next post and attacked the earth with his shovel. Finn remembered a day in the third grade when one of the Rude boys had accused Finn of stealing his Swamp Thing action figure, and the boys had jumped Finn during recess. Miguel charged the boys, pin-wheeling his ridiculously long arms, taking out at least three Rudes before a teacher could put a stop to it. Miguel said no way Finn would steal. Finn wasn't a stealer.

Truth was, Finn *had* swiped the Swamp Thing. His mother never had enough money for toys. Sean made him give it back the next day.

Finn picked up his shovel and started digging alongside Miguel. For a while, they didn't speak.

Then Finn said, "I'm meeting Petey at the Chat 'n' Chew later. I could ask her about Amber."

"We're not in fifth grade."

"You don't want me to ask her?"

Miguel stomped on the edge of his shovel, levered up a wedge of earth. "I didn't say *that*."

As he sat at the counter of the diner waiting for Petey, nervously drumming his fingers, the black mare huge and agitated at her tether outside, Finn wondered what the hell he'd been thinking. The lights were too bright, the seat beneath him too worn and loose, ready to dump him to the floor. He'd wanted to meet Petey in public so that everyone could see them, could see how real they were to each other. Now it seemed as if he was just asking for trouble.

"Hey! Sidetrack!"

"What?"

A waitress, hair dyed red as new brick, was standing in front of him, holding up the coffeepot. "I been calling your name since the earth cooled. What's a girl gotta do to get your attention?"

"Darla?"

The waitress's mouth twisted. "Now, who else would it be?"

"But, your hair."

"Oh, yeah! You like it? I wanted something different. Better than the blond, right?"

"Right!" said Finn. "It's really . . . red."

"Want some coffee?"

Finn nodded, pushed his cup toward her.

"I didn't expect you to say yes. You never drink coffee," said Darla.

"A little tired."

"For good reason, I hope," said Darla.

A flush burned in Finn's cheeks. "Just studying."

"Studying, my butt," said Darla. "It's the summertime."

"I have tests and stuff. For college."

"Uh-huh," Darla said. "Which is why you're blushing."

"That's sunburn."

Darla lifted the coffeepot toward the window. "That's some animal you got out there. She some sort of racehorse?"

"I don't know," Finn said.

"She's a big girl."

"Yeah."

"I never saw a girl that big. Or a boy even."

"Yeah," said Finn.

Darla put the pot back on the burner, grabbed a dishrag, and wiped the counter. "Heard you ride a lot at night."

"Where did you hear that?" Finn said, his voice sharper than he'd intended.

Darla stopped wiping. "Maybe you should lay off the coffee. You're getting awful jumpy."

Finn pushed the cup back toward Darla. "Maybe you're right. Can I have lemonade instead?"

"Sure thing," Darla said, whisking away the offending cup.

Finn took a deep breath, trying to calm himself. He hadn't been in the Chat 'n' Chew in months, not since Roza. Roza had loved the Chat 'n' Chew. She loved the food, the bustle, the gossip, which she said reminded her of home. Finn didn't know where "home" was, exactly. Sean had never asked how she'd gotten to Bone Gap. Sean said that if she wanted to tell him, she would tell him. Sean said that there are certain questions you don't ask, even if the people of Bone Gap wouldn't stop making up stories.

"People talk," Roza had told Finn once, while they huddled in a booth over ice cream sundaes. "They say which boy does Roza love."

"What do you mean?"

Roza waved her spoon. "Sean, Finn, Finn, Sean."

Finn almost choked on his cherry. "That's stupid."

"They say which girl does Finn love, too."

"They do not."

"Yes. I hear. I listen."

"Most people don't listen."

"People look, they don't see."

“That too.”

Roza plucked the cherry from the top of her sundae, dangled it in front of Finn. “You see bee girl.”

He took the cherry. He knew something, too. “You see my brother.”

“He not see me.”

“Yes, he does,” said Finn, both embarrassed and pleased that they were talking like this, as weird as it was.

She leaned forward. “The people talk right now. They say, look! Roza and Finn! Together! Maybe they go kiss! Maybe they get married!”

Finn laughed. “We’re too young to get married.”

“Maybe we kiss, though.”

The flush burned the top of his ears. “You don’t want to kiss me.”

“No matter. They like story.”

Even though Sean had warned him, he couldn’t stop the words from spilling out: “Speaking of stories, how did you get to America? Where were you before you came to Bone Gap?”

She laid the spoon carefully on her napkin but did not speak.

“Never mind,” he said. “I don’t need to know. I’m sorry.”

She gazed at him so intently that he could not escape her gaze.

Jonas unwrapped a straw, sank the straw in the drink, took a long pull. "Tastes like baby aspirin."

Finn didn't ask Jonas Apple why he'd drink a drink that tasted like aspirin, as concerned as he was about drugs. *Have you been sniffing something? Jeez Louise, it's not meth, is it?* Finn watched Darla dance from one customer to the next, doling out food and drinks and extra ketchup. All around him, the people of Bone Gap jangled ice in their glasses, spooned soup into their mouths, talked about the weather, and how all the warmth and sunshine should have made for strong and healthy crops. But the sky was too blue and the earth was too dry, despite the brief rains that came and went. The days seemed to last too many hours, and the nights were too dark and brought strange dreams. The corn, which had been so green and strong, was now striped with yellowing leaves. The vegetables were small and withered, the flowers leached of their color, confusing the birds and the bees. Something was off, something was wrong, very wrong, and they didn't know what it was, but they knew it wasn't normal because they had never seen anything like it before. Even Charlie Valentine couldn't explain, even Charlie could only look at the sky and the plants and shake his head. And because whatever it was wasn't normal and because none of them had never seen anything like it before, their eyes slowly drifted toward Finn bent like an inmate over his lemonade, the giant black mare jerking at her tether outside.

Yes, this was a very, very bad idea.

Darla slid a plate of fries drenched in gravy in front of Jonas Apple, watching with satisfaction as he popped a fry into his mouth. "How's the crime-fighting business these days?"

It seemed to Finn that Jonas made a show of not glancing Finn's way when he said, "Slow. A few break-ins. A couple joyrides. Some loud parties. We'll get busy when the monster truck races come."

"Brings in the monsters," said Darla.

Jonas laughed and pointed with a fry. "And when we have the fair, and those lunatics come down from Chicago and up from Saint Louis. If you ask me, it's the city types that bring the crime with them."

"Who would want to live in the city?"

"They do have great pizza in Chicago," Jonas said.

"I guess that's no small thing," said Darla.

The rumble of a motor and the subsequent whinny of protest from Finn's enormous horse made everyone in the restaurant turn toward the door. Petey stepped into the diner, blondish hair wild as a thicket, wearing a short white dress that shone like moonlight against her skin. They gaped when she sat on the other side of Finn and gave his arm a squeeze. And such a buzz arose, a murmuring and whispering like the incessant yapping of the corn, that Finn wished he had never asked her here, wished he had never been so stupid as to think the people of Bone Gap would see her, see him, see the two of them the way Finn himself did.

"Why, hello there, Miss Priscilla," said Jonas. "Bringing some honey for Darla?"

"Not today," said Petey. For some reason, Petey didn't seem to be aware of the looks they were getting, or if she was, she didn't care. She was too busy glaring at Jonas Apple.

"You okay there, Priscilla?" said Jonas.

She ignored Jonas. "That's some color, Darla! What's next, a mohawk?"

Darla laughed. "Your fella didn't even recognize me!"

To Finn, Petey said, "Get me a pop, okay? I'm going to try to tame this." She gestured to her tangled locks. She walked toward the ladies' room, waving at this person or that one, thrilling, it seemed, in the attention.

Darla grinned as she poured Petey's pop and refilled Finn's lemonade. "That Priscilla Willis sure looks nice in a dress," she said. "Don't you think, Jonas?"

"I couldn't say."

"Oh, don't be such a grump. You can too say. I bet if she got herself a good haircut . . ." She fluffed her own hair as if marveling over the magic a good haircut could do. "You two kids going somewhere?"

Finn frowned. He'd planned on taking Petey back to his house to meet Calamity's kittens, but he couldn't imagine saying that out loud. "Movies."

Jonas popped another fry into his mouth, leaving a smear of gravy like a question mark on his chin. "Careful, Finn."

"Finn should be careful? Or Priscilla should be?" Darla said.

The lemonade soured on Finn's tongue. If Jonas "Jeez Louise It's Not Meth?" Apple said anything about Petey having a sting, Finn would punch him.

Jonas said, "Women are complicated."

Strange boy, ugly girl . . .

"Or men are simple," said Darla.

Maybe he's taking advantage of her, maybe she'll do anything . . .

"One minute they can't stand the dog and the next day they load the dog up in a van and drive off. No phone number, no address. You don't even know if the dog's all right. I mean, they should tell you that the dog's all right, don't you think? A person should know about his dog." Jonas rubbed at one eye. "Allergies are killing me."

Darla handed him a napkin. "You have gravy on your chin."

Petey returned from the ladies' room and took Finn's arm. "Hi," she said.

"Hey."

"What's wrong?"

"Nothing. Let's find a table in the back."

She let go of his arm. "Why do you want to sit in the back?"

"No reason. Well, I want to ask you something about Amber."

"Amber?"

Darla glanced past the police chief out the window. "Hey, who's that messing with your horse, Sidetrack?"

"What?" Finn said, spinning on his stool, just in time to see the mare rear back, kick her front legs, and charge past the diner.

He flew off his stool and ran out the door. The mare was already half obscured in a cloud of dust. Finn stood there, frozen, staring down the road, until a voice behind him said, "That fool horse is headed right for the highway."

The highway? With the speeding cars and the semis and the SUVs . . .

Petey's moped leaned up against the building, key in the ignition. Finn jumped on the machine. He turned the key and kicked the start lever the way he'd seen Petey do. It didn't work. He tried again, this time squeezing the brake handles as he kicked. Still nothing. One more kick and the moped fired up. He took off just as Petey's hand grabbed the back of his shirt, almost pulling him off the bike. He struggled to hold the bike upright, then gunned the engine, breaking free of her grasp.

He sped the moped after the runaway horse, fighting to keep his seat as the tires caught on the edge of the road through town. Flying gravel tattooed his skin with hot pricks of blood.

The mare was moving so fast her shoes sent up blue sparks when they struck the pavement. Ahead of her, brakes squealed as cars jerked left and right. The sound reminded Finn of an earlier time, a time when another car was jerking left and right, Roza's pale hands slapping at the back window.

The mare sped up. The highway was only a few miles down the road. If she reached it . . .

Sirens blared in his head. He gunned the engine as hard as he could, racing around the galloping horse. Once in front of her, he suddenly swerved the moped, tacking from one side of the road to the other. His hands pumped the brakes. She'd have to slow down. She'd have to.

She didn't.

The next time he swerved left, she banked right, galloping by him before he had the chance to react. He could see the white foam gathered at her mouth, the dark sweat on her flanks, the raw terror in her eyes. Something had scared her. Something had scared her so badly that she was going to run out onto the highway and—

Again Finn flew around the horse. This time, he dropped the moped into a slide, leaving yards of his own skin on the pavement as the bike sparked and squealed and finally stopped. Finn could only lie in the road, pinned by Petey's bike, as his horse, his beautiful, magnificent, impossible horse, thundered toward him. The mare reared up, shrieking, hooves hammering the air. When those hooves came down, they came down right on his heart.

His first thought was: *I'm broken.*

His second: *No, I'm burned.*

Third: *I'm broken and burned.*

A cool hand touched his cheek. He opened his eyes to see Petey's anxious face hovering over him, her hand squeezing his. On the other side of him, Mel Willis's long brown hair swung gently as willows in a breeze. Beyond Mel and Petey, the squeal of brakes, the slamming of car doors. The people of Bone Gap coming to see for themselves. They'd all followed him here.

"Finn?" said Petey. "Are you okay?"

"Describe the time you were run over by your own horse using only interjections." He coughed, fought to sit up. His chest was burning as if he had been branded.

So, broken, burned, and branded. *But not high!* he wanted to say. *I'm not sniffing glue, people, and for that—*

"You should stay still," Mel said. "The mare stepped on you. She stumbled off at the last moment. As scared as she was, she knew it was you. You're lucky. She didn't want to hurt you. But you could have some cracked ribs."

At this, Petey abruptly dropped his hand, stood, and stomped off.

"I'm fine," said Finn. "Where did she go?"

Mel pointed. Her truck was parked a few feet away, blocking any traffic. The mare stood quietly in the middle of the road, lathered and exhausted. Petey took the reins and knotted them in her fist. Her angry fist. She was breathing hard, chest heaving.

Mel followed his gaze. "Priscilla called me when you took off on the moped."

"She looks mad."

"She always does."

"No, she looks really mad. Did I break the moped?"

"I don't think she's worried about the moped. People sometimes get mad when someone they care about throws himself in front of a charging thousand-pound animal wearing steel shoes."

"Sorry," he said, though he wasn't sure what he was apologizing for. "Is she okay?" And he wasn't sure if he was asking after the horse or the girl.

Mel sat back on her heels. "I don't know, Finn. That horse just ran flat out for miles and barely missed getting turned into dog food. She stomped on your chest and she almost stomped on your head, so *you* barely missed getting turned into dog food." She raked her hair from her face. "I think you should have the vet check her out. The vet should check you out, too. And maybe give you some kind of shot so you never, ever do anything like that again. Do you know how dangerous that was?"

Finn grunted. He didn't think it was any more dangerous than playing with millions of stinging insects and risking anaphylactic shock. He straightened his leg. His thigh and calf were sanded raw as a T-bone at the meat counter. Then he really was sorry, sorry that he'd looked at it.

Mel sighed. "Just rest for a second."

He ignored her and sat up. He'd been roadkill many times. What was one more?

"You're one giant pain in the Buddha," Mel said.

"I'm fine."

"Stop arguing with me. You look like you lost a battle with a thresher."

By then, some of the people of Bone Gap had gathered behind Mel. Someone whistled. "Whooeeee. That's going to hurt later."

"It hurts now," said Finn.

"Whaddya expect?" someone else said. "Pulling a stunt like that."

"Yeah," said another. "Who do you think you are? Evel Knievel?"

"Evil *who*?" Finn said.

"Kids today don't know nothing."

Petey said, "Some of us know not to use a double negative."

"Priscilla Willis," Mel said. Her tone was warning enough.

"Sorry," Petey mumbled, not sorry either.

"Don't mind her," Mel explained. "She's just worried about Finn."

Petey tossed her wild hair. "Who says I'm worried?"

Mel pressed a palm to her forehead. "Anyone want to adopt a couple of teenagers?"

"They're all yours, Sweet Melissa," a man said.

"Groovy," said Mel.

Sirens blared. Actual ones. An ambulance. Usually, EMTs worked in pairs, but only Sean jumped from the driver's side with a black bag. He always made his own rules. He strode toward Finn, one long drink of water, not a drop spilling out. Mel stood and caught his arm, whispered in his ear. Sean nodded.

He set his bag next to Finn. He didn't say a word, just pulled up Finn's T-shirt. In the middle of his chest, right on the breastbone, a furious red horseshoe was indented in the skin. Sean grabbed his stethoscope and touched it to the left of the mark.

"Breathe in," he said. Finn did.

"Breathe out," he said. Finn did.

Sean felt each of Finn's ribs with expert fingers. Then he laid his palm flat in the center of Finn's chest. "Does it hurt when I press down?"

Finn gasped. "A little."

"How much? Scale of one to ten."

"One."

"I mean it."

"Fourteen."

Sean inspected the scrapes. "These aren't too bad," he said. "Considering." He put his stethoscope back in his bag. He glanced up at Mel.

"Can you sit with him? I have to get the gurney."

"Sure," said Mel.

"I don't need the gurney," Finn said. But it was like talking to a bees' nest. Nobody heard him. And if they did, they didn't care to listen, because they all had things to do. Sean went to the ambulance and got the gurney. Mel and Petey said they would take the mare home while Finn was being checked out at the hospital. They would make sure she had food and water. They'd call the vet.

Sean helped Finn lie on the gurney and wheeled him to the ambulance. One push and Finn was inside. Sean closed the double doors, moved around to the side of the truck. He hopped into the cab and started the engine. This time, he didn't bother with the sirens.

The hospital was twenty minutes from where the horse had stomped Finn. For most of this time, Finn could feel Sean gathering himself to ask one of his questions. Finn knew not to rush him. Finn shifted on the gurney, trying to ignore the sting of his cuts and scrapes, and the dull ache that bloomed in his chest with every beat of his heart. He counted the boxes of medicine on the cramped shelves. He counted the freckles on his arms. He imagined Petey visiting him in the hospital, slipping into the bed with him, letting him bury his nose in her hair, letting his hands roam where they would. He thought about Roza sitting in the back booth at the Chat 'n' Chew, waiting with two ice cream sundaes and a lot to say.

Nineteen minutes into the ride, Sean asked, "Were you trying to get that horse killed?"

Finn almost swallowed his tongue in surprise. "What do you mean? I saved her."

A pause. "You chased her."

"She was running toward the highway," Finn said. "I had to try to stop her before she got there." He tried to turn his head to look at Sean, but the gurney was too low for him to see over the front seat.

"So you thought the best way would be to go after her on a really loud machine?"

Finn said, "Something scared her and I—"

"Horses are prey animals. She thought some smoke-belching monster was trying to eat her for lunch, so she did what prey animals do. She tried to escape."

"But—"

"Don't you see?" Sean didn't sound angry, just tired. Tired beyond tired. The kind of tired that worms its way into the bone and stays there, feeding on the marrow. "You were the one who scared her, Finn. She was running away from *you*." Sean stopped the ambulance and leaped from the cab. When he threw open the back doors, the sunset was blinding.

Petey

The Whole Picture

Petey and her mother got to Finn's house about an hour after Finn attempted to grate himself into sausage and his brother had to cart him off to the hospital for reassembly. They led the mare back into the slanted red barn. They fed and watered her and spent some time petting the desperate little goat that kept the mare company, a goat that promptly tried to eat the eyelets off the bottom of Petey's dress.

Though they could detect no injuries to the horse, Mel decided to call the vet anyway. They let themselves into the O'Sullivan house, where Mel made herself a cup of tea and sat at the kitchen table, sipping quietly while they waited for the vet to arrive.

Petey wasn't sipping, wasn't waiting for anyone. She

moved around the house, examining family photos, opening and closing books, and peeking into drawers. If there had been a computer, she would have booted it up, but the O'Sullivans, it seemed, didn't have a computer anywhere.

"You're not looking through their things, are you?" her mother called from the kitchen.

"No," said Petey. She wasn't looking through *their* things as much as she was looking through *Finn's* things. And considering what she and Finn had done—how real things had become—and considering the fact that Finn had tried to get himself killed right afterward, she had a right to snoop. She could still feel his arms around her, still feel his lips on her neck, hear the hitch in his breath, and yet when she'd seen him bloody and limp on the ground, she'd wanted to kick the crap out of him. It had been his idea to meet at the diner, but as soon as she'd put on this dumb dress, she knew she wanted to do all the things everyone else did. She wanted to go out for ice cream, she wanted to go to the movies, she wanted to hold hands while running through the rain, she wanted to get in idiotic spats over idiotic things, she wanted to make out until she didn't know whose tongue was whose. But none of these things would happen if Finn were too good to be true, if he were some character out of a tale, if she'd made him up through loneliness and sheer will: *And so the young lovers had a month together before he was stomped to death by his magical horse.*

That wasn't the real reason she was snooping, though. The real reason was what he'd done at the diner, how he'd acted before his horse ran off. Cagey and strange, as if he didn't want to be seen with her after all.

Didn't want to be seen with her.

"Mom?" Petey called. "What was Finn like as a really little kid?"

"Spacey. Just like he is now. Why are you asking?"

"No reason," said Petey, who had no real reasons but a gnawing worry in her gut that Finn was hiding something from her, from everyone, and she had to know what it was.

Petey pulled a photo album from a shelf above the couch. In the beginning, the photos were of a very pretty woman holding a pretty little baby, and later, a small boy and another, even prettier baby. Finn's mother, Didi, and her sons. The people of Bone Gap talked a lot about Didi, about how lovely she was, but unstable, and how her husband was devoted to her anyway, speculating as to whether she was the reason that Finn was so lost and so spacey, that maybe Finn was too much like her. They said that it was a shame that Roza had run off, too. Women, said the people, were always running away from the O'Sullivan men, and wasn't that a shame, particularly for Sean, who could do no wrong.

She slid the album back into place and selected another. Lots more pictures of the boys growing up, skinny boys with dark curling hair, Didi as lovely as ever, no pictures of Hugh anywhere. Maybe he was the one with the camera. She wondered if Finn had forgiven his mother for leaving. He hadn't sounded angry when he spoke of her, but what did that mean? Sean, she thought, Sean probably hadn't forgiven Didi. The people of Bone Gap worshipped him, but Petey knew what Sean thought of her, knew what he thought he'd seen at that party last year. He hadn't been any wiser than anyone else.

Sean was a hard man.

But lots of people ran away. Petey's father had also run off, and when Petey was only a toddler. Her mom said it was because they'd had Petey so young, and he couldn't handle the responsibility. Petey thought that was a lame excuse and had decided long ago she would never look for him, let alone forgive him.

So maybe Petey was hard, too. Wasn't that why she was looking through the albums?

Someone knocked at the back door, and Petey heard her mother talking to the vet.

"Priscilla? I'm going out to the barn with Dr. Reed."

The door slammed. "Don't call me Priscilla," Petey

told the furniture, in case it had a mind to address her. She pored over the bookshelves, found lots of biology and physiology and animal science books, some agriculture, only one little book on myths, which she pulled out; she had this book, too. Once, she had asked Finn what his favorite book was, and he'd blushed and wouldn't answer the question. She'd said, "What? Is it a romance or something?" and still he wouldn't say. She wouldn't have minded if it was a romance or one of those books about a really awesome golden retriever that ends up dying at the end, but she minded that he wouldn't tell her. She read and reread all kinds of books for all kinds of reasons, complicated reasons. When she was little, someone gave her some weird book called *The Wife Store*. It was about a very lonely man who decided that he wanted to get married. So he went to the wife store, where endless women lined enormous shelves. He picked himself a wife and bought her. She was bagged up and put in a cart. He took her home. After that, the two of them went to the children store to buy a few kids.

Petey read this book over and over. Not because she liked it, but because she kept waiting for the story to change, kept waiting for the day she'd turn the page and a *woman* would get to go to the *husband* store. She kept waiting for justice. But, of course, the story never changed. She never got justice. If Petey were keeping one of her lists of the things she hated, she would have to add: the fact that there was no justice. But *The Wife Store* was still on her shelf at home, if only to remind her that there were assholes in the world who would write such things, believe such things.

What did she believe?

She believed Finn had a secret.

She headed for the bedrooms. There were two in the house—one in the front, one in the back. One neat, one messy. Petey stepped into the tidy room first. Though this was a violation, though she would be furious if a stranger did this to her, she couldn't help herself. It was like opening up that graphic novel about the brothers and the blankets and getting a peek into the lives of boys, lives that had always been so closed off to her, had always been such a mystery. The tidy, tiny room was furnished sparely—a large bed with a plain blue cover, a dresser, a nightstand, groups of old family photos on the walls. On top of the dresser, some sort of instrument that could have been a police scanner or radio next to a picture of Hugh O'Sullivan tossing a laughing boy in the air, the boy himself a grinning blur. The air in the room was cool and crisp, like pine trees, but there was another scent underneath, the scent of a person—a man—a scent that got stronger when she moved toward the bed. On the nightstand, a lamp with a ragged shade and a worn anatomy text.

I shouldn't be doing this, I should not be doing this, Petey thought, as she opened the drawer of the nightstand. But her hands dipped into the drawer anyway and came out with a fat spiral-bound sketchbook. Loose pencils rolled around in the drawer. She sat on the bed—she would have to remember to straighten the cover later—and flipped through the book. The drawings at the beginning were of trees and corn and things, some animals and people, drawings lovely but crude, as if they had been drawn by a younger person just figuring out his talent and skill. But as she leafed through the book, the drawings got more sophisticated, more detailed, more artistic. Through the middle of the book, Petey found nudes of various women in various poses. Not pornographic but beautiful, worshipful, as if the artist was trying to understand a woman's body from every angle. Her skin flushed as she examined these drawings, the lines of thighs and rise of breasts—were they imaginary women? Did he know these women? She didn't recognize any of the faces, but Sean wasn't a kid anymore, he was a man, he had a job and a life outside Bone Gap and could know all sorts of women from all sorts of places.

Face still burning, Petey turned the pages. She was looking at a chronicle of Sean's artistic life; even the nudes got more sophisticated and intimate as she progressed. Toward the last quarter of the book, she did find a face she recognized. Roza, laughing. Not a nude, but a picture of her crouching in the garden, laughing as a butterfly flitted by. After this picture, another of Roza's small hands kneading dough, Roza chopping firewood, Roza knee-deep in mud, Roza curled up in a chair reading a book, Roza, Roza, Roza, Roza. Petey stopped at a close-up of Roza's face, drawn with such loving detail that Petey felt like the worst sort of intruder, like a monster who peeps in windows in the dead of night. But she could not stop staring at it. Though the drawing was done in black pencil, Roza's smile blazed, her hair seemed to glow with dark, unearthly light, the hollow of her throat pulsed with a private invitation. The page had bumps in the paper, and Petey ran her fingertips over them, reading what must have been tearstains.

Petey closed the book and slipped it back into the drawer. She straightened the blue cover on the bed to erase the evidence. Sean wasn't a hard man. And Petey wasn't hard, either. She was just a nosy, presumptuous jerk.

She had decided that she would leave Finn's room alone; she had intruded enough for one day and found nothing, no reason not to trust Finn. But as she strode past the messy room, determined to act like a decent human being, she heard a strangled little squeak. She stopped, listening for it. Another small squeak lured her into the room. On the floor, a rag rug in blues and reds. Random piles of clothes. A cluttered desk. On the walls and dresser, photos of horses. Of cats. Of the cornfields right before harvest. Of stones in the creek bed, all of them different shades of gray. One single bed, unmade, the quilt bunched, the sheets rumpled. Curiously, no pictures of any people, anywhere. Not Miguel Cordero, who was Finn's best friend. Not his brother or his mother or father. But maybe it wasn't so odd. What did Petey know about boys?

Petey floated like a ghost toward the rumpled bed, drawn to the outline of Finn's body in the old mattress. As in Sean's room, the smell of skin, salty and sweet, was stronger by the bed, but the smell in this room was slightly different, more familiar, and not overwhelmed by pine-scented cleaner. She told herself that it was not so terrible to lie down on the bed, not so terrible to wrap herself in the sheets and the quilt, not so terrible to sink into that Finn-shaped space, not so terrible to put the pillow on her face and breathe in the scent. It was a narrow bed, like hers, and she imagined Finn on top of her, murmuring something about how beautiful she was, and her whole body flushed with the knowledge that she wasn't just a nosy jerk, she was a *weird* nosy jerk. And then she was jerking for real because something crawled across her feet. She yelped, tossed the pillow aside, and sat up to find a tiny kitten, ears like little tufts sticking from its head, getting ready to pounce. He must have used his claws to climb up the bed, because there was no way he could have jumped that high. She laughed as the teeny thing attacked her toes, but tried not to move too fast so that she didn't hurt him, this brave thing, this new thing. A larger striped cat leaped onto the bed. With great dignity, the mother cat took her baby by the scruff and jumped down. The cat padded over to the closet and sat, peering at Petey.

"You want me to open it?" said Petey. She got up from the bed and pulled the closet door wider. At the bottom of the closet was a pile of towels. The striped cat slunk inside and dropped the tiny kitten onto the pile. Then the cat stalked from the closet and crawled under the bed. She came out again bearing another striped kitten, which she also dropped into the nest at the bottom of the closet. She did this four more times, until six kittens wriggled in the towels. The mother cat walked around her babies a few times, rounding them up in a tight writhing ball of fur. The cat flopped down, too. She started to clean each kitten methodically, running her tongue over their stubby ears.

Petey went to the kitchen and found a saucer in one of the cabinets. She filled it with water, just an inch or so. She returned to Finn's room and placed the saucer on the floor by the closet door, where the mother could find it. Finn wouldn't mind if she went into his room to see the kittens, to give them water. She sat by the open door, pressed against the jamb, listening to the purring sounds of the cats. They sounded like a slower version of the hum of bees, and she felt the sounds in her skin. A lump curled in her throat, and her eyes prickled. The sight of the drawings and the sound of the kittens and the smell of Finn everywhere sapped her, made her ache for these brothers in different ways, confusing and strange and overwhelming ways, and she was again afraid that something was wrong, and she was missing it, and it would do her in.

She looked again at the kittens, each of them the same size, each of them marked with the same mottles and stripes. Petey wondered how the mother cat told them apart, if she ever needed to. They didn't look different. Maybe they smelled different? The lump and the ache grew larger, fought her attempts to swallow them down, choke them back. She glanced around the room, at the pictures with no people in them anywhere. What had Darla said, that Finn didn't recognize her with the dyed red hair? She remembered watching Finn sign her yearbook, how instead of scanning the page for his own photograph, he'd found his name first, counted from left to right to get to his picture. The swarm at the diner weeks and weeks ago, how Finn had mixed up Derek Rude with Frank. How distracted he always seemed. How he would never quite describe the man who stole Roza, at least not in the way that other people would. But his vision was fine. There were some people who were bad with faces, but . . .

She stood abruptly, fingers itching for a keyboard. But there was no keyboard here.

Except for the one on her phone.

She had a cheap phone and the internet was slower than smoke signals, but she searched anyway. She stood in Finn's room with the kittens purring and the musky scent of Finn in her nose, fingers flying, lump rising, hot tears threatening to spill over as she followed the threads, found what she never wanted to find. She stared at the tiny screen, trying to make herself accept it for what it was, for what it meant. Then she went back into the living room and opened one of the albums. She pulled a few photos and tucked them into her pocket. She replaced the album, straightening the spines so that no one would be able to tell she had been here, so no one would know how soft she really was, and how easily broken.

Finn

Questions

At the hospital, Finn was poked, prodded, X-rayed, plucked free of embedded gravel, rubbed down with stinging antiseptic, and swaddled in bandages. Then he was deposited in his own room for observation overnight. Just in case, Sean said.

What Sean didn't say: *You had me scared there for a minute, but I'm glad you're okay.* Or *It might have been a stupid thing you did, but at least it was brave.* Or *You'll feel better tomorrow.* Instead, before he left, he told Finn not to give the nurses any trouble, turned on his heel, and walked out.

Finn tried not to give the nurses any trouble. Without complaint, he ate his dinner—a dry brown sponge that he thought was supposed to be meat loaf and gelatinous mashed potatoes, though he left the hockey-puck roll alone. He took the pain pills he was offered, gulping them down with plenty of water the way he was instructed. He spent most of the evening stabbing at the remote control, trying to find a show that wasn't too boring or confusing. He settled on a documentary about a lost tribe found living deep in the Amazon, a tribe that had never before had contact with the outside world. The pictures showed the tribesmen, their bodies painted red, pointing bows and arrows at the approaching helicopters. When they saw those helicopters, did they realize what it meant? Did they know that they could never go back to the way things used to be, that their only future was one of flying monsters and strange white men with clipboards and cameras?

After a while, he pressed the power button on the remote and the TV went quiet. Sean had left him some horse magazines, but he didn't feel like reading. Despite the pain pills, his whole body felt raw, the horseshoe in the center of his chest etched in angry purpling bruises. The mare hadn't meant to stomp on him, she was just scared. But the idea that it could have been Finn who'd scared her made that mark in the center of his chest throb.

He drifted into a restless, drug-induced sleep. The steamy green jungles of the Amazon morphed into the barren cornfields of Bone Gap in the last weeks of winter. January and February had seen no snow, and March had come in like the world's sweetest lamb, but that evening—the evening that changed his life and Sean's—was chilly and gray, the lightest rain falling like glitter, the whole sky hanging low enough to drape the cornfields in gauzy gray fog. But Finn and Roza and Sean were warm as they drove to the festival that marked the approach of the spring, warm as they toured the garden of giant wood sculptures carved from logs with chain saws. Lincoln and Washington plus lions and tigers and bears. Warm as they looked at quilts and handmade furniture in a heated barn. The three of them a kind of family. Roza liked one of the dressers and Sean bargained for it. Finn moved to take one end so they could carry it to the truck, but Roza was faster and more insistent. She and Sean lugged it all the way to the parking lot. Sean asked her if she was an Olympic weight lifter.

"No," she said. "I am Polish."

Then, the beep of Sean's phone. Someone having chest pains by the hot dog stand. Sean raced off, calling over his shoulder that everything would be all right, he would take care of it, he would find them later. Roza wandered back to the sculptures while Finn went to get them cookies and warm cider. But when he returned to the sculpture garden, Roza wasn't there. He circled

Washington and Lincoln, lions and tigers and bears, but no Roza. He went back to the tent with the quilts and the furniture. After that, the maze of stalls. The cider sloshed over his hand, the cookies crumbled in his fist as he jogged, then ran to the hot dog stand, and then—when he couldn't find Sean either—back to the parking lot.

And that was when he saw her. And him. The man. Tall, thin, gray. He had her arm. He was murmuring to her, he was holding something in his palm. Finn had never seen him before. At least, he didn't think so.

"Roza!" Finn said.

Roza turned. She was smiling.

She said, "Finn. I am sorry. Please. I go now. Tell Sean . . ." She stopped talking, blinking against the icy rain.

Finn said, "What's going on? Who is this guy?"

She closed her eyes, kept smiling.

The tall man said, "I'm her husband."

"What?" Finn said. Roza had never told them where she'd come from, she'd never said what happened to her. "You're married? Is he the one that hurt you?"

"No, no," said Roza, smiling even wider. "He not hurt me."

The man let out a long and heavy sigh, as if he'd been in this situation many times before and couldn't believe it was happening again. He put a heavy hand on Finn's shoulder. "You are young, but you will learn. Beautiful women lie, just because they can. It's a sickness, really."

Finn said, "Roza?"

Roza swung her head from Finn to the man back to Finn. She opened her mouth to speak, but before she could, the man interrupted her.

"Let's not toy with this poor boy more than you already have. We don't want anything to happen to him." He looked at Finn then, a look Finn could not read. Roza looked, too. The man squeezed Finn's shoulder, squeezed too hard. Finn tried to knock the arm away, but the man was carved from stone.

Roza said, "Stop."

The man said, "Do you understand now? Do you see?"

Roza nodded. The man let Finn go. She gave Finn a last smile, didn't protest as the man steered her away. She didn't protest as he opened the passenger door of a black SUV parked sideways in the lot.

Finn rubbed his shoulder. He didn't understand, he didn't see. The laughing girl, the girl who chopped wood and danced in the dirt and talked to pigs and carried dressers and grew enough vegetables to feed a city would leave? Without a sound? Without an explanation? Without a good-bye? Without Sean?

Finn thought: *What kind of secrets has Roza been keeping?*

Then: *What if she really wants to go?*

A wave of heat, of useless rage, rushed over him, for himself, for his brother. The people of Bone Gap were right, he was a stupid moonface, a spaceman, a poor motherless boy, to think that a magical girl could show up in a barn and fix everything, to think a magical girl would stay.

Finn had crossed his arms over his chest and didn't say a word until the door slammed behind Roza, until she pressed both hands to the glass, eyes wide, wide, wide enough to fall into.

The rage melted like snow in the sun. Something was wrong.

"Wait!" Finn said.

A foot slammed into his gut so hard that the air exploded from his body. Finn dropped to the ground, arching his back, trying to make himself breathe, breathe, BREATHE. The first inhalation felt like a lungful of razors. He gasped, inhaling cold, powdery dirt. He rolled to his knees, the icy rain stinging his skin. The man stood just a few paces away, so still, so unbelievably, completely still, that he barely seemed to be alive. Maybe he wasn't. Maybe he was a scarecrow. Maybe he was dead. Maybe *Finn* was dead. Behind the man, Roza slapped at the glass, scratched at the door, trying to find the lock.

The man moved, a series of skittering twitches like

a ghost in a movie, his face inches from Finn's. He was holding a knife, a corn knife, in the moonlight, and he stared into Finn's eyes for what seemed like hours. The temperature around Finn dropped twenty degrees, and Finn's skin burned with the cold. The man pulled up, hovering over Finn, darkening Finn's world with a shadow too big for just one man. "She is mine, and she will love me," the man said, deep voice barely audible over the wind. "And when your brother cries for her, I will feed on his tears." As Finn fought to breathe, fought to *fight*, the man was gliding over the dirt, he was sliding into the car, and the car was driving away, disappearing down the long, gray throat of the storm.

Finn didn't know how long he knelt in the rain, frozen. Sirens flashed, and Sean and Jonas Apple helped Finn to his feet, his legs so stiff he could no longer feel them, the air outside him and the air inside him foggy and thick. Jonas guided Finn to the patrol car. Finn shivered, unable to get warm though the officer blasted the heat as high as it went. At the police station, a cup of hot tea with three long squeezes of Hippie Queen Honey was thrust into his hands. Books were stacked in front of him, books made entirely of faces. "Look carefully at each one," Jonas Apple was saying. "We've got time." But they didn't have time, they had no time at all, and

Finn knew it. He had to pick out the man from the pictures so that they could find Roza, so that they could save Roza. But he couldn't find the man in the pictures, the pictures all looked the same, the faces swirling and blending as if every one of them was made of nothing but sleet and wind. When Jonas Apple grew tired of the books and the waiting, and he asked for a description, every detail Finn could remember, Finn couldn't remember anything about the man. Not the color of his colorless eyes, not the shape of his nose or lips, not even the shade of his skin. Jonas Apple sat back in his chair, and the tapping of his pen on the chipped desk grew louder and louder as the doubts about what Finn had seen, doubts about what Finn had done, doubts about Finn himself, came creeping in.

Soft footsteps, the rolling of wheels. Finn's eyelids scraped open. The world was still foggy. The pills maybe. Or the memory of Roza. Or both. A face swam in front of him. Finn tried to focus but saw only a beard so thick it reminded Finn of wall-to-wall carpeting.

"Sleepy?" said a deep voice.

"What?" said Finn. It was hard to keep his lids up; they kept falling down like malfunctioning shades. His muscles wouldn't obey.

"Everybody needs rest," said the voice. "But you also

need to eat." Cool fingers circled Finn's wrist and lifted his hand to the table in front of him, to the plate on top of it.

"I ate already," Finn mumbled. His eyelids weren't working and his lips weren't working either; the words sounded garbled even to him.

But whoever this was—a doctor, a nurse—didn't seem to have any trouble understanding him. "That was hours ago. You need to keep your strength up."

"Why?"

"Your brother said so."

"My brother hates me," Finn said.

"Now, now. You know that's not true."

"It is. He does. He hates me because I lost her. I didn't mean to. I didn't know. I thought she wanted to leave." The words were nothing more than mutters and mumbles and strange hissing sounds, but the man answered him.

"But she did want to leave," said the doctor or nurse or whoever.

"No, I don't think so. I think she loved my brother. At least, I think she liked him a lot."

"Hmmm. Why?"

"What?"

"Why do you think she liked your brother?"

"I don't know."

"You must have some idea."

"I . . ." Finn's brain swam along with his vision. Why did Roza like Sean? Why did anyone like anyone? If he could answer that question, he could go on talk shows and make a million dollars.

"Think," the man said.

"Everything is blurry. Why is the room so cold?"

"Why did Roza like your brother?"

"He's big and strong."

"What else?"

"He saves people."

"What else?"

"He doesn't ask the wrong questions."

"What else?"

Finn racked his foggy brain. "He listens."

"He . . . listens?" said the man. "He listens to what?"

"To the answers to the questions. Even when he doesn't understand the answers. Especially when he doesn't understand. He keeps listening. At least, he used to. And he notices things. Things that other people don't. Things that I don't." Finn's stomach roiled and his eyelids ticked and the horseshoe burned over his heart. He opened one eye as wide as he could, which was not very wide at all. The walls of the hospital room seemed to be made of stone, the beard on the nurse's or doctor's or whoever's face dense and shaggy as moss. Finn's eyelid fell. "Are we still in the hospital?"

"No."

"I don't like this dream. I'm cold, and that's a fake beard. Who wears a fake beard in a dream? Why do you sound like you're talking underwater? What did you give me?"

The nurse or doctor or fake-beard-wearing person said, "So, your brother asks the right questions and you ask the wrong ones."

"What?"

"This has been very instructive."

"What?" Finn used cold and trembling fingers to peel back his eyelids, forced his reluctant eyes to focus.

But when he did, there was nobody there.

Roza

The Lamb

The sun touched her face like the softest caress. Roza sat up in bed, feeling for the familiar warmth of Rus. He was there, as huge and shaggy and ugly as always, but the castle had vanished. Instead of the cavernous chamber with its oversize hearth and red velvet curtains, the room in which Roza awoke was small, simple, neat, and so familiar.

Roza threw back the covers, flew to the window. She looked out not upon a moat teeming with monsters or guards marching back and forth, but on streets indifferently paved with cobblestones. Long-faced horses and chocolate-eyed cows wandered past houses huddled right at the edge of the road. Beyond the houses and the street, rolling green hills frilled with clumps of trees and flowers brushed up against a brilliant blue sky.

"Here," Roza breathed. "Rus, we're here." But even as she said it, she knew it wasn't true. The hills were too green, the sky too blue, the cobbles too indifferent. And Rus, dear Rus, was with her, and how could he be if this whole thing had been a dream?

Still, the vision was close enough to the real thing to bring her hands to her chest, to fold them as if in prayer. She turned from the window, went to the wardrobe in the corner of the room, and flung the doors wide. She grabbed a summer dress from a hanger. She didn't have to check the stitching to know that it had been made by hand, just the way her babcia used to do. Roza changed from the nightgown to the dress, not even caring that there were still no shoes for her to wear, for this was not the place for shoes. Her feet felt fast and light as she slipped from the room and smelled the rich smell of coffee and of bacon sizzling in an iron pan. With Rus at her side, she entered the kitchen. Her breath caught when she glimpsed the old woman with silver hair standing at the stove. *It couldn't be, it couldn't be . . . could it?*

The woman turned.

It wasn't.

The woman gestured toward the table, told her to sit. Roza slowly lowered herself into the chair. *Where is he?* she wanted to ask. *Did I kill him? And if I killed him . . . ?* The kitchen was so much like her babcia's kitchen, but then, the coffee mug with the red rooster on it was not a mug owned by her babcia, and the plate on which the woman laid the strips of bacon and one perfectly fried egg was beige instead of white. Roza asked for toast and the old woman smiled and cut two large slices from a fresh loaf on the counter. While the woman dug around in the cupboards for a tray, Roza slipped the bacon and egg to the dog. But the toast, when it was pulled from the oven, was delicious, and she was so hungry.

Roza got up from the table, unsure of what to do next. She had gotten used to the rhythms of the enormous castle—the bustle of the cooks in the kitchen, the marching of the guards, the falconers with their swooping birds of prey, the cats chasing the mice along the stone floors, even the restless splashing in the moat. The sounds were so different here. Low moos and whinnies from outside, the buzz of gossip, the clatter of heels on the cobblestones. The smells were different, too—earth and grass, flowers and milk. She went to the front door, laid her hand on the handle. She expected the door to be locked, but when she pulled on it, the door opened. Roza stood there, too surprised to move, until Rus nudged her forward onto the porch. The bare wood was comfortable and familiar under her feet. But her feet wanted more than just the sensation of bare wood, her feet wanted to *go*. Her feet took her down the porch steps and onto the stones already warmed by the sun. She walked down the street past the chocolate-eyed cows and the long-faced horses, unable to keep a smile from twitching at her lips. She didn't know if she was dying in some hospital bed somewhere or if she had slipped into some dark chasm from which there was no return, but if cobbled streets and cows and rolling hills were the last things she saw, maybe she could bear it.

She sped up to a jog, heading for the green hills filled with wildflowers so tall and thick they waved like new corn. She splashed through a stream and Rus splashed with her, dancing around her, great wet mouth curving up in his own version of a smile. The cows and the horses and the sheep watched her as she ran herself out, as she fell in a heap at the top of a hill. But the flowers and grasses *shush*ed, *shush*ed in the gentle wind and her worlds blended—she could be here, wherever here was, and she could be flinging herself from a black SUV into a vast and endless cornfield, a field that caught her, held her.

The earth had been hard, and she had been hurt—cheek, wrist, ribs, foot—but not nearly as badly as she'd expected. The corn itself seemed to shield her as she ran through it, impossibly growing taller, denser, reaching outward and upward, *alive*, alive, whispering for her to run, run, not to stop, never to stop. The professor—that madman—must have been chasing her, but the cornfield was so dark and seemed so determined to save her. It was as if she had passed from one dimension into another where no man would ever find her—unless she wanted to be found.

When she could not run any harder, any longer, she'd fallen from the thick jungle of corn plants onto a bare, grassy field, trees all around. Strange lights shot through the trees, and she stayed low to the ground, trying to figure out what they were. She heard voices, and the panic rose in her throat, and she ran until she came upon the cars. A row of them—trucks, vans, sedans—parked in the crushed grass. She ducked behind a bush as the voices got louder.

"That sucked, Mom."

"Shhh! These people work hard to arrange the orienteering courses."

"But I took a day off from school. And this isn't even a real forest. There wasn't anything to find. Look at the map! We had to locate a rock. And some stupid spindly tree. No waterfalls, nothing cool."

"Well, were you the first one over the finish line?"

Silence.

"Then I guess this course wasn't so easy, was it?"

Some low grumbling. "It still sucked."

"Shhh!"

The people came into view, a mother and two children, one boy near to Roza's age and another some years younger. The three held flashlights, the beams pointed at the ground. The younger boy giggled. "You're just mad because that girl already had a boyfriend."

The mother said, "What girl?"

"Never mind," the bigger boy said.

"No normal girl is going to want some guy with Hulk arms," the younger boy said.

"Better than having a Hulk *face*."

"Stop it," said the mother. "Your arms and faces are perfectly normal arms and faces, and I don't want to listen to the two of you bickering the whole way home."

"Maybe we can put him in the trunk," said the older boy.

"Was that supposed to be a joke, Miguel?"

"No," said Miguel.

The woman pulled a key fob from her pocket, and the red lights of a minivan flashed. "Before you get in the car, I want you to scrape your shoes. If I find dirt in my car, you're going to be the ones vacuuming it."

The boys grumbled some more but sat in the grass to remove their shoes, clap them together to rid them of the dirt. The mother wandered over to another car, began chatting with another family. Roza looked from her, to the boys, to the minivan. A stiff breeze hit the cornfield behind her, the whispering sound urging her on.

Miguel said, "Doesn't it sound like the corn is talking?"

His brother said, "Only if you're loco."

Roza cracked the rear door and crawled inside, burying herself in tarps and cleats and empty shopping bags. She pulled the door closed, wincing at the noise, hoping no one had heard it, that no one would check. No one did. The boys and their mother got in the minivan, and the boys bickered the whole three-hour ride. By the time the mother stopped, told the boys to shut up and get out, and everyone did, and left the van dark, engine still ticking, Roza was afraid she'd stay folded like a pretzel in the minivan for the rest of time. But, after a long, long while, as long as she could stand it, long enough for the evening to shift into night, she rose out of the pile of tarps and empty shopping bags, pushed open the door, and stepped out into the crisp air. Wherever she was, it was clear and full of stars. Her wrist and ribs and cheek and foot hurt, but it was her stomach that was making the most noise: she was starving. She limped around the perimeter of the house, looking for a garden, some carrots she could dig from the earth, a tomato she could pluck from a vine, but these people didn't keep a garden. She peered into the back window, into a dark kitchen, where a pile of apples sat in a bowl on the table. Her mouth watered and she tried the back door. Unlocked. She crept into the kitchen, took an apple, and ate it in just a few bites. The fridge beckoned. She rifled through it, devouring a chicken leg, a piece of cheese, a handful of grapes. She closed the door and almost fainted when she saw the older boy standing there in the kitchen, swaying slightly. He was wearing striped pajama bottoms that made him appear much younger, as did his dazed expression. He did have big, powerful arms, which might have scared her had she not had the most peculiar thought: those arms would allow him to give some lucky girl excellent hugs if she wanted them.

"Sorry," she said. "I pay?" Though she had no money, nothing to pay with.

"I heard the corn talking to you," he said.

"What?"

He didn't seem to hear her. He lurched forward and she stepped back, only to realize that he was not grabbing for her, he was opening the fridge. He pulled a container of cooked spaghetti from the shelf and shoveled the tangled nest into his mouth with his fingers. His glazed eyes were focused on the window behind her. As if he was asleep.

"Who are you?" he said.

"No one. I am ghost."

"Okay." The boy frowned at the empty container in his hand. There was a strand of spaghetti sprouting from the side of his mouth. "Was that a sandwich? I wanted a sandwich. La Reina Pepiada."

"That was sandwich," Roza said. "Good sandwich."

The boy's expression was mournful. "It was a bad sandwich. No chicken or avocado or anything."

"No, good. Very good. The best."

The boy put the empty container back into the fridge. "Okay. I need to go to bed now. Good night, ghost."

"Good night."

He turned, stopped. "The corn told me that if you follow the stream going east, you'll find a red barn with a slanted roof. Did the corn tell you that?"

"No," she said.

"You should always listen to the corn. You don't want it to get mad." His eyes were still focused on the window behind her, but he leaned in and whispered, "I think it walks around at night. The corn. It doesn't like the Scare Crow." And then his eyes slid back in his head, his body swiveled, and his legs walked his sleeping brain from the kitchen.

Corn or no corn, she'd had no intention of following any streams, but when she stepped outside the stone house and got a lungful of the crisp, clean air, and an eyeful of the winking stars, she felt freer than she had in a long time. The professor was gone, the city was gone, and here she was under the beautiful stars—alone, alive. She smiled as she found the stream and followed it. The full moon watched her with a warm and approving eye as she hobbled along, slowed by the injured foot, pained by it, but not troubled. She didn't know how long she walked, or how far, and it didn't seem to matter. There was the cool water, the smell of flowers and honey, the sparkling, winking stars that told stories of little bears and big bears, Orion and Andromeda and Hercules, even if she didn't know which star was which. And finally she saw it as if the moon was illuminating it just for her: a barn slanted to the left. She left the stream and made for the barn, which sat right next to a peeling white house, now dark and sleeping. She opened the barn door and peered around inside. Not much, but there was an old pile of hay in the corner that didn't smell too awful. It was as good a place as any to sleep.

"A barn needs a horse," said Roza under her breath. A blur of movement caught her eye. "Or a cat."

The cat, a tiny thing with brown and gray stripes, wound around Roza's legs, joined her in the pile of hay, curling up next to her face, breathing the same breath.

Though her foot throbbed and her ribs and wrist ached, she fell asleep in the hay.

When she woke up, the barn was bright with sunlight, the cat was gone, and a beautiful dark-haired boy was standing there, gaping at her. Weirdly, he wasn't gaping at her face, but rather his eyes darted from her hair to her dirty sweatshirt and back to her hair.

"Are you okay?" the boy said. "Are you hurt?"

She struggled to stand, straightened as best she could, and limped past the boy toward the open door. He reached out—to help her, she guessed—but when he touched the skin of her elbow, she was so startled she stumbled. Instead of hauling her back to her feet, or scooping her up like a sack of cabbages, he turned and ran.

She crept out of the barn and around the side of the structure, seeking the stream that had led her here. Maybe she could go back to the stone house, back to Miguel with the long arms and the kind face. Maybe she could hitch a ride to somewhere with an airport and stow away on a plane. Maybe she could ask about a police station and allow herself to be deported.

She heard footsteps and fell against the wood, then into a green bush. The footsteps came around the barn—the first boy with another boy—a young man—tall and muscular as an action hero. Not handsome like the first boy, but rugged and compelling, with huge, powerful hands.

The man crouched next to her. "Hello."

She didn't answer.

"Can you tell me what happened? Are you injured?" He didn't stare at her face or her breasts or her legs the way other men had. He was looking directly into her eyes, seeming to see straight into her, as if he knew something about her already and was not that surprised. Or impressed. The effect was so disconcerting that when he held out one of those enormous hands, she slapped it away.

The two boys talked about hospitals, but she didn't want to go to the hospital. She didn't want to go, period. She was sitting in a bush, yes, and she'd walked miles with an injured foot, she'd barely escaped a psychopath, she was done with America, she'd had enough of men, she'd had enough of adventure, she needed to get home to her babcia, she had hay in places she didn't want hay, but suddenly, suddenly, she didn't want to go anywhere. She was too hurt, she was too tired. And though these two were men, and young, she felt seen and unseen at the same time, and it was such a relief. When they offered her the keys to an apartment in the back of their house, she almost cried at the kindness.

So she stayed, telling herself it was only for a day

or two. They showed her the "apartment," gave her some threadbare sheets for the bed. She locked the door behind them, tucked a chair under the knob. She fell into the bed and slept like a princess under a spell.

When she emerged from her coma, she was so stiff that she thought there was a danger of her limbs cracking off if she moved, so hungry that her stomach was willing to risk it. She let herself out of the apartment and hobbled to the back door of the house, lifted her hand to knock, hesitated. The kitchen light was on, but the room was empty. And then one brother, the big one, stepped through the doorway and into the kitchen. He had half a bagel clamped in his teeth as he buttoned up his shirt, some sort of uniform. He finished buttoning and took a bite of the bagel, set it down on the counter while he poured himself some coffee. The tiny striped barn cat trotted into the kitchen, whirled around his ankles. Absently, he reached down, scooped her up, and perched her on his shoulders. He leaned against the counter, eating his bagel and sipping his coffee, the cat frantically rubbing his hair with her little head. Despite her stiff body, her embarrassment at her predicament, Roza laughed.

He turned, saw her through the window in the door. His cheeks went ever so slightly pink as he pulled the cat from his shoulders and set her on the floor. When he opened the door, the smell of strong coffee wafted out with him. Already, the blush was gone and she wondered if she'd imagined it.

"Sorry," he said. "Have you been there long?"

She shook her head.

Again, he looked straight into her eyes, his gaze oddly weightless, demanding nothing. "You slept a long time. How are you feeling?"

She shrugged.

He dropped to one knee in front of her and she stumbled back, clutching the top of her sweatshirt.

He held up both palms. "Just checking these feet, okay?"

The striped cat rubbed along his thigh, covering his uniform pants with fur.

"Okay," she said.

He inspected her toes—one foot, the other—then stood. "They're not any more swollen than they were yesterday, so that's something. How are your ribs? Your wrist?"

She shrugged again. Her stomach rumbled. She wrapped her arms around her middle.

Again, the oddly weightless gaze. "If you're hungry, we've got plenty of food," he said. He pointed to the fridge, various cabinets and drawers. "Milk and eggs in there. Bread right here. Other stuff in the pantry. And the coffee's still hot, if you drink it this late. I'm on my way to work, so take what you like. But I wouldn't stay on your feet too long."

She nodded. He nodded back—crisp, professional, as if he were talking to a patient.

Before he left, he said, "Get some ice on those toes."

She nodded again, and then he was gone. The cat mewled and head-butted her. Roza remembered the pink blush on the man's cheeks. She tried perching the cat on her own shoulders, but they were too thin. She settled for carrying the cat like a baby as she poked in the cabinets. There was a lot of food that came in boxes and jars, but she found some good dark bread and some butter and jam. She poured herself a cup of the strong coffee and ate her fill with the cat on her lap. Then she filled some plastic bags with some ice and hobbled back to the apartment. She crawled into the bed and laid the bags on her feet. She had one last thought before she fell asleep again: she had forgotten to lock the door.

She slept, she woke, she ate, she slept again. She carried the cat like a baby. The big one checked her toes and asked after her ribs and wrist, and then dashed off for work. The younger one was shy and awkward and seemed much more comfortable simply bringing her things: bags of ice, glasses of water, tea with honey. She asked to borrow a phone to call her babcia, so he brought her that, too, waving off her offer to pay them back. Eventually, her toes felt better, her ribs began to heal.

She still didn't want to leave.

They were kind to her, but that wasn't it. She felt so light around them, as if the eyes of others had a heft and a pressure that she couldn't comprehend until the pressure was gone. She ignored the boxes and the jars and cooked her favorite foods, she baked tray after tray of cookies. She worked the dirt in the garden—rich dirt wriggling with worms—bringing a sad patch of vegetables to life.

"Looks good," said the big one, Sean.

She glanced up from the tomato plants. They had been planted too close together, and she had decided to replant a few in the hopes they would flourish even this late in the season. The day was hot and she had taken off her sweatshirt and tied it around her waist, baring her shoulders to the sun. She had been enjoying the feeling until she heard his footsteps.

But he wasn't looking at her. He was looking at the root ball she cradled, at the garden all around her.

"It's never looked this good," he said. "The plants, the whole garden. Everything's so green. Green as . . ." He didn't finish.

"Green as?" she said.

"Really green."

Her eyes were green, but that couldn't be what he'd been going to say.

"Where did you learn how to do this?" he said.

"My babcia."

He frowned at the unfamiliar word. "Bop-cha?"

"*Babcia.* Is grandmother. She has garden. She teach."

"A garden in Poland?"

"Yes."

She was sure he'd ask how she came to be in America, and then how she came to be in his barn, how she could trust him so fast, and she was trying to figure out how she wanted to answer when he said, "Do you miss it?"

"What?"

"Poland."

"Yes," she said.

"Will you go back?"

"I will be back," she said. "But . . ."

"But?"

"I stay here," she said, embarrassed by her need, by her inability to put it into words he could understand, that *she* could. "For little while? Is okay?"

Again, she was sure he'd ask about her feet and her ribs and her wrist, and how she'd hurt them, or maybe who had hurt her, but she didn't think she could explain that either. There had been little hurts and big ones and she could hardly tell them apart, and it all sounded crazy anyway. The sun was warm here, she knew that. The garden was green. The dirt was good. She could bury herself and be happy.

He said, "Do you want help?"

Heat burned her skin—anger or embarrassment or some mixture of both. When she'd first come, she'd overheard him talking to the younger one, Finn, about counselors and doctors and shelters for girls like her.

Girls like her.

"Toes better," she said. "I better."

"No, I mean, do you want help with those tomato plants?"

His eyes were dark brown, just like the earth under her feet.

She sprawled in the grass, Rus beside her, wondering what Sean was doing now. Was he looking for her? Had he found someone else to work the garden?

A shadow fell over her. Rus growled. She squeezed her eyes shut.

Of course it was the man.

Of course she had not killed him.

Of course he could not be wounded.

But she could be. He could kill her right now, she supposed, though she could hardly gather up enough energy to care.

She sat up, opened her eyes. He was a dark figure blotting out the sun.

"You're crying," he said.

That he said these kinds of things made no sense to her. "So?" she snapped.

"Perhaps this will cheer you up."

Because the sun was behind him, it took her a moment to realize that in his arms he held a wriggling black-faced lamb.

"Oh!" she said, the sound escaping before she could pull it back.

He smiled that smile of his, and she knew he would ask the question he always asked, and despite the sun and the cows and the hills and the wriggling black-faced lamb, she buried her hand in Rus's fur, steeling herself for her answer.

The man scratched the little lamb between the ears and did not ask the question he always asked.

He said, "Would you like to hold him?"

Roza's hand dropped to her lap, the tears still wet on her skin.

"Yes," she heard herself say. "Yes, I would."

Finn

Blindside

Finn spent the night wrapped in fevered dreams that he could barely remember upon waking, so he spent the next morning and the rest of the day refusing the pain pills and insisting to anyone who would listen that he was fine, he was absolutely fine, he didn't need skin on his legs, he was ready to go. He was released in the early evening, and not soon enough. Sean picked him up, drove him home in a silence so absolute Finn felt as if he were wearing a helmet packed with lamb's wool. He was relieved when Sean dropped him off, when Sean didn't bother stopping inside to eat.

Finn went first to the fridge to get a couple of apples, then to the barn to check on the mare. If she'd been scared of him yesterday, she wasn't today. She nosed his forehead and snorted into his hair and stomped her hoof for her treat. He fed her the apple and stroked her mane and said he was making it official, her name was Night. She nodded her royal head and then shook it, as if to say, *I told you my name a long time ago, and you're just figuring it out? I like your apples, but you're not very bright.*

"As for you," Finn said to the goat, who had eaten his apple in one gulp, "you are what you do. You are Chew."

"Meh!" said Chew, which Finn took as agreement.

After he'd fed and watered the animals, he hobbled to the garden. And a sad, sad garden it was. Leaves droopy and yellowing, rabbit holes everywhere. He had worked as hard as he could on that garden, and yet everything was dying. Just one more way he'd disappointed his brother. But he plucked the weeds and filled in the rabbit holes and watered the garden, too, just in case there was something to salvage, something under the surface that couldn't be seen.

At least the horse wasn't mad at him.

He went into the house to check on Calamity and the kittens, kittens he found sleeping in a messy, boneless heap at the bottom of his closet. They would need names too, but right now they were simply the Kittens. He grabbed the saucer of water Petey must have left on the floor, refilled it. He scraped out a can of cat food onto a plate and set the plate by the closet door. Then he stripped off his dirty clothes and wrapped his bandages in plastic. He showered as best he could with one leg sticking out of the bathtub, dried off, dressed, and tried to occupy himself with dinner and with books and with Kittens until the darkness came and he could see Petey again. Petey was mad at him, but maybe she wouldn't stay that way for long. He should bring something to her, a gift, but what? Some of the Kittens would need homes, but they were too little to give away. And he had nothing else.

But wait. He did have something. He went to the bathroom and took the jeweled box from the shelf. He took out all the bandages and swabs and put them in an old mug from the kitchen. Sean kept the bathroom so clean that the box didn't have a speck of dust on it, but Finn wiped it down anyway. He opened the lid. He couldn't give her an empty box, even a nice empty box.

He brought the box to the kitchen table, sat with pen and paper, all those stupid prep books. He wrote, then crossed out, balled up the paper, threw it in the trash. Wrote some more. Wrote again until he had something that could work, something that said a little of what he felt, even though he was just scratching the surface.

When the clock read ten thirty-five, and Finn

couldn't wait anymore, he folded the sheet of paper and slipped it into the box. He went back to the barn and led Night into the yard. Despite his wounds, and the ache in his bones, he hauled himself up on the mare's back and rode to Petey's house, happy to see the glow of the fire in the beeyard, calmed by the hum of the bees. Petey was sitting cross-legged on a blanket, poking at the fire with a stick.

"Hey," he said as he sat down next to her.

"Hey," she said. "I thought maybe you wouldn't come."

"Why not?"

She shrugged and jabbed the fire. "Because of your leg."

"My leg's fine." He brushed the hair from her face. He'd been here a total of nine seconds, and already he couldn't keep his hands off her.

But her eyes glittered in the firelight, her expression unreadable. He said, "Are you still mad?"

"Mad at what?"

"You were mad yesterday."

She shook her head. Jabbed the fire.

"Is it something else?"

Again, she shook her head. Jab. Jab.

"Are you sure?"

Jab. Jab. Jab.

"I have something for you." He held out the box.

She dropped the stick and took it, stared at the

jeweled box winking blue and red and purple in the light of the fire.

"It was my mother's. She called it her beauty box. She kept makeup and stuff in it."

"I can't take your mother's box."

"Sure you can. We weren't using it anyway. I mean, we were, for bandages and whatever, but I thought it would look better in your room. I thought it would be better with you. Look inside."

She did. She took out the piece of paper, opened it. Read. She touched her mouth with her fingertips. Her voice was softer when she said, "Thank you."

He put the paper back in the box and set it aside. He turned one of her hands palm up and, with his thumb, drew little circles where the lines formed a star. "Thank *you* for taking care of Night for me."

"Night?"

"The mare. I finally named her."

"Night," she said, testing the name. Petey looked over at the horse, standing some yards away next to a tree. "I bet that's what she wanted all along."

"Probably," he said. "I'm sorry about her. About chasing her. I mean, I scared her, I think. And maybe I scared you. I didn't mean to."

Petey didn't say anything, but she didn't pull her arm away either.

"And I hope I didn't wreck your moped."

"You didn't. That thing's a tank."

He pressed his lips against her wrist, then her forearm and the inside of her elbow. "I missed you. I know it was only twenty-four hours, but . . ."

A pause. Then, "I missed you, too. Are you . . . are you sure your leg's okay?"

"Are you sure *you're* okay?"

She blinked, and for a second he thought she was blinking back tears, but then she leaned forward, cupped his face in her hands, and kissed him, so he must have been wrong, must have been seeing things.

"You brought a blanket this time," he said.

She nodded, hugging herself. "I know that we were inside last time, but since we met outside—"

"We met in nursery school."

"I mean," she said, "this is where we first—"

He interrupted her with another kiss. "Are we celebrating something?"

"Just . . ." She seemed to be having trouble getting the words out. "Just that you're here."

His wounded leg burned, but not as much as the rest of him, and he pressed her back onto the blanket. They kissed until his brain spun, until her limbs fell loose and soft and open, until the moon hid its face behind a veil of clouds. She pulled off his shirt and he pulled off hers, and the bra with it, lingering over her breasts, tasting the salt and sweet of her. She was so beautiful in the firelight, glowing like an ember, and he thought he said it out loud, *beautiful, beautiful*, but he couldn't be sure. He wanted to hear her say his name, he wanted to make her feel so good she'd never leave him, he wanted so many things he lost the words for them all. He unbuttoned her jeans and slid them away, and the wisp of white cotton she wore underneath, his lips tracing a path across her belly, the half-moons of her hip bones, down one thigh, up the other, and back to the center, where he kissed, and kissed, and forgot where he was and who he was and who he had hurt and who he had not saved. She clenched the blanket in her fists, and sighed, and breathed his name, and if she hadn't said it out loud, he wouldn't have known what to call himself, because everything was her.

When it was over, he kissed his way up her body and reached for her face. Felt the tears on his fingertips.

"Petey?"

She pressed both palms over her eyes and started to cry, and kept crying, and he didn't understand, he didn't understand. He thought he had done it right, or at least done it okay, but maybe he had done it wrong, maybe it wasn't what she wanted, maybe he should have asked her out loud, he'd never thought of asking her. He didn't know how he would have asked that kind of question—how do you ask that kind of question when you've completely lost the power of speech?—but maybe she hadn't wanted anything at all, maybe he'd . . . *made* her, and the thought of that brought on a wave of nausea so strong he wished the horse had stomped him to death. "Petey, I'm sorry. I'll never . . . If you didn't want . . . I'm sorry, I'm sorry."

Finally, wordlessly, she grabbed for her clothes, tugged them on. He didn't know what else to do, so he did the same, wishing she would just say something. But Petey swiped at her cheeks, reached into the shadows beyond the blanket, and pulled a worn canvas bag onto her lap. She dug around inside the bag and found a stack of pictures, which she handed to Finn.

"What are these?" he said.

"Just take a look."

"Okay," he said, flipping through the pictures. He had no idea what he was looking at, or who he was looking at, or why he was looking at pictures when the taste of her was still on his lips, when she had just wept like someone had died.

She tapped a particular picture. "What do you think of this one?"

It was a dark-haired kid in a grade-school graduation cap and gown. It meant nothing to him. "It's okay."

"I think Sean looks cute." She seemed to be watching him intently, her body—all softness just moments before—coiled and tense.

"Okay," he said again. Where had she gotten an old picture of Sean? Since when was Sean *cute*?

"Don't you think so?"

"Think what?"

"That Sean looks nice in that picture?"

"I don't know. I guess."

She sprang forward and ripped the stack from his hands, her expression so triumphant that not even Finn could mistake it. "This isn't Sean."

He stared at her. "Well, who is it, then?"

"What?"

"If it's not Sean, who is it?"

Her breath burst from her in a huff, as if someone had wrapped his arms around her and performed the Heimlich. "Who . . . ?" she began. "It's James Pullman. From school."

Finn held out his hand, and she placed the photograph back into it. "It's hard to tell. It's dark out here. It's an old picture. And because of the cap and gown. You can't see his ears. Sean's ears stick out a little."

"But I knew it was James," she said.

"Petey, why did you bring these pictures out here? Why are you showing them to me?"

"Do you have problems with your eyes? Maybe you can see things better when they're far away?"

"Huh?"

"Can you see me right now?"

"What are you talking about? Why wouldn't I be able to see you?"

"Right," she said, mostly to herself. "Right. You could pick out the queen bee. So you can see just fine. But . . ." She shook her head and flipped through the stack of photos. "Who's this?"

"Enough with the pictures already," he said. "Tell me what's wrong."

She thrust the photo at him. "Who is it?"

He sighed and glanced at the photo. "Miguel."

"How do you know this is Miguel?"

"What?"

"Just humor me for a second. How do you know it's Miguel?"

"Well, he's brown. And the biceps."

"And that's it?"

"Huh?"

"You just look for the arms, and you know it's Miguel?"

"Well, yeah. I mean, the hair helps, too. It's really dark. But mostly, I look for the arms. Don't you do that?"

"What if you met someone else with the same brown skin who also had big arms? Would you be able to tell that it *wasn't* Miguel?"

"I . . ." Finn's mind raced. Then he said, "Would you?"

"Yes. I'd be able to tell."

"You're better at faces, then. Lots of people are." He thought of Roza, of her kidnapper, and bitterness sanded his tongue. "Believe me, I know I'm not so good at faces."

"I don't think that's all of it," said Petey. She flipped through the pictures again. "What about this one?"

"He looks familiar," Finn began.

Petey nodded.

He brushed a finger over the image as if that could provide more information. "He's wearing a cap, too."

Petey nodded again.

"But you think I should be able to tell who it is anyway?"

"Yes," Petey said.

"Why? Why do you think that?" He reached for her hand, but she pulled away. "Petey?"

She took a deep breath. "Finn," she said. "It's a picture of *you*."

He watched her carefully. She seemed to think this was a very important thing to say, but he didn't understand her, he didn't understand any of this. "And you think I should have been able to see that right away. Even though he's—I've—got that cap on, I should have been able to see?"

She rocked backward as if assaulted by a strange wind. "Yes."

"Just by the face alone?"

"Yes," she said.

"And that's . . ." He paused, his mind churning, stumbling onto it, feeling for it, the thing that made him odd, the thing that made him different. "That's how everyone else does it? They see someone's face and they just *know* who it is? Without having to see their hair or their clothes or the way they move or anything?"

"Yes!" she said, almost shouting. Then she softened her voice. "Finn, I think you're face blind."

"I'm . . . *what*?"

"It's a condition." She dug around in the bag, pulled out papers, printouts from the computer, articles, a library book with the name Sacks on the cover. "You can see as well as anyone else, but you can't recognize faces the way other people can."

He sat very still on the blanket, his wounded leg suddenly stiff and itchy. "I don't know what you're talking about."

"You can't process the image of a face, you can't store the image so that you can remember it later. Some face-blind people learn to recognize themselves and close family members, but some can't even pick their own children from a crowd. And some will never recognize a face, even their own."

Before, he'd wished she would just say something,

and now he wished she would stop talking. But she didn't.

"It's why so many people look the same to you. It's why you don't look people in the eye. Why you couldn't describe the man who took Roza."

He felt as if he were unraveling like a ball of yarn. "I *did* describe the man who took Roza."

"Not like someone else would. You couldn't see his features. You couldn't put them together. You talked about how he moved, which is the way some face-blind people recognize others. They use other cues like facial hair or body type. Here. I found lots of stuff about it." She thrust the papers at him.

He didn't want the papers. He didn't want any of this. It had never occurred to him to ask anyone how he or she recognized another person. And why would he? It would be like asking people how they knew that the smell of coffee was the smell of coffee. A stupid question. Everyone knew what coffee smelled like. Everyone.

"But . . .," he said. "I can see you. I always know it's you."

One side of her mouth curved up into a smile, no kind of smile at all. "Yeah. Because I'm ugly."

"Stop it," he said.

"It's true. Face-blind people can sometimes recognize really unusual-looking people, and they're attracted to them." She pawed through the damned papers. "This article is about a teenage girl with prosopagnosia—that's the technical name for face blindness—who ran away with a middle-aged circus clown. But she was attracted to him because she could see him, recognize him in a crowd."

Again, she thrust this article at him. He pushed it away. He didn't want the stupid article. "You're not a circus clown."

"No, not a clown. But I'm hideous. Everyone thinks so."

"I don't think so," Finn said, angry now. He had some sort of crazy disease and Petey was talking about being ugly after he'd been coming for her every night, because he couldn't stand to be away from her, and she was throwing papers and books at him as if it proved something about *her*, and not about him.

"It's true," she said. "I look like a giant bee. And that's why you can tell it's me. And that's why you're here." She shrugged, but the tears came again, wet tracks down her cheeks.

"That's not why," he said.

She said nothing.

He said, "I love you."

She shook her head. "You can see me, that's all."

But wasn't that love? Seeing what no one else could? And yet if it wasn't enough for her that she was beautiful to him, if she couldn't believe him . . .

And who would? If what she said was true, and he had this thing, who would believe anything he said about anyone, ever?

He clutched at the horseshoe branding his heart as if he could will away the terrible ache that threatened to crush him, the terrible knowledge that told him that the people of Bone Gap had been right all along. *They* had recognized him for what he was. Spaceman. Sidetrack. Moonface. Not like other people. Not like them.

"Petey," he said, but she held the box up to him. "Petey." Her head dropped, and the tears spilled onto her knees, droplets soaking into the fabric of her jeans, and she would not look at him, would not speak. He took the book and the papers and his mother's box and got to his feet. He stumbled to the mare. He had no idea how he had the strength to haul himself onto her back, how he got home, how long he sifted through the articles, how he got into his bed, how Calamity sensed the calamity. Cat and Kittens surrounded him, buried him, and their thick and rumbling purrs reminded him of the hum of the bees, and the taste of honey. He wrapped himself in the sound and drowned in the warmth. He plummeted into sleep, the only place he could pretend he wasn't blind, the only place he could pretend he still had everything he'd lost.

Roza

The Dead

Without planning it, Roza settled into a routine, awaking each morning in her simple bedroom, greeting the iron-haired lady in the kitchen, eating the nutty toast hot from the oven, walking through town toward the hills, splashing through the streams, decorating Rus with flowers until he looked ridiculous. In the afternoons, the man would visit, and he would bring a lamb, and she would hold it, and kiss its soft woolly head, and smell the wool on her hands the rest of the day, the smell like a promise. He did not touch her, did not approach her. And the question he asked her when she was holding the lamb was not the same question. Now he asked her other things: her favorite food (jam-filled cookies), her favorite color (brown), her favorite game as a child (hide-and-seek). He even asked her if she wanted to play it, and she snorted despite herself, imagining this tall, strange man with ice-chip eyes crouching in the boxwoods.

So she asked *him* a question: Could she have a garden? The next morning, she awoke, ate her toast, walked into the field, and found a patchwork of the greenest, healthiest vegetable plants she had ever seen, beds of flowers so carefully arranged they could have been in the courtyard of an English manor. The sight of these things disappointed her so greatly that even the lamb couldn't cheer her, so the man asked her what was wrong.

"I wanted to grow the plants myself," she said.

"Yes, yes, of course," he said, and nodded, and the next day, the vegetables and the flowers were gone, and in their place was a bare expanse of rich dark earth, sacks of seeds and tiny pots of seedlings, a shovel and spade, a watering can.

Roza had her garden. And if the earth smelled a little too rich, and the plants grew a little too easily and looked a little too vibrant, the worms in the soil too fat and happy, the praying mantises too pious and too plentiful, she told herself that she was surely dying in a hospital somewhere, and that the garden was a gift from her own wasting mind, a last vision of happiness, and there was nothing to fear anymore, as this was her last adventure.

But she could not help—as she dug in the dirt, and sang to the worms, and prayed with the mantises—comparing this garden, this field, with her other gardens, with Sean's garden. For a farm boy, he was not a very good gardener. But he did everything that she told him to do and seemed just as happy as she when the tomatoes finally turned fat and red. Sean helped her hill the potato plants so that they didn't get sunburned and helped her dig up the tubers once the vines died. When the fall came, and the garden didn't need them so much anymore, she taught him how to make pierogi, to fill the purses of dough with potato and onion and pinch them closed.

"Must be tight or will leak in pan," she said, demonstrating. "Now you."

"Like this?" he said. But he was not looking at the purse of dough in his own hands, he was staring at *her* hands. Of all the things to stare at. Her hands were rough skinned, broken nailed, small but strong. Her hands had rolled dough and chopped potatoes and milked cows and prepared slides and made things grow. She'd even sewn stitches in his finger when he'd cut himself with a kitchen knife.

She liked that he stared at them. She liked him for staring.

She tucked a stray curl behind an ear, and his eyes followed the motion.

Soon, she was sneaking glances, too. At the pink scar on his finger. The curls on the nape of his neck. The furrow between his brows. The veins in his forearms. And the more she looked, the more she wanted to see. On a warm day in the late fall, they were adding compost to the garden to prepare it for the next spring, and he stopped to rest. He used the bottom of his T-shirt to mop the sweat from his face. The pale exposed flesh of his belly froze her. He dropped the edge of the shirt and there she was—gaping, humiliated—but unable to tear her eyes away in case he decided to do it again.

The next time he rushed into the kitchen, late for work, fumbling with the buttons on his uniform shirt, and found her leaning against the sink, coffee cup hovering an inch from her lips, he stopped buttoning, stood stock-still, let her look.

When she reached out with her rough-skinned hand and touched the dark hair that dusted his chest, he let her touch.

And when she stepped up on a chair and leaned down to kiss him, he let her do that, too.

And when she stepped down, stepped back, chewing hard on the inside of her cheek, terrified and overwhelmed by all that looking and touching and kissing, he buttoned up the shirt and tucked the chair under the table. As if he understood. As if, maybe, maybe, he was just as terrified and overwhelmed as she was.

She had been wandering around the spring festival, thinking about the weird combination of safety and terror she felt around Sean, when the man with the ice-chip eyes—the teacher who wasn't a teacher, the man who wasn't a man—had appeared out of nowhere. There was a tug on her elbow and he was in front of her, smiling the bland smile.

"Here you are," he said. "I've been looking all over."

"How . . .," she stammered, "how . . ."

"It might take me some time. Weeks. Years. Eons. But I'll always find you."

Behind the man, she saw Finn running for her. She would have screamed, she would have screamed bloody murder and never stopped screaming, but the man opened his fist and showed her a handful of white baneberry, white berries with black dots.

"Remember these? Doll's eyes? If you eat them, they cause a heart attack. There are so many ways to die. A bit of bread lodged in the windpipe. A strike of lightning. A falling tree. A clean twist of the head. If you don't come with me, don't come quietly, those boys who took you in will die of heart attacks, or accidents, some ravenous parasite or flesh-wasting disease that causes the body to eat itself from within. I am creative when it comes to death. It is a science and an art. Do you believe me?"

He said all of this in perfect Polish.

She believed him.

So she'd smiled and she'd lied, she'd gone with the man to save the boys. But she'd wanted Sean to come and save *her*.

Sean hadn't come. Maybe he couldn't. Maybe it was too much to ask of another person—*I'm too tired to save myself, you do it!* But the more she thought about it, the more wrong it felt. Had she gone with the man to save those boys, or had she gone with the man because he was like all the others wrapped into one—Otto and Ludo and Bob and and and and and, the men who wanted to use her, own her, burn her up—and they were everywhere, and escape was impossible, no matter how hard she ran? When she thought about it that way, Sean felt like a dream she could never hold on to. She was too used to running.

Maybe Sean was sitting next to the hospital bed, willing her awake right now, and here she was, standing in her kitchen, baking her favorite jam-filled cookies the way her babcia used to; the table was already covered with four trays of them. Later, she would pack up the cookies in her burlap sack, she would dig in her imaginary garden with the worms and the praying mantises and the dog. The dog would eat the cookies. The dog loved cookies.

The man came in the afternoon, holding a new lamb. He placed the lamb in her arms and she kissed the top of its woolly head. Before he could ask a question, she asked him one: "What is this place?"

"Does it matter?"

"It matters to me."

"These are the Fields. They are everywhere and nowhere. I can make them look any way you wish."

"Has anyone ever left here?"

He didn't respond right away. Then he said, "Did *he* always answer your questions?"

"Who?"

He sighed, steepled his fingertips. "Once, a young man lost his wife and went to the Land of the Dead to find her. He said his life wasn't worth living without her, and played the loveliest song to prove it. The song was so moving, the Lord of the Dead granted his request, though he had never done it before. He said the young man could go, and his wife would follow him, she would be right behind him. But he couldn't look back at her, he had to trust she was there. But he didn't. He didn't trust, he looked back, and so the woman had to stay. Obviously, he didn't love her the way he said he did. But then, I have found that people never love the way they say they do. They can't. They are just people. Full of lies and sentiment and fear. There is no reason for you to leave here, and no way for you to go. No one will come for you, and even if they did, I am not the sentimental sort."

A chill washed over her at the telling of this tale. She had heard this story before. But it was a myth. An old, old myth.

She was not in a hospital bed. And she was not in a garden.

"So," she said, hugging the lamb close, "I'm dead, then, is that what you're saying?"

"Of course you're not dead," the man said, chucking the little lamb under its chin. "That's just a story among so many other stories. If that world ever existed, it doesn't anymore. But the point is the same. You are not dead. But everyone else here is."

"What—what do you mean?"

"This lamb, of course. These people. This world. All dead, all dead."

The lamb wriggled in her arms and Roza squeezed tighter. The warmth of the creature, the smell of the wool, the tension in its body all said that the man was lying. How could this lamb be dead? But then, how could this man have built her a house, then a castle, then brought her *here*? How was any of this possible?

"But where did they all come from?" Roza said.

"I have lived a long time, known many people. You could say I collect them. But their hopes, their dreams, even their nightmares have become so tiresome. You can't even imagine. It's been a long time since I've been back to the Fields. I've been a visitor to so many places, I had forgotten what I was looking for. Whom I was looking for. You have made me want to come back. You have inspired me to build something new."

"Why do you want me?" she said.

"Because you're the most beautiful."

"Stop saying that!"

"It's true."

"That can't be the only reason."

"People have gone to war over a beautiful woman. Why not move heaven and earth for one?"

"Because I don't want it!" The lamb spilled from her grasp and tottered around the grass, bleating for . . . what? A mother butchered for sausage long ago? Roza clapped a hand over her mouth as if it could stay the words coming from his.

"You've been content here. You have your garden. And I have asked you all the right questions." He stepped closer, and her heart froze around the edges. "I know what kind of foods you prefer, I know what color is your favorite, I know you like simple things. The house was an error, the castle was an error."

"An . . . *error*?"

Rus began to growl, and the man regarded him with an amused expression. "You've charmed my most fearsome beast."

"You have to let me go."

"I wanted you to choose this. To choose me. But it isn't always possible for two people to want the same thing. I want you, and that will have to be enough for both of us."

"It is not enough!"

"If you cannot love me, you must accept me. There is nothing else."

"I will kill myself," Roza said. *"I will kill myself."*

But the man only laughed. "I thought you understood. It's all the same to me."

July
Thunder Moon

Finn

Punched

He didn't want to read the papers, he couldn't stop reading the papers. They yapped and murmured at him, telling him about themselves, telling him about himself:

Imagine looking into the face of your much beloved wife and not being able to recognize her. That's what happens to thirty-seven-year-old Jack Donovan every time he sees Michelle, his partner of ten—

And:

For years, Wesley thought he was "bad with faces." As a child, he wouldn't be able to pick his mother out of photographs. He had trouble telling one classmate from another. When a favorite teacher shaved off his beard, Wesley no longer recognized him. Later, as an adolescent, Wesley recalls other teens marching up to him in the hallways, demanding to know why he didn't say hi to them at lunch or—

And:

Things came to a head for Yolanda Hughes some four years ago, when her son Max was three. She'd taken Max to the store to shop for shoes. She bent down to try on a pair of sneakers, but when she looked up, Max had wandered off. An hour later, a frantic Hughes was approached by a security guard with a young boy in tow.

"He asked me if it was Max. And I didn't know. I was so upset that I didn't remember what Max was wearing that day. And Max was crying too hard to speak. I just couldn't recognize his face. I just couldn't. My own son, and I didn't know who it was. The security guard thought I was a lunatic and said—"

And:

Edwards had to weigh things carefully before agreeing to do this interview. "I might be inviting potential criminals to take advantage of me if they find me," she said. "How do I know if the person who tells me he's a friend isn't a stranger out to hurt me?"

And:

Beyond the social awkwardness are everyday issues that are not as obvious. Plots of certain movies and TV shows are too confusing to follow: "If I watch a movie with three dark-haired actors, I often think they're all the same guy. And when the movie's over and everyone else is talking about the bad guy, I say, What bad guy?"

What bad guy?

So he wasn't just a careless, spacey, moon-eyed idiot who'd witnessed a crime and couldn't identify the man who did it. It should have made him feel better. Of course he couldn't identify the man, and here was the proof. He should bring these papers to Jonas Apple and say, *Look! Here! Read this!* He should bring the papers to his brother and say, *Don't blame me anymore! Don't hate me anymore! It's not my fault!*

But this new idea about himself—face blind—didn't make him feel better. He wasn't going through a phase.

He wasn't going to grow out of his strange distraction. He had something wrong with him, wrong deep down in the bone.

Tell us about the day you discovered you were not like everybody else. Use a language other than your native tongue.

Either way, Roza was still gone. Rain beat on the roof, thunder growled. Finn spread the photos Petey had given him out on the table, trying to guess who was who. He could separate women from men, young people from old, white from brown, but nothing more specific.

> *"I remember looking in the mirror when I was little and thinking, Who are you supposed to be?"*

He went to the bathroom and looked at himself. He saw a mussed thatch of black hair. Dark eyes. Cheeks, nose, mouth. He'd never really tried to see the whole before, keep a picture in his head. Maybe it was a matter of effort? Of practice? He stared at his own reflection, memorizing every detail. If he tried, if he really tried, could he remember his own face?

After he'd spent five minutes with his image, he went back to the table. He mixed the photos like a little kid mixes playing cards, smearing them together with the flats of his hands. Then he stared at the photos, trying to pick himself out. A thatch of black hair, he told himself, brown eyes. He pawed through the photos looking for boys with dark eyes, found one. Out of habit, he scanned the clothes. Cap and gown. No clue there. His attention drifted back up to the face in the picture. The eyes were dark. His own eyes were dark. So was this a picture of him? Or was it just some other guy?

He pored over the photos, trying to latch onto something familiar, anything that looked like the face he'd seen in the mirror. But he couldn't. He couldn't.

He swept the photos off the table and slumped into a chair, but his leg felt stiff and awkward, and he popped back up and circled the table like a restless horse. He was still pacing when Sean came home from his shift, shaking the rain out of his hair. Sean raised a brow at the piles of papers and photographs and said, "Art project?"

"Right. That's what it is," Finn said.

"Make sure you clean up when you're done."

Like a robot, Finn bent and began gathering the pictures and papers. Here was his chance. He could show Sean all this stuff right now. He could explain. But what good would that do? What would it prove? That he was weird? That he was different? Sean knew that already, knew it better than anyone, even though he never talked about it with Finn, never asked the right questions.

Sean walked past the table and was almost out of the room when Finn said, "Is that the only thing you care about?"

Sean stopped but didn't turn around. "What?"

"I said, is that the only thing you care about? Cleaning up?"

Sean's head swiveled like an owl's. "What the hell are you going on about now?"

"You can't even look at me, can you?"

Sean turned, his broad shoulders a wall in the blue uniform, the gold name tag glinting. "All right. I'm looking."

"You're not. You didn't."

"I didn't *what*?"

"You didn't look for her. Everyone thinks you did. Maybe you told yourself you did. You held on to her stuff for two months, you pretended. But you gave up. And I—" Finn stopped.

There it was. The worst part.

His affliction, whatever it was called, hadn't prevented Finn from helping Roza when she had needed him. He just hadn't trusted her. Hadn't trusted that she wanted to stay. Because of his mother or his father or the way she had appeared in the barn, Finn hadn't believed in Roza. Or maybe he hadn't believed in Sean, or himself.

Finn said, "I thought she wanted to go, too."

"Don't," said Sean, voice low.

"That's why I let her get in the car. Why I didn't try anything or do anything until it was too late. I mean, who would want to be with us? Mom didn't. She left you to take care of me. Poor, poor Sean, stuck with his weird brother, whole life ruined."

Sean's face went red, and his chest heaved. Finn would have had no trouble picking Sean out of a crowd. Even Finn couldn't miss someone that big and that red and that angry, someone whose fists clenched and unclenched and clenched again.

"You want to hit me," Finn said.

"I'm not going to hit you."

"But you want to."

"It doesn't matter what I want."

"That makes two of us."

Sean laughed, an ugly laugh. "The two of us? What do you know about it, Spaceman? What could you possibly know? What have you *ever* had to give up for anyone else?"

"Yeah, you gave up. And you keep doing it. You tell yourself it's for other people, but it's not."

"Like you would have survived on your own."

"That was years ago. What about now? What about Roza?"

Sean crossed his arms. "What about her?"

"Jesus, are you really that stupid?"

Sean said nothing. Finn ground his palms into

his forehead, trying to rub away the dull ache there. Talking about Roza made him think of Petey. He saw Petey. But she didn't see him. It was almost funny, except it made him feel like throwing up.

Finn scooped the photos from the floor and the articles from the table and stuffed them in the trash. He opened the back door.

Sean's voice was honed to a cutting edge when he said, "Going to see your girlfriend?"

Finn gripped the handle so tightly he could imagine crushing it. "I don't have a girlfriend."

"That's not what everyone says."

"Everyone is an idiot."

"You want to know what else they're saying?"

"No," said Finn.

"That you're using her. She's desperate, she's angry, she's homely, she's—"

Finn flew across the kitchen, punched his brother in the face. Sean didn't go down—he was too big and too solid for that, too ready for anything—but he rocked on his feet. When Sean caught his balance, a tiny flower of blood bloomed at the corner of his mouth. He didn't look so big anymore. He didn't look so strong.

"You know why she's gone, you chickenshit," said Finn. "You *know*."

Sean wiped the blood from his lip. "Because she wants to be."

"If that's what you think, you're more blind than I am," Finn said. And he then took his newly mangled hand and recently mangled leg and limped stiffly from the kitchen, expecting to be followed, expecting to be seized, expecting to be tackled to the dirt, expecting to be beaten within an inch of his life, wanting all of that. But neither he nor Sean would get what they wanted. Sean didn't believe in Finn, either; Sean let him go.

And so Finn went. Not to the stable or to the police chief or even to the beeyard to find Petey. He went to where he'd last seen the man who twitched like a cornstalk in the wind. Because by punching his brother he'd knocked some sense into himself.

Finn had a few more questions for Charlie Valentine.

Charlie

The Ballad of Charlie Valentine

Charlie sat in his favorite chair—his only chair—a chicken on his lap, waiting for the knock on the door. He knew who was coming, but he couldn't be certain what he, Charlie, could possibly say, other than "I'm sorry" and "Go home."

Charlie himself had had many homes, going so far back that he only had the vaguest, haziest memories of them. A man, even a man like Charlie Valentine, had limited room for memories, and the new ones kept kicking the old ones out, the way slang replaces the proper names for this or for that, cheapening the nouns and the verbs until they were barely recognizable. For

of his time spent on a horse farm. He told everyone who would listen that his grandfather kept Belgians, huge working horses, and boarded horses for others. But that old man wasn't his grandfather. And Charlie wasn't there because of him anyway. Charlie loved the horses, every one of them. He couldn't remember his own name, but he remembered theirs: Blackbird. Babe. A retired Chicago police horse, Gladiola. A foal with a parrot mouth called Sweetheart. A gelding named Pippin. Horses were like dogs, sometimes calm, sometimes playful, sometimes mean as snakes. Sometimes the horses would try to rear back their heads and smash their riders with the tops of their massive skulls. When the horses did this, Charlie was supposed to take a bottle filled with water and crack them between their ears as hard as he could. The water would run down. The horses would think they were bleeding, and they would never rear back again. But no matter how mean they were or how much they reared, Charlie refused to hit the horses. Refused to even fill the bottles. And the old man who was not his grandfather would shake his head in disgust. "Tchórz. Królik," he would mutter. Coward. Rabbit.

As soft as Charlie was, however, it was his job to exercise the animals. A long trail snaked through the property, marked with different-colored mile markers. A blue marker. A white marker. Green, yellow, orange, red. Every day, that old man would tell him, "Take Gladiola out and run her to the blue marker." Or "Take Pippin out and run him to the white marker." The old man wanted Charlie's favorite new horse, a thoroughbred named Thunder, run out to the green marker. So that was what Charlie did. Every day, he took Thunder out and rode him to the green marker and back. But instead of staying fast and strong, the horse grew thinner and thinner and thinner. No matter how much Charlie fed and watered him, no matter how much Charlie whispered in his ear, Thunder's ribs showed pitifully. The doctors thought that Thunder had some kind of terrible blood disease. One bright morning, they came and took him away. Charlie never knew where. He would spend nights in the stables, crying over Thunder. Years later, doctors would tell him that he was color-blind. Red-green color-blind, specifically. He'd been running Thunder to the wrong marker for months, running him so hard and so long that Thunder had just wasted away to nothing.

That was how Charlie learned that he couldn't protect the things he loved. Not even from himself.

In despair, he left that farm and came to Bone Gap when it was a huge expanse of empty fields, drawn here by the grass and the bees and the strange sensation that this was a magical place, that the bones of the world were a little looser here, double-jointed, twisting back on themselves, leaving spaces one could slip into and hide. He had the place to himself for years, but he wasn't so stupid as to keep horses. He kept goats. And when he loved the goats too much, he gave them up for sheep. And when he loved the lambs too much, he gave them up for chickens.

Then the people came. A woman named Sally came. She was neither beautiful nor wretched. She laughed a lot. She laughed so much it cracked him open, swapping his insides for his outsides, as if he were wearing his own nerves for a coat. He couldn't give her up. He married her. They had a child, they had thirty-six years together. For most, that would have been quite a long time. For him, it was a few minutes.

He couldn't protect the things he loved.

He still had his daughter, everyone reminded him. And four grandkids. And great-grandkids. They terrified him, especially the littlest ones. Each of them so young and so easily ripped away. He had no idea how to protect them, how to keep them safe. It made him furious. He yelled at them all the time, waving his broom, stamping his feet, trying to make them understand. The wounded expression in the children's eyes broke what was left of Charlie's heart. Better not to see them at all. Better to hunker down in his house with his chickens and forget.

And that was the way it stayed until Roza. She was Polish, Charlie could hear it in the curve of her voice, but she was also so familiar, like a painting on a wall by an artist whose name he had forgotten. Charlie was rusty, but he could still speak her language. The first time he'd said dzień dobry, hello, she seemed scared and relieved at the same time. He visited her, offering some stories about his home on the horse farm, about Gladiola and Sweetheart and, later, Thunder. He asked her about her home in Poland. She told him of the green rolling hills, the cries of new lambs in the spring, the smell of her babcia's homemade soup. Sometimes they'd talk for an hour before Roza realized how much time had passed, and she ran back to the O'Sullivan house to perform whatever chore demanded her attention. The scent of her, the bright sun scent of her, lingered in the air long after she left, making him feel cleaner somehow, new and brave, a green shoot pushing through the earth, ready to greet the morning and whatever came after. She seemed to have that effect on many in Bone Gap, the people opening up like seeds after a rain. But Charlie never asked her what had happened to bring her there. He thought it was safer, considering.

She *had* seemed safe with Sean and Finn O'Sullivan. Charlie Valentine would watch them sometimes from his yard. Roza tending her garden,

Finn digging along beside her, Sean O'Sullivan trying so hard to keep his heart from leaping like a trout out of his throat. Some people seemed to show up just when you needed them, and Charlie had no idea who needed whom more—Roza, those boys, those boys, Roza. It all felt fated somehow. But Charlie had never been comfortable with the idea of fate. He didn't like knowing that something else, someone else, held all the cards.

Then Roza had disappeared. Sean O'Sullivan had locked up tighter than a nut. Finn drifted around, rootless and aimless as dandelion fluff in the wind. And the horse, that magnificent horse! Just showing up here as if she wanted to remind him of every stupid mistake he'd ever made, all the ways he'd been disloyal and blind. Fate again, Charlie supposed. And here *he* was, alone with his chickens, waiting for a knock on the door, thinking that you can't protect the ones you love, you have to hope they're smart enough to save themselves. And hope, well. Who had any of that to spare?

The door flew open. Finn O'Sullivan limped straight through the living room to the kitchen and back again, tracking water and mud everywhere.

Well, that was a surprise. Charlie was sure it would be—

"Where is he?" Finn said.

"Who?"

"You know who. The man who moves like a cornstalk in the wind."

Charlie thrust out his dentures, sucked them in again. "I don't know where he is."

Finn's breathing got harder and deeper, as if his very *breath* was angry and was attempting to launch an attack from the depths of his lungs. "You know this guy, you know he took Roza, you knew I wasn't lying about what I saw, and you didn't do anything? You didn't say anything? You let people think I was crazy! And Roza! What about Roza?"

"It's complicated."

"What's complicated about it?" Finn yelled. "Who is that man? Where did he take her?"

"Not a place where you or anyone else can go. And even if you could make it, who knows if you could find your way back?"

"What are you talking about?"

"I'm sorry. I thought maybe the horse would cheer you up."

"The *horse*? You thought you could swap a girl for a horse and that we'd just forget about her?"

Charlie would have kept the horse. He wanted to so badly. But he couldn't do it. He had the feeling that he had tried to hold on to things that weren't his before, or helped other men do that, and maybe this was why he was holed up in a broken-down old house with nothing but chickens to keep him company. "You can't swap what you don't own. She's her own horse," Charlie said. "She does what she wants to do."

"What the hell are you talking about?" Finn shouted. *"What the hell is going on?"*

The chicken flapped in Charlie's arms. "All right, all right, just calm down and I'll tell you what I can."

"You'll tell me everything."

"I'll tell you what I can."

"You'll tell me what I need to know to find Roza."

"Valentine's not my real name."

Finn began to pace—step-drag, step-drag. "Who cares about your name?"

"Are you going to let me talk or not?"

Finn clamped his mouth shut and jerked his head, motioning for Charlie to go on. And Charlie did. He talked about the horses, about Gladiola and Pippin and Thunder, ignoring the way Finn rolled his eyes and sighed and muttered under his breath. Charlie talked about Bone Gap before the people came. He talked about Sally. How much she laughed. How it cracked him open. "And she was smart, too," Charlie told Finn. "Sally said it seemed dumb to name a place 'Gap' when there weren't any gaps anywhere. No ravines or cliffs or stuff like that."

Finn stopped pacing. "I've seen a cliff."

"Did you?" said Charlie. "Can you say that for sure?"

"I—"

"Because we don't have your typical gaps around here. Not gaps made of rocks or mountains. We have gaps in the world. In the space of things. So many places to lose yourself, if you believe that they're there. You can slip into the gap and never find your way out. Or maybe you don't want to find your way out."

"Roza didn't slip anywhere. She was taken."

"But maybe she wants to stay now. Maybe he convinced her. I know stories like that."

"Who is he?"

Charlie tried to remember, he tried, but all he had was fog and haze and a parade of loss that numbed and shamed. "I know him, but I can't name him. I think of him as the Scare Crow. Seems as good a name as any."

Finn said, "Fine, just tell me *where* he is."

For a moment, there was only the sound of the two of them breathing, the chickens worrying their feathers, clucking nervously. "You're not the one I expected," said Charlie.

"Yeah, but I'm the one who's here."

"Why?"

"I . . . ," Finn began. His lips worked, his hands worked, struggling for the answers. Charlie had asked the question, but the answers were obvious. Finn was here because he was the one who had seen the earth swallow Roza. He was here because he had done nothing to stop it. Because he had fallen in love, and it had made him brave and stupid and desperate. He was here because Roza was his friend. Because his name was Finn and he didn't want to be called anything else.

But—another surprise—the boy, the young man, said none of these things. What he said: "When I lost Roza, I lost Sean, too. I'm here because he can't be."

Charlie Valentine, whose name wasn't Charlie Valentine, who hadn't been called anything else for as long as he could recall, who had lost more than even he could remember, said, "The chickens have been plucking out their feathers. They haven't been laying, but when they do, the eggs are small and gray as stones. They talk to each other. It sounds like *fox, fox, fox*. It's their word for nightmare. Do you understand what I'm saying?"

"I know it's dangerous. How do I get there?"

"You know how. You're the one who's here."

"I don't know what that means!"

"It means you can find her if you can find the gap."

"What?" Finn said. He started pacing again. "Maybe the horse can—"

"The horse can't take you there," said Charlie. "You have to go alone." Not the horse. He wasn't willing to sacrifice the horse.

Finn drew himself up to his full height. He was

getting so tall and broad, more like his brother every day. Stern. Determined. "So, you won't help me?"

"I just did."

Finn half laughed, half swore. "Fine." He limped to the front door, opened it, slicing the room with a beam of moonlight, blasting through the fog of Charlie's memory, of his many pasts.

"Wait!" said Charlie. "I can tell you one more thing!"

"Yeah? What's that?"

"The Scare Crow is a betting man."

Finn

The Fields

The rain stopped, leaving the air thicker than it had been before it started, both soupy and charged. The light had retreated at the insistence of the darkness—a scrap of cloud lidding the blank eye of the moon—and Bone Gap was still. No cars traveled the roads, no creatures howled or sniffed or chuffed, and the wind, a constant in the cornfields of Illinois, pulled in on itself and snoozed like a cat. Finn's leg itched under the bandages, and his hand throbbed; he should have known his brother's jaw was made of iron.

He had no idea where to go.

Never had Bone Gap seemed so large, so full of hidden spaces. If what Charlie Valentine said was true, Roza was here and there, everywhere and nowhere.

And if Finn hadn't ridden the Night Mare, hadn't glimpsed the gaps for himself, he would have thought Charlie was crazy.

But he wasn't riding the mare, and he had no one else to trust. He almost screamed at the unfairness, at the injustice—*the blind in charge of finding the hidden, sure, that made so much sense.* Still, he walked from Charlie Valentine's house to the main road, racking his brains for some way into another world. The mare had taken him past the Corderos' and into the graveyard, and he had seen the mists rising and pooling, coalescing into vaguely human shapes. Ghosts? Maybe that was where the skin of the world thinned, and he could slip through.

So Finn turned down the lane to Petey's house, expecting to see the Dog That Sleeps in the Lane, but it seemed that the Dog also had other business, because the lane was empty. When he got to Petey's house, he forced himself not to stop at her window, not to knock, not to whisper her name as he trudged through her backyard, past the hives with the bees humming so low Finn barely heard them at all.

He passed by the Corderos' house and, after some time, entered the graveyard. The ghosts that he and Petey had seen or imagined on their rides were sleeping, perhaps, and Finn had the graveyard to himself. He wound around the rows of graves, hands brushing against the cool, rough stones. Strangely, he wasn't afraid, but he wasn't hopeful either, which felt much worse. A willow tree, branches caressing the tops of the mausoleums, anchored one corner of the yard, and Finn sat beneath it, just for a few minutes, just to watch and see, just to get off his feet. He thought he heard a soft, collective sigh when he collapsed into the grass, but when he looked up, looked out over the gravestones, he was still alone. Five minutes, ten minutes, twenty minutes later, his leg was stiff, the backside of his jeans damp from the grass, and the graveyard hadn't revealed itself to be anything more than a graveyard. All of a sudden, he felt stupid. Roza wasn't a ghost. If she was—he squeezed his fists against the possibility—she was beyond his help.

He hauled himself off the ground and walked back to the main road. A tired half hour later, he could see his own house, the roof of the barn canting as if leaning a bent elbow on a dark line of cloud. Maybe Petey was right and there was something magical about it. Roza had turned up there, the horse had turned up there. Sean could turn up there, too, but Finn needn't have worried; the house was dark. Stranger still, the barn was empty—no mare, no goat either.

"Night?" Finn whispered. "Chew?" Their smells were strong, musk and hay and dung, but it was as if someone had just carted the animals off, leaving the mess for someone else. Finn scratched for the flashlight Sean kept by the door, but the light was weak and yellow, casting the barn in sepia. As in the graveyard, Finn wasn't sure what he was supposed to do. He felt around the edges of the barn, wincing at the splinters, searching for . . . for what? A slat of wood that wasn't actually wood? A trapdoor? A curtain behind which stood the wizard of Oz? What in the hell was he doing? The gaps weren't in the town, the gaps were in *him*, the gaps were in his eyes and in his brain and in his soul—he wasn't built right. He could not be trusted.

Something twined about his ankles and he jumped, fell over into a rather fragrant pile of feed. A soft *mrrrow* calmed him. "Calamity?"

The cat climbed onto his chest, and despite the pain of his bruises, he didn't push her away. "I've kept you alive, that's something, I guess. How are the kids?" He stroked her back and she purred, and slid her cheek against his cheek, and kneaded his flesh. Then she stopped, standing at attention, ears cocked.

"What do you hear?" he asked. "You look like Miguel when he talks about the corn running around. He says the scarecrows—"

—weren't made to scare the crows, they were made to scare the corn.

The corn.

He hugged the cat, who uttered a surprised mew,

and released her with a rushed "Bye, kitty." He got to his feet and half ran, half shambled out of the barn. He didn't even think about which direction to go, he let his feet take him to the nearest cornfield, any cornfield. He'd already plunged into the yellowing, crisping plants, dying plants, he'd already stumbled forward several dozen yards, when he began to feel stupid again, wrong again, worried again. But the corn whispered, *here, here, here,* so he kept running, crashing through the plants, not certain where he was going or what he was doing but trusting—not himself, but the plants that had always sung to him, the plants that had always made him feel safe.

It took a second for him to register the cold and the damp leaching into his sneakers. He kept walking, slipping on rocks here and there, righting himself, slipping again, walking, walking, walking. He had just begun to question his own sanity in a serious way when he noticed the stream carved into the plants. Waterways used to channel runoff from the fields. He followed the channel as it got wider and wider, cutting a little more deeply into the earth, and the water deeper, first splashing up around his ankles, then his knees. Soon, he was wading through the water, the current sucking at his legs, pulling him forward. The water was waist level, then chest level; he couldn't see over the banks of the stream, the river.

His feet no longer scraped the rocks on the bottom, and the current lifted him, carried him. The water churned and rushed and sucked and tossed him, and strange yellow eyes watched him from the sky and from the tall banks, and black shapes writhed under the surface of the river and brushed and bumped against his body—ridges of bone, sandpaper skin, the brief press of teeth that tasted, tested. He would have screamed if he could have, but he was too busy trying to breathe. He was sure he saw a boat, and a skull-faced man glaring from the prow, but then he was past it. The water surged forward, powerful as spring rapids. His foot kicked a rock, his knee hit another, and he was running along the bottom as he tried to keep pace with the rushing water, and ran, and stumbled, and ran some more, and then it was not the water sucking at him, it was the wind whipping, and the cold air chilling him and the leaves grasping at him and the plants whispering *here, here, here,* and he opened his eyes, which he must have screwed shut, and saw he was in a river no more, he was in the middle of a field, the plants reaching upward, *alive* alive. He stopped running and slowed to a walk. He moved through the field, the plants turning from corn to wheat to thick grasses back to corn. The sky overhead brightened, and turned from black to blue, like the healing of a bruise. He pushed through

was already in full swing, as if time had condensed, collapsed, and only seconds were needed to set up the coasters and games.

"Excuse me, pardon me, excuse me," Finn said, as he barreled through the throngs of people, thousands of people, more people than he'd ever seen at the fair, or anywhere in his life. The streets of Chicago couldn't have held more faces, the faces of strangers, bobbing like flowers in a breeze, each one indistinguishable from the next. Was Roza hidden somewhere at this fair? And if she was, how would he ever find her, when the fair seemed to stretch out for miles and miles and miles, bigger and wider and denser than any city, when there were so many people, when his lungs squeezed and would not let him breathe? He searched for the familiar, for Miguel's long arms, for Petey's angry bee face, for Sean the giant, for a chorus line of wishbones, but if the Rudes were here, he couldn't see them.

"I can find you," Finn said, to himself, to Roza, to everyone here, whoever they were. "I can."

A woman glanced his way. "I am Roza," she said, with a Polish accent.

Finn stared at her, stared at the green eyes and the inky hair and the bright smile. "No you're not," said Finn. He shouldered the woman aside and plowed through the streams of people.

"I am Roza," said another woman.

"I am Roza."

"I am Roza."

"I am Roza."

"No," said Finn. "No, and no and no." He waved off a clown selling cotton candy and a mime pushing against an imaginary wind and a pimpled teenager braying, "Three ring tosses wins you a prize for your girlfriend. Do you have a girl? Where's your girl? Where's your girl?"

"She's her own girl," said Finn.

"Roza is mine," a voice buzzed. Finn whipped around, scanning the endless waving, twisting bodies, a vast sea of faces, searching for the pocket of stillness. There, there, *right there*, next to a man on a unicycle juggling swords. Finn charged forward, but the crowd surged with him, pushing him and dragging him at the same time. He punched and kicked his way to the juggling man, but by the time he got there, the pocket of stillness had been swallowed up by the undulating crowd.

The juggling man dropped his bowling pins and grinned with graying teeth. "You will never find her."

Finn shoved the juggler off the unicycle and snatched up one of his swords. He pointed the sword at the juggler. "Tell me where she is."

The juggler only grinned wider. "You should be more careful when you handle snakes."

The sword in Finn's hands writhed and he dropped it to the ground, where it twitched like a cornstalk in the wind and slithered into a nearby tent. Finn dove into the tent after it, landing on his elbows, pain ringing up to his shoulders. Inside the tent it was dark and hushed. He rose up onto his knees and found himself face-to-face with a young man with black hair.

"Who are you?" Finn said.

The young man said, "Don't you know?"

Finn scrambled to his feet. It didn't matter who the young man was. He passed the young man and was cut off again by another young man, also with black hair.

"Get out of my way!" Finn said.

"Get out of your own way," said this young man.

Finn shouldered the young man aside but slipped when his shoulder hit not flesh, but a slick surface, and he spilled to the dirt. He reached up and touched glass. The young man in front of him also put up a hand.

A mirror.

"The House of Mirrors," said Finn. "Cute."

His reflection laughed at him. "Who the hell are you supposed to be?"

"Shut up," said Finn, hauling himself back to his feet. He kept his eyes on the ground, searching for the snake, and not on the dozens of young men appearing in mirror after mirror after mirror, the young men who would not shut up, whose voices washed over him like the voices of the people of Bone Gap, except they all had the same voice, his voice, the voice inside his head that chattered at him and would never let him sleep.

"You are a joke."

"You are a freak."

"Your mother left you."

"Your brother hates you."

"Petey doesn't trust you."

"Nobody believes you."

"You couldn't save Roza."

"You can't save her now."

"You couldn't recognize her . . ."

". . . if her life depended on it."

". . . and it does,

it does,

it does . . ."

Finn lowered his head and crashed into the next mirror, knocking it over, sending it into the mirror behind, and the next, like a series of dominoes, the last mirror ripping a hole in the tent on one side. He scooped up a shard of mirror and held it in his palm like a knife. He stepped through the tear in the tent, once again carried along by a current of people.

"You won't find her," said a little girl with ice cream melting all over her hand.

"You'll never find her," said a little boy with a giant stuffed bear.

"You'll never find her," said a woman with a bright pink mohawk.

"I bet I can," Finn said. "Do you hear me, wherever you are? I bet I can see her better than you can!"

The crowd stopped moving, turned toward him in unison. His hand tightened around the makeshift knife until he felt the edges bite into his skin. Warm blood dripped.

A voice hummed in his ear. "Put that away before the people get hungry."

"What?'

The man, the Scare Crow, tall and still, stood beside him. Without thinking, Finn thrust the mirror shard at him, but the Scare Crow didn't move; he was that still, that fearless, that invincible. "You're only hurting yourself. Besides, the citizens like blood, don't they? They smell it."

The familiar rage rattled Finn's bones, but rage would not help him now. He slipped the glass into his back pocket, wiped his palm on his jeans. "I bet I can find her."

"Interesting," said the man. "I've never understood why people choose to do the things that are hardest for them. You've heard of the Tilt-A-Whirl?"

Finn didn't even have time to say "Yes" when the

world around him began to spin, faces blurring one into the next, the tents and trucks and people tilting on an axis until the ground and the sky switched places: the earth above him, white cloud beneath. Worse than the spinning, the nauseating flip of earth and sky, was what happened to the people. They now hung all around him, unseeing, unconscious, as if their feet were stuck fast to the ground over his head, arms and hair dangling, bodies swaying like animals hooked in a slaughterhouse before their throats were cut.

Finn's stomach lurched, and he fought to keep from getting sick. The world stopped spinning, but earth and sky were still flipped, the bodies still dangling. "Put them back!"

"They don't mind."

"If I find her, then you have to let her go."

"Do I?"

"Yes."

"Hmmm. Perhaps you're right. I'll accept your wager. But tell me, what do you want with her? You can't even see yourself. You'll never be able to appreciate beauty like hers."

"What would you know about beauty?"

"This story won't end the way you expect it to."

"Maybe it won't end the way you expect it to, either."

"You'd best begin. There are a lot of people here. This could take a while. Maybe forever." The Scare Crow backed away from Finn, vanishing into the tangle of bodies like an eel retreats into a bed of river weed.

Finn slowly turned in a circle, taking in the immensity of his task. How could he do this? He couldn't even recognize himself right side up. How was he to recognize anyone else upside down?

He dug his fingernails into his wounded hand. No. He would do this. He had to. But they all looked the same. Or did they? Bees looked the same, and he had picked out the queen not because of her special stripes or even her size but because of the purposeful way she moved. She might be the only one fighting. But maybe Roza wouldn't be able to move either, maybe she was as docile and unknowing as the rest. He closed his eyes and tried to picture her, but her features jumbled in his head, everyone's and no one's. He opened his eyes and let his vision go slack and loose the way he had back at Petey's house. He walked slowly, carefully among the dangling bodies, touching one after the other, observing the pitch and sway of their arms and hair and hands, saying, *I'm sorry, I'm sorry* as he did so, because it was his fault, because he *was* sorry, and because this could take forever, and forever was a very long time.

Petey

Crows

In her favorite novel, a brokenhearted boy burns everything his ex-girlfriend ever gave him, including a photo of her as a child. But Petey had no childhood pictures to burn. All she had were the images burned on her brain and the sensations burned into her skin, and how did you erase those? Stuff yourself in the freezer? Move to the Arctic? Turn yourself inside out and scrub them off in the shower?

She pulled out a folded piece of paper she was using as a bookmark, unfolded it, smoothed it on the bed. It was a poem called "Essay."

Describe the shorts that changed your life.
Moonlight on skin, warm under fingers.

The color red: why or why not?

Not. Her eyes are black as stingers.

Her mother peeked into Petey's doorway. "You're awfully mopey this morning. What's up?"

Petey crumpled the paper, closed the novel. "Nothing."

"Didn't Finn visit last night? I thought he was here every night."

Images burned in her brain, a flush burned in her cheeks. "How did you know?"

Her mother smiled. "I look stupid to you?"

"No," Petey said.

"I hope the two of you are being careful."

The flush turned nuclear, scorching her flesh. "There's no such thing as careful."

Her mother frowned, took a step into the room. "Petey, do you have something you want to tell me?"

Write a story that includes a new pair of loafers, the Washington Monument, and a spork.

I'd rather tell you about a new horse, a forest of glass, and a long good night.

Petey plucked at the old blanket on the end of her bed, the one that she'd brought outside and laid by the fire, the one on which she and Finn had been together.

She loved this blanket. She hated this blanket. "I'm not pregnant or diseased or anything like that, if that's what you're asking."

"I wasn't," her mother said. "What I'm asking is, are you all right?"

Was she? She had been so sure. Sure that Finn was face blind and that it explained everything, including his feelings for her. Sure that it meant that his feelings were broken somehow, the way his ability to recognize faces was broken. She had read that it was incurable, but what if, one day, they learned how to fix it? What if Finn saw her and saw how hideous she was? He knew already what other people thought of her. He'd heard what they said. And he'd changed his mind about being seen with her in public, he'd wanted to tuck her in the back of the café like a dirty secret. So, what if he started looking at her the way so many other people did, with a mixture of fascination and confusion and repulsion? She wouldn't be able to stand it.

But she couldn't stand this, either. Maybe she should burn the blanket. Maybe she should make a dress out of it and wear it for the rest of her life.

"Petey?" said her mother.

"I'll be fine."

Her mother took a great lungful of air, let it out, as if she were settling into a particularly challenging yoga pose. "If you want to talk about it—"

"I don't."

Her mother tucked her hair behind her ear and nodded, worry creasing the skin around her eyes. "I love you, you know."

An ache gathered at the back of Petey's throat, and she was afraid she would burst into tears. "Did you need me for something?"

"Oh. Well. If you refuse to confide your deepest, darkest secrets to your very receptive and very cool mom, and if you're not doing anything else, you can bring Darla at the café some more honey and cookies."

"I can do that," Petey said, grateful enough to have some kind of task, something to take her out of her house, away from the beeyard and the hum of the bees and the soft trickle of the stream and the smell of the grass and everything that was telling her that maybe she'd made a mistake. She and her mother hooked the wagon onto the back of the battered moped, loaded the wagon with the honey and cookies. Petey jumped on the moped and drove past the Dog That Sleeps in the Lane, who didn't bother lifting his head. She stopped at the intersection of the lane and the main road, waiting for a truck to pass before she turned. Her feelings shifted from gratitude to amazement that honey would still have to be delivered and dogs would still sleep in lanes and people would go about their business after a girl had ripped out her own heart and crushed it under her boots. It seemed as if there should be a ceremony to mark such an occasion, a day of mourning, maybe even a week or two during which no one would eat or rest or work, and instead sit sadly wearing black and pondering all the ways that people annihilate themselves.

Describe someone who has had the biggest impact on your life using only adverbs.

Furiously, smoothly, ferociously, surprisingly, deliciously, quickly, slowly.

But instead of finding sad and mournful people pondering all the ways that others annihilate themselves, Petey found the Rude boys lurking around the front of the café. Then Petey found herself pondering the ways in which she might annihilate other people and get away with it.

Frank Rude started in on her as soon as he saw her. "Where's your boyfriend, Petey?"

"Where's yours?" said Petey.

Frank flushed and made a sort of jerking motion forward, then fell back, like a dog that suddenly remembered his choke collar.

His brother Derek shoved Frank aside. "Don't mind him. He's an ignorant dumbass. You let us know if you need something, okay?"

Petey said, "Huh?"

"It's not cool, that's all I'm saying. Right? It's not cool." All his brothers except Frank nodded. And Frank nodded when Derek elbowed him in the ribs.

"What's not cool?" Petey said.

"Stupid Moonface. Doing, you know. What he did."

Petey's stomach roiled, as if she could feel any worse. "You mean Finn O'Sullivan? What did he do?"

Derek jammed his hands in his pockets so hard they threatened to burst through the fabric. "It's just not cool, that's all. And I . . ." He looked as if he wanted to say something and that it was choking him. "I feel bad."

"You feel bad," Petey said.

"You want help with that box?"

Petey looked down at the box she was holding; she didn't remember hauling it from the wagon. "No, I'm fine."

"I'm just saying, is all," said Derek, saying very little that Petey understood.

"Okay," said Petey.

"Okay," said Derek. He and his brothers walked away, but not before Frank tossed one last glare over his shoulder.

Petey watched them go, each of them as bowlegged and as strangely endearing as a toddler. Now, what was that about? And what was she turning into, thinking that the Rude boys were endearing?

Explain a moment that changed your worldview, written in recipe format.

Two graham crackers, one square of chocolate, a marshmallow, a jar of honey. Roast marshmallow over a fire, press between crackers, dip into honey, take a bite.

She backed into the door of the café and carried the box of honey and cookies to the counter. Darla stopped chatting with Jonas Apple and hurried over to her.

"Priscilla! Oh, that's too heavy! You should have asked for some help!"

"But I always bring the box in myself."

"It's too heavy," Darla insisted.

"For who?"

"And it's honey! And honey clusters!" Darla exclaimed, as if Petey hadn't been delivering such things to the café for years. "Isn't that nice, Jonas?"

"Sure is," said Jonas Apple.

"Here, I'll take that box," said Darla. "You want something to drink? Or something to eat maybe?"

Jonas Apple said, "Fries are real crispy today."

"No, I'm okay," said Petey. Clearly, everyone had decided that there was something endearing about *Petey*, a thought that was a little disconcerting. Petey didn't want to be endearing to anyone. At least not anyone here.

Darla laid a hand on top of Petey's. "Are you sure you don't need something to eat or to drink?"

Petey frowned at Darla's hand. "I guess an iced tea would be nice. To go."

"You got it!" said Darla. She grabbed a waxed paper cup and filled it with iced tea and a lemon, capped the cup, and brought it back to Petey. "That's on the house. And let me pay you for the honey and the cookies." She opened the register and counted out some bills. When she handed the bills to Petey, she said, "Sooooooo," drawing out the vowel with such forced casualness that a first grader would have been suspicious. "You meeting Sidetrack here today?"

"No," said Petey.

"Well, that's probably for the best," Darla said.

"What is?"

Darla's lips pursed. "Not meeting Sidetrack."

Petey tucked the bills into her back pocket. "And why is that for the best?"

Darla unpursed her lips, repursed. Glanced at Jonas.

Jonas said, "That boy's a few Froot Loops short of a full bowl, you know what I mean?"

"No," said Petey. "I really don't."

"He's not right in the head. He's never been right. You don't need a boy like that playing you."

"Playing me?" said Petey, a lot louder than she'd

intended. Anyone in the café who hadn't been paying attention was now paying attention.

Write about the moment of your most dishonorable intentions in the form of a fortune cookie.

One tumble in the weeds will never be enough.

Petey repeated, "Who said he was playing me?"

"Uh, no one exactly," Darla stammered. "I mean—"

"Is that what you all have been talking about? Is that why the Rude boys were so nice to me just now? The *Rude* boys?"

"Well," said Darla, "you know we're not ones to gossip. We're just concerned, that's all."

Petey gritted her teeth. "No one is playing me."

"Whew! That's good to hear!" said Darla. "Isn't that good to hear, Jonas?"

Petey said, more to herself than to anyone, "He said he loved me."

Darla caught it. "Oh, honey, is that what he told you? That's what they all say."

"Is it?" Petey said. But she wasn't really asking. She left the iced tea on the counter and ran out of the café. She hopped on her moped. A half mile away, she saw the paper festooning the trees and bushes in front of Finn's house. How many rolls of toilet paper had they used? Dozens? Hundreds?

Sean was outside, hands on hips, surveying the mess. Petey dumped the moped in the middle of the drive and stomped over.

"Finn here?"

"No," Sean said. "Left in the middle of the night."

"You know where he went?"

Sean shook his head. "I figured he was with you."

"No." She nodded at the trees. "Rudes?"

Sean shrugged his broad shoulders. "Your guess is as good as mine."

A murder of crows had gathered on one of the trees, cackling and flapping. "The crows like it," Petey said.

"I guess that means they're not going to help me clean it up," Sean said. He kicked a rock. If this weren't Sean O'Sullivan, Petey would have guessed that the man was annoyed. But Sean O'Sullivan didn't get annoyed. Not outwardly.

Sean kicked another rock.

But maybe he did now.

Sean started tearing paper from the branches, bunching it, and dropping it to the ground. After a minute, Petey joined him, pulling the paper off bushes and out of flower beds. The flowers looked sad, drooping and dispirited. Petey could sympathize.

Would you rather be a robot, an alien, or a wolf?

Wolf. All the better to ...

"These flowers don't look so good," she said.

"They haven't since . . ." He trailed off.

"Since Roza?" Petey said.

"Since Roza," said Sean. Petey wondered when he'd last said her name out loud. All those drawings in Sean's sketchbook flipped through her head, and her cheeks went hot. She bent to scrape the paper into a tighter ball.

"You don't have to do that," Sean said.

"I should help. Whoever it was, I think they did it for me."

"Oh yeah?"

She yanked some paper off a prickly holly that didn't seem to want to give it up, threw the pile of paper to the grass. "People think Finn's playing me."

Sean stopped tearing and bunching. "Which people?"

Petey's turn to shrug. "People. Suddenly, Bone Gap is full of concerned, chivalrous types with lots of extra toilet paper. Who knew?"

Sean made a little sound. A laugh? Then he touched his mouth.

"Wait," Petey said, taking a few steps closer to him. "Is that a fat lip?"

"No."

She stepped closer to him. He was large, sure, and not half as pretty as Finn, but handsome in a different way, handsomer now because of the puffy lip. Made him look human.

She said, "Did someone hit you?"

"No."

"Someone hit you. Who would be that dumb?"

Another little sound.

"*Finn* hit you?"

Sean glanced down at Petey, the tiniest, barest hint of a smile playing on the bruised lips. "He was a little pissed."

"About what?"

Sean hesitated. Then: "Turns out he's one of those chivalrous types."

Petey took a step back. "Oh."

"I'm sorry," Sean said. "He was . . . I mean, I know how he feels. And I was wrong. About a lot of things."

Compose a haiku in honor of a person you admire.

You are spiky spring,
humming summer, wings that beat
back ghosts of winter.

They unwound more of the toilet paper in silence. Then Petey said, "So I guess he told you about his condition."

Sean frowned. "What condition?"

Petey stopped unwinding the paper. "Oh. Nothing."

"Did the doctors find something at the hospital?"

"No. Forget it."

"You need to tell me."

"You can ask Finn when he comes back. You guys should talk anyway."

Sean took both her shoulders in his hands and turned her around to face him. Petey wasn't short, but she barely came up to his chin. "Priscilla. *Petey.* What are you talking about? What condition?"

"I don't know if he has one. I don't know if I'm right about it. And he should be the one to tell you."

He let go of her. "The trash. He was reading a bunch of stuff and he threw it in the trash. I didn't even—" He jogged away from her and ducked into the house, the screen door slamming behind him.

Propose a theory to explain one of these eternal mysteries: Mona Lisa's smile, crop circles, or Velveeta.

Here is a theory of love:
you find a sister, you gain
a brother, you lose
a sister, you lose
a brother, you lose a cat,
you find a girl, you kiss
a girl, you find the cat,
you hope
that there is nothing left to lose, and
all there is, is there to find

Petey pulled more paper from the tree trunks, the bushes, the flowers, whatever wasn't strung up too high. She looked up at the canopy of yellowing, even crumbling, leaves. How did they get the toilet paper all the way to the top the way they did? Sean was going to need a ladder.

Just then, a crow darted down from one of the branches, a streamer of paper in its mouth. Soon, another crow was doing the same, and another, and another. The crows darted and dived and cackled, the streamers of paper raining down upon Petey's shoulders, and on the lawn and on the flower beds all around her, the birds helping her with this one small task, and telling her with their shining wings and knowing laughter that the truly impossible ones were yet to come.

Roza

Slaughter

At first, she fought. She jerked and squirmed and screamed. But there was no point. Her feet were stuck fast, the way the lamps in the suburban house had been stuck to the floor so she could not use them as weapons. Her feet were never going to be weapons. They ran when they shouldn't, and stuck when they should run.

And then she saw the others. She had no idea where they'd come from, all these people hanging upside down. No ropes held them either, but they didn't bother to jerk and squirm. They didn't even seem to be conscious.

But of course they weren't conscious.

They were dead.

Or close enough.

She might have thought she was dead, too, but she knew she wasn't. The blood rushed to her head, making her woozy, but not woozy enough that she wasn't aware her dress fell around her waist, exposing her legs, her underthings, her *body*. She fought the dress, too, couldn't help it, fought to keep it in place, but her arms got tired, and soon she let her hands dangle, fingers reaching for the cloud beneath. How was it that cloud was beneath her? Why was it that she kept asking *how* when the man could do anything with this place, including turn it upside down when it suited him? The more time passed, the more powerful he got.

Would it be better or worse to be dead? Even if it was better to be dead, she had nothing with which to kill herself. Maybe hanging here would kill her.

Her fingers toyed with the clouds and she imagined Sean striding up to her, releasing her from this horrible prison. She hadn't allowed herself to think of him too much, because thinking of him made her sigh and the man would ask her about it, and he would touch her and she would remember the way she had touched Sean, and the sadness would grip her throat the way the icy-eyed man gripped her throat, and the touching would get mixed up in her head until the thought of anyone touching her ever again would make her want to rip off her own skin.

Sean had never told her he loved her. He'd given her

his drawings, he had eaten her food as if he had been taking Communion, he'd trembled when she kissed him, but he had never said it. And neither had she, the two of them hiding behind their mother tongues as if there was no way to bridge the gap.

She was sorry she hadn't been braver when she'd had the chance.

Nearby, a body swayed and her gut clenched, her pulse pounding in her ears and temples. He was coming, and he wouldn't bother to ask questions anymore, because what and who she loved didn't matter. But she had already decided. She would still say no, even though she could not escape, even though the world was flipped on its axis, even though her feet were bare and unlovely and useless, even though she was practically half naked and so humiliated there wasn't a word to capture it, even though she couldn't be sure if Sean had ever loved her, even if this was the end of her, or just one of many terrible ends, she would say no, no, no, no, no.

"No," she said. A low hiss came from one of the hanging bodies. Her left foot felt loose, and she peeled it from the grass above her.

"Roza!"

She opened her eyes. Someone was pushing through the sea of bodies, coming toward her, someone tall and dark and . . .

"Finn?"

"Roza!" Finn fumbled with the hem of her dress, pulled it up to cover her. "I knew it was you. I knew it. I saw your hair, and I thought . . . maybe? But it was your hands. I remembered that drawing Sean did. The drawing of your hands. Isn't that crazy?"

It was more words than Finn had ever spoken to her at once, all shooting from his mouth in a heated burst, and she understood almost none of them. "Sorry?"

"Never mind." He tugged at her leg. "How the hell are you stuck like this?" He stopped tugging at her legs and yelled, "I found her! You hear me, you creepy shit? I found her. Now you let her go!"

Whatever force was holding Roza's sole to the earth above suddenly gave way, and Roza would have dropped headfirst into the clouds had Finn not caught her, setting her on her numb feet. Then there was another sickening flip of grass and sky, and the world was right side up again. The people, the thousands of people who had dangled so peacefully and quietly, now surrounded Roza and Finn, crouching like animals, needle teeth bared.

The icy-eyed man appeared, standing on top of a nearby stage as if he was about to make a speech. He looked taller and more icy-eyed than ever.

Finn took Roza's arm and started to pull her away when the man said, "I'm impressed. But this changes nothing."

"What?" Finn said.

"You bet that you could find her, and if you did, I had to let her go. But you didn't mention anything about yourself. So if she goes, you must stay." He turned his eyes on Roza, the scraping, knowing, awful eyes. "But Roza will never allow this."

Finn looked at Roza and dropped her arm. His jaw was set. He had already decided long ago. "Tell Sean that I—"

"No!" Roza said.

"Roza, you can send back help or something."

"Send where?" said Roza. Once she left this place, if she could find a way out of this place, she knew she would never be able to find her way back.

And if the icy-eyed man was powerful enough to build castles overnight and flip the world upside down, couldn't he come for her anytime he wanted? How safe would she be? How safe would she ever be?

And if she ran now, left Finn here, she would never forgive herself.

The icy-eyed man seemed to understand this, so serene was his expression. He thought he knew how this story ended. He thought he had written it.

He said, "But if Roza agrees to stay in your place, well, then . . ."

Finn shook his head, swearing under his breath. Roza caught a glint of silver in the overbright sun. A shard of mirror winking from Finn's back pocket.

When are you going to do something with that knife?

In Polish, Roza said, "Why do you want me?"

"You know," said the man.

"I want to hear it again."

Again, the serene smile. His story, written his way, with the ending he always expected. "Lovely women are so vain. You pretend you're not, but you can't pretend for long."

"Tell me," said Roza.

"Because you are beautiful."

"The most beautiful?"

The man nodded, enjoying his moment, the moment when he got to keep his prize, the one he had stolen, the one he thought he deserved. "The most beautiful woman of all."

"If I weren't, you would let me go?"

"If you weren't, you never would have been here in the first place."

"And you would let him go?"

"He wouldn't have been here either," said the icy-eyed man.

"Roza," Finn whispered. "What are you two talking about? Why don't you get out of here? I'll think of something, okay? Tell Sean I'm sorry."

"You will tell Sean," said Roza, in English. She pulled the shard of mirror from Finn's back pocket and held it up to the light.

The icy-eyed man said, "Beautiful women are so—"

Roza sliced her face from one ear to the corner of her mouth.

"Roza!" Finn yelled.

"No!" the man howled. "No, no, no, no, no!" He said it again and again as if it were the only word he knew how to say.

Roza whispered, "Yes."

Seconds ticked by before the pain registered, white-hot pain, a line of fire, blood that burned its way down her face and neck. Despite the pain and the blood, Roza took in the icy-eyed man's expression of frozen, stony horror and reveled in it, delighted in it. It was delicious, his horror. She wanted to see it up close.

She wanted to *eat* it.

She walked toward the stage and stood right in front of him, letting him see the wound, her red and seething insides, the place where her fury pulsed, where her fire lived.

She said, *"Do you love me yet?"*

He recoiled from her, from the look of her. "You don't love me because you can't see me," she said. "Look! Look! I am beautiful now. *I am beautiful.*"

The icy-eyed man said, "You are mine." He waved a hand at her face. But the wound did not knit, did not heal, and the blood kept pouring down her face and neck, hot and thick. The man waved his hand more and more frantically. "What do you think you have done?" the man said. "You have ruined yourself. No one will want you now."

"Then I don't want them," said Roza. "Foolish boys who drop you in puddles. You are the puddle."

Finn moved close. "I don't know what you're saying, but I think we've got some other problems here."

Roza turned. The fields—wherever they were, whatever they were—had gone darker, the grass yellowing under their feet, the rides rusting, the candy apples moldering, the smell of rot and wet and damp assaulting her nostrils. The people, thousands of them, crept forward, their limbs stretching, elongating as they limped and crawled and skittered like insects.

"Stop!" the icy-eyed man said as the creatures advanced. "I collected you. You're mine. You do what I say."

Finn said, "I don't think they believe you."

"Stop!" the man roared, as a buzzing arose from the crowd. Wings burst from backs, mandibles from mouths. The buzzing got louder and louder as the man was swarmed.

Roza grabbed Finn's hand. "We go!"

They turned and ran. The creatures lurched after Roza—attacking her or trying to help her, she couldn't tell. Finn beat them off as best as he could, but they tore at her arms and dress, their black tongues flapping and flailing. One latched onto her—maybe it had been a man once, but it now looked like some kind of wasp—and Finn and this creature tugged at her as if she were a length of rope. She screamed, and a giant reddish blur slammed into the wasp-man, yellow teeth tearing off its dark, chitinous face.

"What was that?" Finn shouted.

"My friend," Roza said. She and Finn and Rus ran from the fairgrounds. Roza almost shrieked with relief.

"The corn!" Roza said, just as Finn said it. At the sound of its name the corn seemed to grow taller, greener, thicker, reaching upward, *alive* alive. They threw themselves into its lush green arms and it drew them in, hiding and sheltering them, delivering them from one world to the next. They ran until they could run no farther, till a river of green was a river of blue, blue water that crashed and swept them in a wild torrent. Roza kept one hand knotted in Rus's fur and her other hand in Finn's as the water carried them, until their feet brushed upon the rocks at the bottom, until they were running again, then walking, the waters receding to a brook, a stream, a wild tangle of plants. They slowed, stumbling, holding on to one another as they broke through the wall of plants and spilled onto a familiar road.

They stood, panting in the dim light, jumping when something else crashed from the corn. Rus, dancing alongside Roza like a monstrous, bedraggled pony. She fell to her knees in the road, not minding the scrape of the pavement on her bare skin, and threw her arms around his shaggy neck.

"Is that a wolf?" Finn said.

"Dog," said Roza.

"I don't think so." Finn watched the cornfield as if expecting an army of monsters to burst from it.

"Not coming," Roza said. She couldn't have explained how she knew, but she did. The man was not going to follow. He couldn't.

A sudden breeze made Finn's hair dance. "You mean, that's it? We're done?"

"Not done," said Roza. "Free."

Finn

Sunrise

They stood in the road for a while—Finn keeping an eye out for lurching monsters and Scare Crows, Roza hugging the strange beast that had followed them out of the gap. Amazingly, Finn had forgotten what Roza had done to free them until he saw the dark smear on the beast's reddish fur.

"Roza. Your face. We need something to ..." He patted his pockets, but he had nothing to stop the bleeding.

She bent down, tore a length of cloth from the bottom of her dress. She pressed it to her cheek.

"I live," she told him, standing. She smiled at him, even though it must have hurt. "I live."

They started to walk. "Did he ... did he ..." He

couldn't say it—*Did the Scare Crow touch you? Did he hurt you worse than that cut on your face?* He examined his shoes, laces dripping water onto the pavement. Any other time, he might have said something about the impossibility of what had happened, how it was some kind of horrible nightmare that they, that *she*, needed to forget. Instead, he said, "Sean would have come if he could have."

She laid a palm on the dog's head. "No matter."

It wasn't the time for this, she was hurt, it was stupid, but he kept talking. "It does matter," Finn said. "It's just . . . he couldn't come. Because of me. And when I told them what I saw, that a man took you, he didn't believe me. It's not his fault. No one believed me. I didn't describe the man so well. I'm not good at faces."

Roza nodded. "I know."

"You know? You know I'm not good at faces?"

She took his hand, squeezed it. "Who does not know this?" she said, as if it was the most obvious thing in the world.

"Right," he said. "Who doesn't?"

She let go of his hand, instead slipping her arm around his, elbows linked like a chain. They kept walking down the dark road toward town. He felt every step—the rub of his wet socks in his shoes, the burn of his wounded leg, the ache in his hand—but he also felt more himself than he ever had before. So he tried again.

"About what I saw, about what happened to you," he said. "It's not just because I'm bad at faces. I didn't understand you went with that man to save me. That's what you did, right? Because that would mean you didn't want to leave us. That would mean you didn't want to leave *Sean*. And everyone leaves Sean. Do you understand?"

"Dumb," she said.

"Dumb is cutting yourself like that."

"I save you, you save me, I save you. We save, we will again. Circles."

"If you wanted to stay in Bone Gap, it would mean Sean was worth staying for. And he doesn't know that. But maybe you can forgive him for it?"

"No," said Roza.

"That's fair, I guess. I don't blame you. If it's any consolation, I punched him before I came to get you."

"Good," Roza said. "I punch, too."

"You already did," said Finn. "He won't ever be the same."

They walked in silence for some time, arms still linked, considering who wasn't the same anymore, and in what way. They had almost reached Finn's house when they heard the buzzing. Not the terrifying buzz of nightmares, not the low buzz of sleepy bees, but the buzz of the people of Bone Gap, all of whom seemed to be gathered in Finn's front yard. Jonas Apple. Charlie Valentine. Amber Hass. Miguel Cordero. Mel Willis.

Petey.

And then everyone started talking at once, voices rising in a crescendo of relief and alarm:

"There they are!"

"Oh, thank God!"

"Is that a coyote?"

"Is that a werewolf?"

"She's bleeding!"

"Her face! Oh, no! Her face!"

"Someone get a blanket!"

"Someone get them to a hospital!"

Finn and Roza walked past each person, some of them reaching out and pulling back as if they were afraid that she wasn't real, that this wasn't happening. Roza stopped to touch one of Miguel's arms, to nod at Petey.

"You were right about the bees," Roza said.

Petey's eyes had never seemed so big. "What?"

Sean shouldered his way through the crowd, running toward Finn and Roza. He stopped short at the sight of Roza, the bloody cloth she held to her cheek. "Oh," he said. "Oh, no."

"Yes," she said. She let go of Finn's arm and stepped forward. For a second, Finn worried that she was going to punch him, or tell him that she wouldn't forgive him, or scream at them all for not looking long enough or hard enough.

But she dropped the bloody cloth to the ground,

took Sean's big hand in her small one and laid it on that terrible wound. "You fix."

"We'll get you to the hospital right now. I know a doctor who—"

"No, *you* fix."

Sean shook his head like a dog shaking off water. "I drive an ambulance, Roza, I'm not a surgeon, I'll never be a surgeon, I can't . . ."

"You love me."

"What? I . . ."

"Is not question. You love me."

Sean swallowed hard. "Yes."

"I love you. Even with you so stupid."

His mouth dropped open. Then, "Okay."

"You fix."

"Roza, please. I'm not . . ."

"What?"

Sean shook his head, no, no, no, just like Roza had when they'd found her in the barn. "I couldn't come for you. I didn't come for you."

"No, you wait for me. And I come back for you. You see me. You see."

Sean blinked—frozen, terrified—until Finn said, "Come on, brother. Let's get your bag."

Dawn was spreading her rosy fingers in the sky when Sean finished twenty of the smallest, neatest, most careful stitches his big fingers could manage, would ever manage. It was only after he laid the curved needle on the kitchen table that his hands started to shake, then his shoulders. Finn had never seen his brother cry before and wasn't about to now. He left Sean with Roza, and they tended to each other as they would have tended any garden, running their hands through each other's hair, as if to make something inside them both burst and bloom, whether they were ready for it or not.

Finn drew the curtains in the living room so that the people choking up the lawn wouldn't gape. Then he collapsed on the couch next to Petey. Rus, the wolf-dog-coyote, sprawled out on the carpet while Calamity Jane gave him the evil eye from the hall.

Petey said, "Are you going to tell me what happened?"

"Maybe," he said. "Eventually."

"You should have let Sean take a look at you, too. You're a little mangled."

He was mangled in all sorts of ways. "Sean's in there *crying*, which, I'm sorry, is really screwed up."

"It's like watching a superhero cry."

"Yes! And besides, I'm stronger than I look."

"I know," Petey said. She bit her lip. "So if you're not going to tell me what happened to you, how about I tell you what happened to me?"

Finn was doing his best not to look at her. Looking at her hurt, and too much of his body hurt already. "Sure. Whatever."

"It was the Rudes."

"What was the Rudes?"

"I went to deliver some honey to the Chat 'n' Chew? And I was thinking that it was so weird that the world could keep turning. I mean, that honey would still need to be delivered and vegetables would have to be picked and laundry would need to be done when I was so miserable."

"You were miserable," said Finn.

"But the world does keep turning even when you're miserable, in case you didn't know that, so I went to the Chat 'n' Chew with the honey the way I always do. And Frank Rude started in on me the way *he* always does, and you know what happened?"

"You ran them over with your moped?"

"No. *His brothers* defended me. His own brothers! They told me that it was wrong, what you did to me, and they were sorry."

Now Finn looked at her. "Wait! What I did to you? What *I* did to *you*?"

"Just listen for a second. Then I went inside the diner, and everyone there was trying to console me—the Rudes, Darla, Jonas, everyone. They thought you used me and dumped me, and that's why I seemed so sad. Like we were all living in some nineteenth-century novel or something, and men are the ones who go around breaking hearts."

"Plenty of heartbreaking girls in nineteeth-century novels."

"They just assumed it was your fault. Because, you know . . ."

"I'm Sidetrack."

"Because I'm . . . because of the way I look. You didn't want to see me at the diner. You wanted to sit in the back."

"That's not—" he began. But he could see it, see how she saw it. He'd heard the crap said about her, but he'd assumed she was too fierce to care. But who was too fierce to care?

He said, "I didn't want them talking about us. I thought I did, but I didn't."

"Why did you care what they'd say?"

He closed his eyes because clearly they were useless. "They would have gotten it wrong."

Petey sighed. "They always do. As soon as the Rudes started talking, the Rudes of all people, I thought maybe I'd gotten it wrong. I came here to find you, and I found Sean instead. He was cleaning up the yard. You guys had been TP'd."

"What?"

"Paper everywhere. In the bushes, trees, and all over

the grass. I think it was the Rudes. Fighting for my honor and all that."

"What the hell would the Rudes know about honor?"

"Maybe they read a lot of nineteenth-century novels, who knows?" Petey told him about her conversation with Sean, noticing the fat lip, and the fact that she might have mentioned Finn's condition.

"You might have?"

"He freaked out, and we remembered that you said you saw the man who took Roza at Charlie Valentine's, so that's where we went. We found Charlie there. He said some crazy things."

"He's old. Old people tell a lot of stories."

"You're a superhero now, too, you know?"

Finn wiped a palm down his face. "Stop it."

"I'm apologizing here."

"You're taking your time."

Petey tugged her earlobe. She had great earlobes. "Do you think it was magic? I mean, when we rode Night and saw all those strange things?"

"I didn't care if it was magic. I just cared that I was riding with you."

"You're mad."

"I'm too mangled to be mad."

"You're mad. I get it, I'd be mad."

Finn plucked at his jeans, which had stiffened when

the river water dried. He needed a shower. He needed a bed. "You didn't trust me."

"I'm sorry."

"You didn't believe me."

"I'm really sorry."

"And that was a lot to lay on me, all that face-blind stuff. Especially after . . . well . . . after . . ."

"I know. I'm sorry. I am! I'm dumb. Really dumb."

"You *are* dumb. Pretty, but dumb."

"Pretty?"

"Don't fish for compliments."

"You're pretty, too," she said.

"And dumb?"

"Seriously dumb."

"I'm sorry, Petey."

Her arm brushed his. "What can we do to make it up to each other?"

Trying to get a handle on what he thought, what he felt, what he thought about what he felt and vice versa, was like trying to open a locked door by ramming it with his head. He wasn't getting through. The only things he was sure of: it sucked she hadn't trusted him, it sucked he was blind, it sucked she wasn't sitting in his lap.

"You're smiling," she said.

"I'm not."

"A little bit."

"This is not a smile."

"What is it?"

"This is my thinking face."

"I think I know what you're thinking."

"You can't. I'm too mysterious for you."

"Is it something dishonorable?"

"Only slightly."

"I'm disappointed, then."

"I forgive you," he said.

She moved close enough that he could smell the mint of her gum. "Do you?"

"Maybe. Eventually."

Petey put her hand on his knee. "I can work with that."

After Petey left, dragging the people of Bone Gap with her—including a vigorously protesting Jonas Apple, who wanted statements, damn it—Finn went to his room to check on the Kittens. He gave them some food and some water and lay on the floor, let them use him as a playground. They hopped over his legs and chewed on his hair, chased his fingers, nibbled his toes. Finn fell asleep draped in Kittens and dreamed that the corn walked the earth on skinny white roots, liked to joke with the crows, and wasn't afraid of anything.

*

He woke up a day or a month or a year later, Rus the wolf-dog snorfling at his face.

"I'm not edible," Finn mumbled.

Rus woofed. Finn opened one eye. Cat and Kittens had retreated to their closet, peering out at the giant shaggy creature.

"This is important," Finn said. "Nobody in this room is edible, okay, dog?"

Rus woofed again, wagged his giant shaggy tail against the bed. It sounded like someone beating a rug.

Finn sat up, groaned. "How long have I been asleep?"

The animals didn't respond.

"Some help you are."

He used the bed to leverage himself off the floor and shuffled to the window. From the light coming through, he could tell it was evening. Outside, Roza stood with the mare, brushing her coat and murmuring to her as the goat tottered around them both.

Finn said, "Hey."

"Look," said Roza to the horse, "boy with eyes great moons of love."

"Where did you find her?"

"Who?"

"The horse."

"I ask brother same question."

"Huh? What do you mean?'

"I know horse. My babcia's horse. This Córka. Means *daughter*."

"That can't be your babcia's horse."

"No?" said Roza. "Why not?"

Finn had no idea why not. The horse snorted as if to laugh.

"Where Petey?"

"She went home. Where's Sean?"

"I say go to work. He say no. I say yes." She shrugged. "He go." She continued to brush the horse. "Soon, I go."

"What? Go where?"

"Poland. See Babcia."

"Now?"

She smiled. "No. Soon."

"But you just got back! And you have to heal, don't you?"

She touched the line of stitches. "I go. Then I come back. You see?"

He saw. As she stroked the horse, the air around her shimmered and danced, and he saw through her to a young woman with black hair, then copper, then yellow, eyes the color of the greenest grass, the bluest sky, the deepest earth, skin kissed gold, white, bronze, night. She was a horse galloping across a plain, she was a mountain spring, she was a shoot thrusting through the earth, a red flower in the barley.

And then she was just a girl petting a very large mare, a goat chewing at the hem of her dress. "What?" she said. "Why you stare?"

He thought about telling her what he had seen, how many faces she had. But maybe he was seeing things again. And it was nothing he could explain.

He said, "That scar makes you more beautiful."

She laughed. "Ha. You not so blind."

August
Green Corn Moon

The People of Bone Gap

What they had heard: Finn O'Sullivan had seen the kidnapper lurking around Charlie Valentine's house and had followed him to his lair, where he had found Roza.

Or something like that.

But the kidnapper found *him*, and threatened to kill them both.

Or something like that.

So Roza broke a mirror and fought with her kidnapper. She was injured, but she and Finn got away with the help of a dog the size of a horse.

Or something like that.

The details were fuzzy, which just made the story that much more fun to tell. Jonas Apple had an all-points bulletin out on the suspect, but Roza said the man wouldn't be kidnapping anyone else ever again. The people believed her, because she had a way of saying things that just sounded true. Maybe it was the accent.

Plus she made such excellent cookies.

Roza brought hundreds of these cookies and trays of golobki to the Chat 'n' Chew. They joined Mel Willis's honey clusters and piles of sandwiches and vats of chili and dozens of bean and tuna and macaroni casseroles on the counter. Halloween wouldn't arrive for months, but the people of Bone Gap were throwing a costume party. Masks required.

The highlight of the evening was the game. Everyone was supposed to guess the identity of the other guests without anyone removing their masks. When a person guessed correctly, Jonas Apple would slap a bee sticker on him or her. Whoever was wearing the most stickers at the end of the night won a prize.

Finn O'Sullivan was covered in bees. He recognized Miguel Cordero (his ghost costume couldn't hide the long arms peeking out from under the sheet). He recognized Amber Hass (her pirate costume couldn't hide the fact that she was hanging on Miguel's big arms). He recognized the Rude boys (the cowboy costumes couldn't hide the bowlegs). He recognized Mel Willis (the devil costume couldn't hide her honey voice). And he recognized Charlie Valentine, who just wore a paper bag on his head (he had a chicken cradled like a baby, and a dozen great-grandchildren who followed him like a brood of chicks).

The people were amazed, especially considering Finn's condition. Wasn't that so strange? And didn't it explain so much? Finn's own face was painted black and white—a crescent moon on one side, the other side dark as midnight. Moonface, as if they would ever use a name like that! The people of Bone Gap called Finn a lot of things, but mostly they said he was brave.

At the food table, where Finn was going in for another round of honey clusters, Jonas Apple sidled up. "How are you feeling, Finn?"

"The scrapes on my leg are healing. Still itch like crazy, though."

"Good to hear," said Jonas. He was also costumed in black and white, though for different reasons. He was dressed like an old-time prisoner, complete with a ball and chain around one foot. His shirt and pants were painted with black and white stripes. "I wish we could catch that guy."

"Yeah," said Finn.

Jonas pulled at his striped shirt as if the collar was pinching him. He was about to say something, maybe apologize again for not listening or not seeing or not doing whatever it was he thought he should have done. But Finn was tired of sorry.

"How's Linus?" Finn said.

Jonas Apple smiled broadly. "He's great. He's just great. I would have brought him, but I don't think he would have appreciated the party."

"Cats usually don't," said Finn. Ever since Finn had given Jonas one of Calamity's kittens, the sheriff's allergies had miraculously cleared up. Mel and Petey had taken another, a fuzzy kitten they called Beebop, otherwise known as the Cat That Sleeps in the Lane. The other four kittens—Frank, Derek, Spike, and Priscilla—had moved to Finn's barn, where the mice were now busily dying of despair. Calamity Jane spent every night sleeping on Finn's bed and had never seemed happier. Rus the dog hopped from bed to bed, because he was a glutton for love.

And weren't they all? Jonas Apple was dancing with Mel Willis. Miguel Cordero and Amber Hass were caught making out in the girls' bathroom. Charlie Valentine stuffed his face with cookies and fed some to his favorite chicken, as well as to his great-grandkids. Mrs. Lonogan pushed her Persian, Fabian, around in a baby carriage, Rus enthusiastically licking the poor cat's pouting face. The room was abuzz with the news that Derek Rude had come out to his family and that his date was a dark-haired boy who bore a slight resemblance to Finn O'Sullivan. And though the party was for Roza, Roza and Sean sat quietly in a corner, Roza chattering away while Sean leaned in to listen, the scar on Roza's face a rosy curve like an extra smile.

The diner got stuffy and the party spilled outside. Finn walked a little farther than the others, till the voices of the people of Bone Gap washed over him the way they always did.

"I used to think that boy was nuttier than a honey cluster."

"You're the one who's nuttier than a honey cluster."

"I always knew he was onto something."

"Jonas should have listened."

"We all should have."

"Speak for yourself."

"Hey! How many cookies have you had? Leave some for the rest of us!"

"Where do you think Priscilla Willis is?"

"Funny-looking girl."

"I'd call her . . . unique."

"You would not."

"Would too."

"Finn would, anyway."

"Finn would."

"She not here?"

Sean stood next to Finn, hands in his pockets, huge and muscular and as superhero-ish as ever.

"Not yet," said Finn.

Sean said, "Nice party."

"Yeah."

"Got a lot of fans now."

"You always did."

Sean laughed. "I meant you. You should have heard the Rude brothers going on."

"Before you say it, Derek's boyfriend doesn't look anything like me."

"How would you know?" Sean said.

"He walks like his pants are too tight."

"His pants *are* too tight. Derek's happy, though. Don't think he's going to beat you up anymore."

"Actually, I think he's the one who always held back."

Sean said, "Listen, I know I said it already, but—"

"Stop."

"I was a jerk."

"I have to warn you, if you and Roza break up, I'm siding with her."

"You might have to move to Poland, then. It's official. She's leaving next month."

"You couldn't convince her to stay?"

"I said there are schools here, and Jonas said he could help with the immigration status, since no one would deport a kidnapping victim."

"That's romantic. A shocker it didn't work."

Sean rolled a stone under his work boot. "I might

have said some other stuff. But she needs to see her grandmother. And she has things to do on her own before, well, before she does anything else."

"Oh."

"Yeah. Oh."

Neither of them saw Roza until she was thrusting a plate between them. "Eat."

Sean and Finn peered glumly at the plate.

"Come on, eat."

Finn and Sean each took one. Finn said, "What are these called again?"

"Kolaczki," she said. Before they could bite into them, Roza said, "You eat cookie, you must visit me in Poland. Is rule."

"Is that so?" Finn said. He popped the cookie into his mouth. "Delicious."

"Secret is pomegranate filling," said Roza. "My own recipe."

"I'll remember that," Finn said.

"I remember always what you do." Roza kissed his cheek. "And what *you* do," she said to Sean, and kissed him, longer. Then she laughed. "You do very different things."

Finn, who never wanted to see his brother cry, now got to watch him blush the shade of pomegranates.

"No more gush," said Roza. "More cookies. I'll be back."

The brothers watched her go.

Finn said, "You'll just have to trust her."

"Yeah."

"You're young, too. Maybe you've got some stuff you want to do."

Sean nodded. "Maybe."

"And I hear Poland is beautiful in fall."

Sean snorted.

They looked up at the sky. It was a warm, clear night, and it seemed that the stars were putting on a show. Which wasn't surprising. The whole town seemed to be doing that, the flowers finally revealing their colors, trees shedding yellowing leaves for shiny new ones, gardens bursting with ladybugs and vegetables as if the spring had never died in the first place, and the summer would never end.

"Hey, what are you guys doing out here?"

Petey could have been a bee or a butterfly with her tattered silver wings veined with gold, the silver mask hiding her face. But because Petey was Petey, she had paired the wings and mask with a white T-shirt, a pair of cut-offs, and Converse gym shoes.

"Nice wings," said Sean.

"Thanks!"

"I think I'll let you guys commune with nature." Sean clapped Finn on the shoulder and ambled back to the Chat 'n' Chew, humming to himself.

Petey said, "Was that Sean O'Sullivan *humming to himself*?"

"He's acting a little crazy these days."

"Distracted?"

"You could say that."

"Sidetracked?"

"Sure."

She poked at his face. "Mooning around?"

Finn smiled. "Quite a bit, actually."

"Huh," said Petey. "Wonder what's wrong with him."

"Some chick."

"Just any chick?"

"Nah. Special."

"Pretty?"

"He thinks so."

"What do you think?"

"I think she's awesome, but I found a honey of my own."

She wrinkled her nose. "Honey? Ugh."

"I'm just getting warmed up."

Petey grinned and backed away, gauzy wings fluttering against a wall of corn.

"Hey," he said. "Where are you going?"

She tapped the silver mask. "If you catch me, I'll let you take it off."

And then a gentle wind blew across the cornfields,

and the corn whispered *here, here, here.* Petey dove into the vast sea of green, and Finn after her, the voices of the people of Bone Gap swelling like a chorus behind them, the moon winking above them, the corn laughing with them, because it would have known them anywhere.

Acknowledgments

The idea for this novel first came to me some seven years ago when my late father-in-law, Raymond Metro, handed me a newspaper article and got me thinking about the way we see the people we love. I miss him still.

But this book would never have come together without the time, help, and support of so many others. First, I must thank the people of Bone Gap, Illinois, who might be surprised to learn that their town is full of whispering corn, quasimythical creatures, and mysterious gaps one can slip through to get to other worlds. (Or not.)

Thanks to my dad, Richard Ruby, for all his colorful tales about the horses on my great-grandfather's farm. Thanks also to Linda Zimmerman and her daughter, Kelly Zimmerman, who invited me up to their beautiful home in Wisconsin to talk about everything from runaway racehorses named Mellow—not so very mellow—to barn cats that won't be confined to the barn.

Thanks to Kathy Lipski for her expert take on Roza's story, and to her parents, Bruno and Sophie Ogrodny, for their assistance with the more obscure Polish translations.

And thanks to beekeeper Mollie Edgar, who patiently weathered all my pesky inquiries about swarming behavior, and to Robin Blatzheim for chatting about the job of an EMT.

Much gratitude to everyone on the Faceblind listserv at Yahoo Groups for answering my questions and for sharing their stories. A special thanks to Malcolm Cowen and Amy B. Mucha for so generously taking the time to read and comment on this manuscript. Their feedback was invaluable; any error in fact or perspective is mine.

I owe the amazing Ellen Reagan an enormous debt for her sharp eye and her encyclopedic knowledge on everything from runoff channels in cornfields to the offspring of the goddess Demeter. And I'm further indebted to the incomparable Franny Billingsley, who read the first draft of this book and said the words that reverberated in my head as I revised it: "I want more magic."

To Tina Wexler, a spectacular agent, reader, and cat lover: I can't thank you enough for taking this book, and me, on. You're a tiny warrior of justice.

And thanks, too, to everyone at Balzer + Bray and

the rest of the folks at HarperCollins, especially my editor, Jordan Brown, whose deep and thoughtful feedback and willingness to go to the mat for his authors is unprecedented. Many thanks also to everyone at Faber & Faber, including my editor Naomi Colthurst, designer Emma Eldridge who designed the gorgeous cover, and artist Melissa Castrillón, who created the beautiful cover illustrations.

For the many words of support and encouragement, thank you, Esther Hershenhorn, Esme Raji Codell, Carolyn Crimi, Myra Sanderman, Jenny Meyerhoff, Brenda Ferber, Mary Loftus, and Carol Grannick. Thanks in particular to Sarah Aronson, Tanya Lee Stone, and Katie Davis for knowing when to call when I most need it.

Thanks to all my brilliant colleagues and friends in the Ham-line MFAC program, including Swati Avasthi for the late-night Googling of cake people and the handouts for every occasion, Miriam Busch and Christine Heppermann for the thrift store outings and the bitch sessions, and Megan Atwood for talking me down from the Tower.

Thanks always, always, always to Anne Ursu, Gretchen Moran Laskas, Linda Rasmussen, and Annika Cioffi—you know why. Melissa Ruby, you do, too.

Finally, thanks to Steve, who sees me like nobody else does.

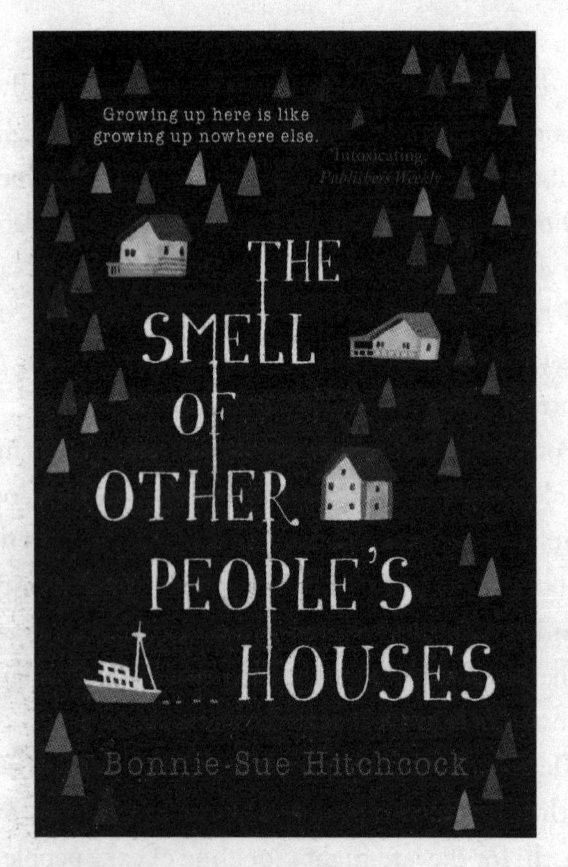

There's one smell that totally catches me off guard. It's the smell of worlds colliding.

Alaska, 1970:
Ruth wants to be remembered.
Dora wishes she was invisible.
Alyce can't bring herself to leave.
Hank is running away.

Four very different lives are about to become entangled.

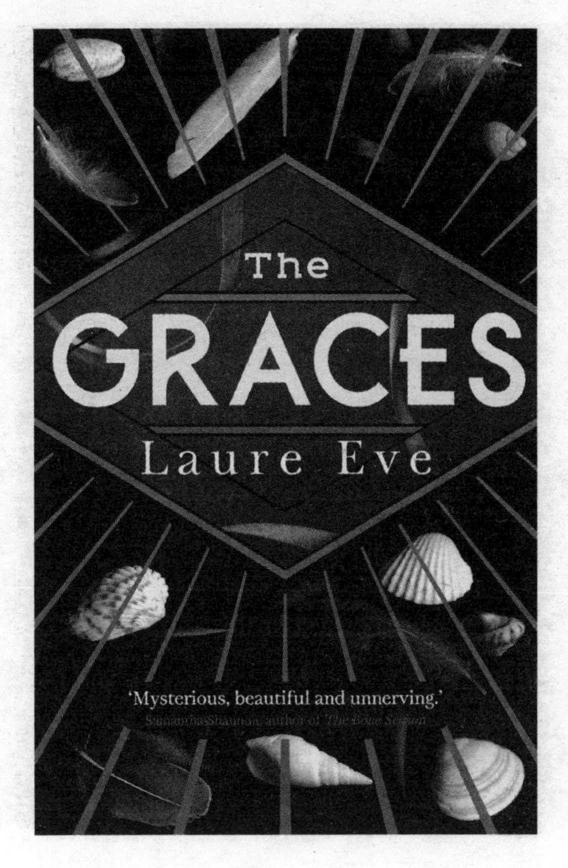

They were waiting for someone different.
All I had to do was show them that person was me.

Just like everybody else in her small town, River is obsessed with the Graces. Just like everybody else, she's been seduced by their wealth, their exclusivity, their beauty and their glamour. And perhaps even their magic. But unlike everybody else, River knows exactly what she's doing.

Doesn't she?

Meet Hel, teenager and Queen of the Dead.

Hel never wanted to be queen, but being a normal teenager wasn't an option either.

Now she's stuck ruling the underworld. For eternity.

She doesn't want your pity. But she does demand you listen. It's only fair you hear her side of the story . . .

It didn't have to be like this.